There are monsters.

There are those who fight monsters

Sometimes they are one and the same.

These are their stories.

<u>*AGENTS OF THE ABYSS*</u>

FRANKENSTEIN: MONSTERS OF THE ABYSS
STARING INTO THE ABYSS
MURDER AT CASTLE DRACULA
HYDE AND SEEK: FURY OF THE WHITE MASK
THE ABYSS STARES BACK
WEREWOLVES OF DERRY

Padwolf 13 Series:

APOCALYPSE 13 Edited by Diane Raetz
MERMAIDS 13 Edited by John L. French
FANTASTIC FUTURES 13 Edited by Robert E Waters & James R Stratton
LUCKY 13 Edited by Edward J. McFadden III
CAMELOT 13 Edited by John L. French and Patrick Thomas

Other Anthologies from Padwolf

BAD COP NO DONUT Edited by John L. French
NEW BLOOD: Tales of Vampires Edited by Diane Raetz and Patrick Thomas

Edited by Patrick Thomas and John L. French

PADWOLF PUBLISHING INC.
WWW.PADWOLF.COM
www.facebook.com/Padwolf

www.theagentsoftheabyss.com

STARING INTO THE ABYSS
edited by Patrick Thomas and John L. French
© 2025 Patrick Thomas

cover by Patrick Thomas

Agents of the Abyss created by Patrick Thomas and all related
characters and settings are © and TM Patrick Thomas

ISBN 978-1-958310-12-0
First Printing.

CONTENTS

From the writings of Abraham Van Helsing, founder and Lord Protector of the Sway:

They say a great genius comes along once in a generation. Minds that made a genius seem a simpliton are far rarer. Rarer still was that two such minds came along not only in the same era but the same country.

The detective and the criminal were two sides of a coin. It is a coin the Sway shall one day spend, provided they do not destroy each other first.

Out of the Abyss

A Baker Street Abyss story

John L. French

from the journal of Doctor John H. Watson

September 9, 1888

There has been another victim in what has come to be called "the Ripper Murders." She has been identified by the papers as Annie Chapman who, like the others, earned her pitiful living on the streets and in the alleys of Whitechapel.

After reading the lurid details of this latest outrage, I lowered my paper and looked over to where Holmes was sitting. His face was hidden by the newspaper he was reading and a dense cloud of smoke was coming from over the top of the paper to be dispersed throughout the room. Before I could say anything I heard, "Yes, Watson, I am aware of it." He then quickly stood and threw his paper to the floor.

"Damn them for their stupidity," he said as he strode over to the large map of London that had pride of place in our chambers. "And Abberline is the worst of them."

Stopping in front of the map, he carefully chose a pin. "A black one, I think."

"Then you believe Chapman is a part of this spree killing, Holmes?"

"Series killing is, I think, is a better term, Watson. And, yes, she is likely part of this series."

As he had been doing several times each day, Holmes studied the map and the pins stuck in it – black pins for the murders he believed to be definitely committed by the Ripper, red for probable. Not all were in the Whitechapel area. And there were more black pins than the papers and the police were ascribing to the killer.

Holmes was looking for a pattern, one that would tell him where the next killing would take place. If there was one, I had not found it. And the fact that Holmes had not either told me that the killer was striking at random.

"I'm going out, Watson," he said and without another word he was gone. He had been doing this almost every night since the murder of Mary Nichols. Hers was one of the first black pins he placed on the map, along with one representing Martha Tabrum. And now there was Annie Chapman.

October 1, 1888

Two more Ripper deaths, Elizabeth Stride and Catherine Eddowes, although Holmes does not believe that Stride's murder is part of the series.

"A knife across the throat, Watson? No, it is more likely that this is someone settling an old score and hoping to place the blame on friend Jack, who will no doubt be happy to take the credit. For their part, the police, in their bafflement, would be prone to blame every such crime on this monster. That way they have only one killer they are unable to catch, rather than several."

More pins on the map, a white one for Stride and a black one for Eddowes.

"Where are you?" I heard him whisper. Then aloud, "I should not have taken the Baskerville case, Watson," Holmes said, again staring at the map and willing in vain for it to give up its secrets. "It will take up valuable time, as did the Sholto case, although that did work out well for you. How is your lovely fiancé, Watson?"

"She is well, Holmes, busy planning the wedding."

A look of melancholy briefly passed over my friend's face. "As they did the last time you abandoned me for a wife, these chambers will seem empty without you, old friend."

November 12, 1888

Another death last night, that of Mary Jane Kelly. Another black pin on the map. Another cryptic whisper, "I will find you, Victor," from Holmes. With no cases of importance, Holmes spent his days on routine investigations and his nights seeking Jack the Ripper. He would go out every evening dressed as a clergyman, or a seaman, or a peddler, and return in the morning tired and disappointed. One night, I jokingly suggested he go out dressed as a street angel. For a moment it seemed as if he was considering it, but then he smiled and said, "I haven't the legs for that, Watson."

As for me, it was days at my practice and evenings with my Mary. And since this journal will only be read by me, I will admit in it that there were some nights spent with Mary as well.

It was the morning after one such night that I returned to Baker Street just as Holmes, disguised as a beggar with a twisted lip, arrived as well.

"A late-night call, Watson?" he asked.

"So to speak, Holmes."

"I trust you had more luck than did I."

There being no gentlemanly answer to that, we ascended to our rooms with Holmes in the lead.

When we entered our chambers, we were surprised by the presence of Holmes's older brother Mycroft. The large man was standing in front of the map, studying the placement of pins.

"An excellent job, Sherlock. If I may make a few corrections …"

"You may not, Mycroft. It is a poor thing but it is my own."

"And it is no longer needed."

"You have him then?"

There was only one person the brothers could have been talking about. My heart leapt at the thought that the killings were over and fell again when Mycroft said,

"Not yet, but we are close. The men of my special section are tracking him down as we speak."

"It is, of course, the Swiss doctor."

"Precision, Sherlock, you mean the Swiss who calls himself a doctor. How did you know?'

"Elementary, my dear Mycroft. Like you, I have read Inspector Vernet's journal. Unlike you, I have been to the Swiss caves and have also read Victor's. When you catch him, do not hang him. The French method is much more reliable, only bury the head away from the body. Better still, burn them both and scatter the ashes."

November 13, 1888.
"For you, Mr. Holmes."
With a quick "Thank you, Mrs. Hudson" my friend all but grabbed the telegram from our landlady's hand and tore it open. On reading it, he crumpled it, threw it to the floor, and with a "Damn them to Hell," stormed off to his room.
As Mrs. Hudson quickly departed the room I bent down to retrieve the message.
"VF has escaped to the continent," it read, "the Directorate of Altérité *Securite* has been alerted but it is believed that our prey has returned to the Alps."
I left the telegram where Holmes might find it and file it, burn it, or tear it into shreds. Instead, he left it until after dinner, when he picked it up and said, "Your first mistake, Professor, and I will have you for it." In the mood Holmes was in I did not dare ask him who this professor might be. Later that evening, I saw him sitting in his chair, staring at the note. As I left to visit Mary, he uttered but a single word, a name I had not heard before.
"Moriarty."

City of London, 1891
In Newman's Court, in that square mile that constitutes the City of London, in chambers that once were occupied by the firm of Scrooge and Marley, a man sat in the main office. His thin, drawn appearance and the darkness of his clothing made him appear much older than his forty-odd years. He had finished the daily accounting. His organization had made a tidy sum that day, more than most men made in a lifetime.
And I may need every shilling of it, he thought, as he once again pondered the biggest mistake he had made in his criminal career. *Why did I help that madman?* he asked himself then promptly answered his own question. *Because I foresaw that he might be needed. What I did not foresee was interference by that meddler Holmes. That was my true mistake.*
"Professor Moriarty?"
James Moriarty looked up. There in the doorway was Sebastian

Moran, *Colonel* Sebastian Moran, as he liked to be called. It was rumoured, although never confirmed, that the Colonel had been stripped of his title and cashiered out of 1st Bangalore Pioneers for unspecified crimes – murder perhaps, or the forcible knowledge of a white woman, or cheating at cards. To Moriarty it didn't matter. True, Moran was a brute and not as smart or clever as his Eton and Oxford degrees would suggest but he was loyal, brave, and an expert shot with any firearm made by man, especially Von Herder's air gun.

Moran thought of himself as Moriarty's second-in-command and the Professor allowed him to do so.

"Yes, Moran, what is it?" Moriarty asked even though the answer was plain on the colonel's face.

"The carriage failed, Professor. Holmes escaped with minor bruises and a torn coat."

Moriarty's head shook from side to side. It was a nervous tic, one that he tried to control, fearing that it would one day give him away. "Who was the driver?"

"Fibbs, sir."

"The same man who missed Holmes with the masonry?"

"The same, Professor."

"Show him the bottom of the Thames. No, show his family the river bottom. Make him watch then blind him and cast him out. Let him beg for the rest of his life, may it be long and miserable."

"Shall I get the air gun, sir? I can rid you of this Holmes ..."

"No, Moran, I do not think so. I fear it is too late for that."

Indeed it was. Moriarty had confirmed this just a few days ago when he left his chambers and confronted Holmes in his Baker Street lair. The exchange between the two men, each of whom respected and feared the other, was brief.

Standing in front of the seated Holmes, a revolver in his pocket aimed at the detective, Moriarty had said, "All that I have to say has already crossed your mind."

Holmes, his pistol within reach on a table, replied with, "Then possibly my answer has crossed yours."

"You stand fast?"

"Absolutely."

"Why did he not use his pistol against you?" Moran asked.

"For the same reason I did not use mine. It would have been the end of both of us. While that was a trade Holmes said he would willingly make, no man wants to die, although sometimes it is necessary.

"That is all, Moran. Prepare yourself for a journey to the continent. Mrs. Stamford will provide you with the details. Please send her in as you go, Colonel."

"Yes, Professor," Moran said with an unmistakable leer.

Violet Stamford was a young woman in her mid-twenties. Her hair was a natural red and she was attractive, but not in the way that would cause men to turn and stare at her in the street. She had been married once, to a forger in the Professor's employ. When Stamford was caught by Holmes and the Yard with a knife in his hand and in the presence of a corpse, he was offered a prison term instead of the noose if only he would give up his employer. Knowing that the price of his disloyalty would be the life of the woman he loved, Stamford chose the short drop and the sudden stop. To reward his man's sacrifice, the Professor took his widow into his employ.

It was believed by many in Moriarty's organization that the position for which the Professor hired Mrs. Stamford was either horizontal, bent over his desk, or up against the wall. Indeed, he had twice used her after she began to work for him but only to establish his dominance and her willingness to do anything he ordered. After that, he left her alone.

Rather than use her for her body, Moriarty used Mrs. Stamford for her mind. She had a first-rate intelligence, a talent for organization that rivaled his own, and a ruthlessness that, on occasion, surprised even him.

"Yes, Professor," she said, entering his office and closing the door after her.

Moriarty looked up at the woman who was his true second-in-command. In her eyes he saw loyalty, admiration, and possibly love. She was the one person outside of that meddler Holmes whom he respected and admired. *And she is not trying to hang or imprison me*, he said to himself and thought, not for the first time, about marriage. But such a partnership would involve sharing power and that Moriarty was not prepared to do for anyone.

"It is time, Mrs. Stamford. A matter of days before Holmes and the Yard bring down the entire operation. Fortunately, we are more than ready for them. We are, in fact, a few moves ahead. You have prepared new identities for yourself and our few key associates?"

"I have, Professor. And there is money enough to sustain us until your return." Then she dared say, "If you return, sir. What you plan entails many risks. Are you sure it is necessary?"

"Yes, Mrs. Stamford. Between Holmes and me there must seem to be a final reckoning. It does not matter if Holmes falls or not, but I am afraid, my dear, that I must die. Only then will they stop searching for me."

"I understand, Professor, and I thank you for putting so much trust in me. How long might you be gone?"

"A year, more or less."

"Then will you allow me to prove my loyalty to you once more?"

Moriarty thought for a moment. He had not been to one of the houses in a while. "Why not? I believe we have time."

"Take all the time you need, Professor."

Meiringen, Switzerland, May 1891

What was believed to have been the final meeting between Sherlock Holmes and James Moriarty took place on a pathway which overlooked the Reichenbach Falls. With John Watson having been lured away, their encounter was witnessed solely by Sebastian Moran. The two men struggled, their physical skills as matched as their mental ones. First one was on the edge of the precipice, then the other. More than once the colonel was tempted to draw his pistol and end things in favour of the Professor. Instead, he obeyed his master's instructions and let the matter play out.

In the end, it was the detective's knowledge of *baritsu* which ended the conflict. Breaking Moriarty's hold with a *jujitsu* move, Holmes then used a *savate* kick to send his opponent plummeting into the abyss.

As his master disappeared into the mist, Moran felt free to act. Holmes had done his part. With Watson as a witness, Holmes was no longer needed. After thrown rocks and launched boulders failed, the colonel tried shooting him but Holmes's devilish luck held. He escaped by climbing down the almost sheer face of the cliff.

No matter, thought Moran. *Two witnesses to the professor's death will serve better than one. I'd best go and see to the Professor.*

Soon Watson returned to the Falls. He read the note and instructions Holmes had left him, studied the scene in the way his friend had taught him, and came to the logical but erroneous conclusion that the best and wisest man he had ever known was dead.

It would be nearly three years before he learned the truth.

Moran searched for two days before finding Moriarty's body. The professor was quite dead, his limbs twisted, his head bent to indicate that the immediate cause of death was a broken neck.

"I should just bury you now," Moran said to the corpse. "Go to Liverpool and tell that Stamford bitch that you couldn't be found. That I'm now the one in charge." But despite his corrupt nature, despite his desire to bend Violet Stamford over a table and show her who was the master, Moran was still a soldier and held to the soldier's creed of leaving no man behind if possible. It may have been the one decent thing about him.

Kneeling by Moriarty's body, Moran took out a padded case. Opening it, he removed a syringe and a vial of what the Professor had called "the Elixir." Filling the syringe, he injected the elixir directly into Moriarty's carotid artery.

"Professor, you were the smartest man I know. You may have been the smartest man in the world," Moran said, "but I hope you knew what you were doing in trusting your life to Jack the Ripper."

Moran waited by his master's body throughout the night. When he woke at dawn he checked Moriarty for signs of life, not expecting to find any. To his surprise, Moriarty was breathing, had a slight pulse, and, despite being unconscious, was moaning in pain.

"Well, bugger me for a uranian, it worked. Come on, Professor, let's get you to that mad Swiss doctor."

Mindful of Moriarty's broken bones and wondering just how a man could be alive with his neck at that angle, Moran picked him up as gently as possible and carried him to a waiting wagon, in the back of which were blankets and bedding to make as smooth a ride as possible.

"I hope you're comfortable back there, Professor," Moran said, "because it's a long road to Zurich."

Zurich, Switzerland, June 1891

"Why the Devil are we waiting so long, Doctor? It's been weeks and all you do is take walks in the woods and write in that damned book of yours."

Victor looked up from his journal. To Moran, the thin, pale man appeared to be in his twenties, not old enough to be a doctor and, judging from his slight frame, not strong enough to have committed the atrocities with which the Professor had credited him.

The truth was, the man was very much older than he seemed, older by about 100 years. And he had done worse things than rip women of low repute, far worse. He was Victor, late of the House Frankenstein, and he had once created a monster. In doing so, he had become a monster himself.

Putting down his pen, Victor looked at his questioner. *A fine body*, he thought. *Would that I could place my brain into it.* But he knew that that could never be, for then he would have to trust someone with his secrets. And governments and men like Moriarty would only use them to make more monsters. And there were too many monsters in the world as it was.

Victor thought of how nice it would be to have a body he could rely on. As far as he knew, he was the only one to have received the elixir while still alive. The others had all died before being given the gift of life. Victor had "died" more than once and was brought back by the lightning, but that did not change the fact that his body would at times fail him, fail him in a way that the elixir could not repair. And so he had to steal life from those who had proven themselves unworthy of it.

"So, *Doctor*, when will you be finished with the Professor? I would like to get back to London."

Moran's voice broke Victor's reverie. "I have told you, *Colonel*," he answered in an impatient voice that was accented with both German and French, "that Moriarty's body was severely damaged and needs time to heal. I gave him another injection of the elixir a week after you brought him to me and a third just two days ago. He should be ready within the week."

"Ready to 'arise and walk'?"

How nice, Victor thought, *the brute has read the Bible. If only he practiced it.* Then, inwardly laughing at himself, added, *If only I had practiced it. I would now be dead and at peace and Elizabeth …*

He pushed aside all thoughts of the woman who had been his wife for only one night.

"No, Colonel Moran. He will be ready for the lightning."

"And what if there were no lightning, Doctor?" Moran asked in such a way that his suggestion was unmistakable.

"Then your master would be trapped in a twilight world, caught between life and death."

Moran nodded as if this would be acceptable to him. "In the state that he is in, can he hear us?" The colonel looked up at the ceiling, at the first-floor room above where Moriarty lay unmoving in a bed.

Victor's mind flashed back to a chalet in Scotland and the body of a helpless woman. She too was between life and death and while in that state he had used her carnally. When he finally awakened her, she remembered and …

"There is evidence to that effect," Victor replied, "but no proof. Still, I would watch what you say around him."

Victor smiled as if in jest but in reality at the pained expression on Moran's face. He had heard the colonel telling the seemingly unconscious Moriarty all the things he would do should the Professor not wake up.

"A proper storm may not come for weeks," Victor said. "You can return to London if you wish. I can manage the rest myself. It would not be the first time."

Moran nodded. The next day he was gone. Soon he appeared in London. While he waited to be contacted by either the Professor or Violet Stamford, he made his living playing cards at various clubs.

Zurich, Switzerland, July 1891

Finally, the storms came. Victor let the first two pass, thinking that they might not have the power he needed. When he heard the rumblings of the third, however, he knew. On seeing the lightning in the distance, on hearing the echoes of the thunder, he knew. The elixir in his body, weak though it was, called out to the power.

Moriarty had stopped moaning. Physically he was healed, all that was needed for his return was the spark of life, the flow of electricity that would ignite the elixir inside him.

Everything was ready. The Franklin rod was on the roof, the cables were attached to the metal netting that enveloped the Professor's body. Moriarty had saved him for this very purpose and now it was time to pay his debt.

The storm was getting nearer. The interval between light and sound growing shorter. *Soon*, he thought. Then lightning and thunder came as one, the netting sparked and the body it covered convulsed as power flowed into it.

The lightning struck once, twice, a third time before moving on. Carefully Victor removed the cables and the netting. Then he waited.

An eyelid twitched, a finger raised, a leg trembled. Not for the first time did Victor think, *Death, I have beaten you yet again.* And not for the first time did he reflect that his victory had cost him everything.

Moriarty moaned. *Napoleon has returned from Elba*, Victor thought as the Professor sat up. Quickly assessing the situation, he said, "Thank you, Doctor Frankenstein."

"You are most welcome, Professor but, please, call me Victor. The title is at best an affectation. And as to my patronymic, I was, like Adam, cast out of my family for my sins."

Still sitting on the worktable, Moriarty looked down and saw that he was naked. He was not, however, ashamed. "Where are my clothes?" he asked.

"On the table closest to you. Put them on when you feel able. They may be somewhat loose, you have lost weight over the past two months."

Moriarty recovered quickly and soon was sharing the meal that Victor had prepared.

"Moran?" he asked between bites.

"Back to London." The Professor nodded as if he had expected that. Victor then said, "There is something of which you should be aware," and told Moriarty of Moran asking, "What if there were no lightning."

Again, Moriarty nodded. "I half expected that. The man is loyal to me in his way, but mostly loyal to himself."

"He did bring you here from the Falls. He could have just left you."

"Yes, he could have. Like all of us, Moran will be judged by his actions rather than his words. But that is a matter for when we return to London."

Victor was surprised by this. He had thought after discharging his debt he would remain in Switzerland for a time, then journey eastward, possibly into Wallachia. "We, Professor?"

"Yes, we, Victor. Despite reports of my death, it is best if I take measures to prevent my being recognized. And for that I need you."

After the Professor explained, Victor said, "It's not as if it would be the first time. And it may be that the lightning would not be needed. I'd need to experiment, of course."

"I would expect nothing less. And you need not worry about the authorities looking for you. My agents have put it about that you were murdered by your creation in the Northern Wastes."

from the journal of John H. Watson
November 9, 1893

It has been nearly a year since my dear Mary died. Since then I have buried myself in my work, both medical and literary. I have been told by Doyle that my reminiscences of the much-missed Sherlock Holmes are quite popular, which may be why my medical practice thrives. They come not to see me but rather the man who was "friend and companion" to the Great Detective. And I am happy to say that, despite the efforts of some of his supporters, the name "Moriarty" has become as synonymous with evil as the name "Jack the Ripper."

Of course, there are those who believe that because I was associated with Holmes that I also have his skills. They come to me seeking help in solving their problems and mysteries. I tell them that I am a doctor not a detective and refer them to those who are, such as Hewitt, Pringle, Carnacki, and the blind Carrados.

Would that I had Holmes's skills. Then I might be able to assist Lestrade in his current investigation, the mysterious disappearances of several Londoners over the past few months.

November 18, 1893

Since the passing of Mary, I have fallen into the habit of having dinner with Inspector Lestrade of the Yard on Friday nights. I think it is our way of keeping the memory of our mutual friend alive. Most of our meals end with "Remember that case ..." then one of us launches into a story about Holmes.

"Any luck on the missing persons case, Inspector?" I asked Lestrade over dinner last night.

He shook his head. "None, Doctor. Other than they seem to come in pairs, two in a week than none for a while, there is no method or pattern to them – man, woman, different professions and walks of life, no one area of the city preferred over any other. Someone suggested that there may be an occult purpose to the kidnappings, so I hauled Crowley in and talked to that Carnacki fellow, just in case. But there was nothing down that street. And I've talked to your colleague Thorndyke. He's quite full of himself but he's helped us in the past, however not this time. Have you spoken with the brother?"

Lestrade was referring to Mycroft Holmes. "Yes, I have, or at least I tried. He told me that if I was unable to apply his brother's methods then the years I spent with him had been wasted. We have not spoken since."

Lestrade let out a harrumph. "I suppose he's too busy doing nothing at that Diogenes Club of his."

Sworn to secrecy, I could not tell the Inspector that Mycroft was indeed busy. Using his club as his headquarters, he kept our nation safe from the external threats that constantly threatened to destroy it.

"It is times like this, Doctor, that I miss Mr. Holmes the most. I fancy myself a good policeman and a better detective than most. After all, I had made inspector before I met him. But whenever I was out of my depth, as I am now, I would go to him. Generous he was with his time and, to be fair, with the credit. I can almost picture it. I'd go to him after the sixth or seventh person went missing. Or some sweet young thing would show up at Baker Street, telling a tale of a brother who cannot be found. Mr. Holmes would investigate and visit the areas where those missing were last seen. Already two or three steps ahead of us, he would lead us to where the missing people, or their bodies, could be found."

"And then," I put in, "he would explain how he did it and it would all seem so simple that we'd wonder why we hadn't solved it."

"It never was simple, Doctor, it was Mr. Holmes that made it look that way" He raised his glass. "To Sherlock Holmes."

As I joined him in our weekly toast, I suddenly heard a voice in my head, *his* voice. "Don't look for where the pattern is, Watson. Look for where it isn't."

"Lestrade," I said, "is there a pin map of the disappearances in your office."

"Of course there is, Doctor. It tells me nothing. Every morning it tells me nothing. And with every pin I add to it, it tells me less."

"May I see it?"

There must have been something in the way I had asked because Lestrade immediately said, "Yes," then "Yes," again when I added, "Tonight?"

Soon we were in his office in Scotland Yard, staring at a map of London. There were twenty-one pins–seven red ones for missing women, fourteen for the missing men.

"I thought the disappearances came in pairs, Lestrade. I count only twenty-one pins."

"A woman, this woman," he pointed to a red pin, "went missing last week. No others since. Perhaps there's one gone whose disappearance has not been reported or noticed."

"Given that, there may be more than twenty-one then."

"God forbid, Doctor. But as you can see, no pattern at all."

I found myself looking at the map not with my eyes but with those of my friend's. Then I saw it, or rather, did not see it.

"Look there, Lestrade, in the City of London."

"The whole damned map is the city of … oh, yes, I get your meaning, Doctor. But there's nothing there."

The case of Silver Blaze came back to me.

"*But, Mr. Holmes,*" said Gregory, "*the dog did nothing in the nighttime.*"

"*That was the curious incident.*"

"I know, Lestrade, and I have to ask why. Your pins are over London. Why are there none here?"

As Lestrade said, he was a better detective than most. He quickly answered, "Because the ones responsible for those pins do not wish to draw attention to … Wait a minute."

He pulled a thick file from a cabinet, leafed through it. "I thought so. Newman Court, where the old Scrooge and Marley place was. That was the headquarters of Moriarty."

Suddenly, the spectre of the man Holmes had called the "Napoleon of Crime" hung over Lestrade's office. But it was soon replaced by the Ghost of Sherlock Holmes, again speaking through me.

"And if Moriarty owned Scrooge's counting-house … Lestrade, gather as many men as you can. Come the dawn we must discover where Scrooge lived, although I fear what we might find."

In a ramshackle building at the end of a court that had long ago seen better days, we found that for which we sought. The smell of death greeted us. There were bloodstains on the ground and first floors. The latter was fixed up as some kind of operating room. There was metal webbing to which was attached electrical cables leading to a massive array of batteries.

A constable called us from below. We heard, "Sir, down here," then there was the sound of him retching.

The cellar was a charnel house, filled with bones and bodies both old and new. Lestrade and I had both skipped breakfast and on that morning we were glad we had.

"As Mr. Holmes would say, your department, Doctor Watson."

"I'll have you know, Lestrade, that these are new shoes."

"Not after today they're not."

More torches were brought in to illuminate the cellar and I began the grisly task of examining the bodies. When I was done, I made my report to Lestrade.

"From what I can tell without moving any of the bodies, all have been decapitated. Their torsos each bear a single knife wound to the heart. The heads uniformly display signs of cranial surgery, with stitching all around the skull. The work of a madman."

"Not a madman," came a voice from the stairs, "but a monster." I looked up to see the great bulk of Mycroft Holmes on the steps. "I will not descend any further, gentlemen. Like you, Doctor Watson, I am wearing new shoes. I will await you outside."

My examinations complete, Lestrade and I joined Mycroft in the relatively fresh air of London.

"Congratulations, Doctor. It seems that the time you spent with my brother was not wasted after all. Sherlock would have been proud."

I felt my face flush from his praise then, "You had me followed."

Mycroft's shoulders moved slightly in what for him was a shrug. "I have lots of people followed. Now, Inspector, if you will withdrawal your people and allow mine to enter I would appreciate it."

"You … have … people?" Lestrade asked. I don't know why he was surprised; he was, after all, dealing with a Holmes.

"Yes, I do. Watson, later on, swear the inspector to secrecy then explain things to him."

An hour later, an hour during which Lestrade and I broke our long fasts as I told him of the true nature of the Diogenes Club, one of Mycroft's "people" came to get us. "Mister Holmes wants to see you."

When we returned, they were bringing out a body. Unlike the others, this body had no stab wound to the heart. Also, his skull had been opened and his brain removed.

"Take a close look at it, gentlemen."

As we peered down at the dead man recognition came slowly. It was not possible but there was no denying the fact that the face was that of …

"Moriarty," both Lestrade and I said at once. "What does this mean?" the Inspector asked.

"It means, Lestrade, that your work is finished. Your superiors will receive word that, thanks to you, a villain whose deeds surpassed Jack the Ripper has been stopped and put down. It means, Doctor, that not a word or a hint of this will appear in the Strand. It means that there is not to be any further investigation by either of you."

Mycroft looked down at the body. "And it means that my work has just begun."

November 19, 1893

My mind still reels from the events of yesterday. To learn that Moriarty somehow survived the abyss was a shock, one only slightly mitigated by the fact that he was, this time, finally dead. Questions abound. Who had killed him and the others, and why? How could Mycroft be sure that the disappearances and subsequent murders would cease? And what of Holmes? Had he also survived? Or were the remains of that great man still at the base of the Falls? I will perhaps never know.

November 25, 1893

My dinner with Lestrade was somewhat quieter than usual. I think we met more out of habit than desire, neither of us wishing to discuss the events that were foremost in our minds.

We were halfway through our meal when Lestrade said, "I received a commendation for clearing up the missing persons case, one that belongs more to you than me, Doctor."

"Enjoy it for the both of us, Inspector. I am sure that in your career you have done finer things that have gone unrecognized. Count this towards them."

"Thank you, Doctor. I also received an invitation to join the Diogenes Club."

"A rare honour. Will you accept?"

Lestrade shook his head. "I'm a copper. I'd rather be chasing criminals than whatever it is Mycroft Holmes goes after. Besides, I still have an open case."

He removed a photograph from his pocket and laid it on the table. It was one of the few I'd ever seen in colour. It was of a red-haired young woman in her twenties.

"The twenty-first pin," I guessed.

"You're getting as sharp as Holmes, Doctor."

"Given recent events, and your showing me the photograph, it was … elementary, my dear Inspector."

"It all sounds so simple when you explain it, Doctor." We then shared a smile in remembrance of our lost, or possibly just missing, friend.

"Tell me about her, Lestrade."

"Her name is Katherine Darcy, no, not those Darcys, rather

an offshoot of that family. I am beginning to believe, given that her disappearance was singular and that her body was not among those found, her being missing has nothing to do with the others. I have circulated her description in the usual places and have asked the constabulary to keep watch for her. I will probably never find her," Lestrade looked at the photo then put it away, "but it's likely I'll never forget her." He raised his glass. "To Katherine Darcy. Wherever she is, let us hope she is happy."

April 6, 1894

It is a joyous day! Sherlock Holmes has returned, not from the dead but from a three-year journey. He surprised me yesterday in my study after which I collapsed in a faint. Once I revived it was as if he had never left and soon the game was afoot. Not only did he survive an assassination attempt but he solved the murder of Ronald Adair, laying both crimes at the feet of Colonel Sebastian Moran, a former confederate of the (definitely) late Professor Moriarty. Holmes called him "the most dangerous man in London." Then added, "Well, the second most dangerous, now that I have returned."

Thanks to his brother, Holmes was, of course, *au courant* with the November case which led to the discovery of Moriarty's body. "Well done, Watson. If I had known you had become this astute I might have stayed away another year."

When I asked him how Moriarty might have survived, Holmes said, "I have my suspicions, Watson, and for once I pray that I am wrong." After that, he never again spoke of the matter.

May 13, 1894

It was slightly more than a month since Holmes's return that the two of us were able to dine with Inspector Lestrade. After the usual greetings, Lestrade said to me, "I still haven't found her, Doctor." After my "Keep looking, Inspector," he explained the matter of Katherine Darcy to Holmes.

With this, a strange expression came to my friend's face, as if his body were there but his mind was elsewhere. Finally, he came back to himself saying, "I see, I see," but he did not explain what it was he saw.

"By the way," Lestrade said, breaking the odd silence caused by Holmes's fugue, "Moran was hung the other day. He went to the gallows like a gentleman. When asked if he wanted the benefit of clergy he said,

'I regret nothing.' Those were his last words. The hood was placed and the trap door sprung. As neat a job of hanging as I ever did see, and one well deserved."

"What became of his body, Lestrade?"

"His sister claimed it."

"Moran did not have a sister," Holmes said as that strange expression again came over him. It was one I would get used to. It meant that his great mind was making connections between what it knew and what it had just learned. "A trick I picked up in Tibet," he later explained to me. "If I had remained I would have learned how to cloud men's minds but where's the sport in that?"

"Of course," Holmes shouted as he came out of his trance. "It is all so obvious. Watson, Lestrade, I have been blind." Then he stood up as he had so many times before, as if he were about to rush out of the restaurant, dragging us along in his wake as he led us to the denouement of another great mystery.

Instead, he sat down again. "It is too late, I am afraid. The chessboard had been knocked over. It has now been reset," he said with the smile that I only saw whenever he was faced with a great challenge.

London, May 1894

"I have his body, Professor," Mrs. Violet Stamford said, adding. "I assume that is still a proper form of address."

The Professor smiled. "It will do for now, Violet. This situation will take some getting used to. Moran, his body is in the cellar? It has been given the injection?"

"Yes, to both."

"Very well. I need two things. Have someone find the most pitiful cripple in London. A real cripple, not a fake from the Beggar's Guild."

"And the second?"

"Locate Victor. Tell him I have one more job for him."

London, June 1894

The last two things Sebastian Moran remembered were the drop and the noise his neck made as it snapped. After that, there was nothing, not until a few minutes ago when he awoke in pain. Although wherever he was being held was in near-total darkness, he could feel that his arms were bent at unnatural angles. His legs were so twisted that he could barely stand. When he did rise, he could not straighten due to the curvature of his spine.

There was in his room a small window through which the dim glow of evening came. Looking up at it he found that he could make out the light only with one eye.

His hearing worked though. He knew this because he heard someone cry out, "He's awake." As he moved toward the sound he fell forward, one of his twisted legs being chained to the wall.

Soon the door open and two people entered, the torch one was carrying hurting and almost blinding his one seeing eye. When it adjusted, he saw that the taller of the two was Violet Stamford, the other he did not recognize, not until he saw the shaking of the head in a familiar nervous tic.

"It can't be," he whispered in a voice that was not his.

"But it is, Moran, it is. You were foolish to have cheated at cards, foolish to have killed the Adair boy. I cannot abide foolishness. And I cannot forgive what Victor told me about your suggesting that he withhold the lightning. You would have deprived me of the spark of life, condemned me to limbo. So I have brought you back from the dead. Enjoy your new body and your pitiful existence. May you suffer for an exceedingly long time."

To the guards, the Professor said, "Turn him loose. Let it be known that he now bears the Mark of Cain. Should any molest him in any way or dare to offer him help beyond a penny or two, they shall share his fate. Moran, it may be that one day I will forgive you, seek you, and put you in a proper body. But do not rely on my mercy, for I have never had any. Now remove him. And put that Swiss madman on the next ship out of Britain."

London, July 1894

In Newman's Court, in that square mile that constituted the City of London, in chambers not far from those once occupied by the firm of Scrooge and Marley, the firm of Barnaby and Stamford opened for business. No one knew what kind of business, but as it was owned and operated by two sisters, no one cared.

In the main office, behind an ornate desk, sat a young woman in her mid-twenties who was now going by the name of Katherine Barnaby. Her red hair was combed forward to cover the scars from the cranial surgery that had placed the brain of James Moriarty into the body of the former Katherine Darcy.

"So, 'Sister,' what business are we now in?" Mrs. Violet Stamford asked her.

"The same as always, Violet, the business of crime, of supplying people what they need and desire for a price."

"And shall I continue to call you Professor?"

Barnaby smiled the smile of the man Scotland Yard believed dead. "Given the circumstances, I think 'Katherine,' no, 'Kate,' will do nicely.

"'Kate' it is then."

There was a knock on the outer door. Violet, acting as clerk and secretary, opened it, and was handed a bouquet of flowers. She took it to Barnaby who read the attached card.

"To Josephine, take care not to involve innocents. SH."

"Josephine?" Violet asked.

"The wife of Napoleon." Barnaby looked down at the flowers. "Well played, Mr. Holmes. First round to you. Let the game begin anew."

Excerpt from Hidden Geography, the Sway training manual:

Monsters have lived among true people for as long as history has been recorded and likely longer. Some form their own communities and pretend that they are like humans and deserve the same rights. This is a dangerous precedent to allow as it gives monsters the idea that they can fight back against their betters.

The legends of Crete tell of the first of one breed of monster stronger and faster than humans who at least have the sense to hide away from their betters. In one instance their delusions of innate rights set them against the worse that humanity had to offer in a time of horrors and death.

A Place of Refuge

Elyssa Mikaela Bolt

Crete, Second World War

"Hurry!" Hanna yelled to her brother Benyamin, not that there was much need for the warning. They had been on the run for three days. She had begun to wonder if anywhere on Crete was safe anymore. By now it was clear that they would never go back to Iraklion unless the war ended and the Germans left the island.

The only sounds either of them could hear were their own footfalls and harsh breathing, but neither of the siblings had any illusions that they were safe on the road. They needed somewhere to sleep indoors. The night before, sleeping out under the stars had been too unsettling. Cars had driven by at all hours of the night. Every one of them had woken the sleeping teens because they couldn't take the chance that it was a German patrol. Now, with the sun setting and what little light still in the sky was fading, another sleepless night outdoors was not a prospect they could handle.

"What about those lights over there?" Benyamin asked. "We're a long way from the coast now."

"I'm glad the island is this big. Imagine if we lived on Naxos or Paros or one of the smaller islands. Crete at least has areas where you can't see the sea."

"I think we've reached one of them."

They stopped running for a moment and caught their breath. Their parents had told them, just before the latest roundup of Jews in the island's major city began, to flee into the mountains and stop running only when they could no longer see the sea in the distance. What they could see was a small village around the nearby hill. The road didn't seem to lead into it. Although they'd never been to one, Hanna and Benyamin had heard that there were villages that were practically cut off from the modern world.

It was a risk they were taking, not knowing who lived in these houses or whether they'd shelter them or turn them over to the Germans, but it was too late to avoid risks. All avenues available to them involved some danger. Most were certain death.

"Seeking shelter in one of the houses in this village offers better odds than hiding in the underbrush," said Hanna. "We'd likely be discovered in the morning anyway."

"And it's better than running any more tonight" agreed Benyamin.

"Going any further makes no sense; we'd just be moving closer to the sea from this point."

"So what, we go up to a door and knock?"

"I guess."

The teens crept into the village. The dirt road, though easy to walk on, had no car tracks anywhere and not a single vehicle stood parked on any streets. Iraklion had cars, as did some of the other towns around Crete. This was the first village Hanna and Benyamin had seen with none.

"We really are in the middle of nowhere," he whispered.

"That's where we need to stay," she concurred.

"Bare footprints all over the place."

"I guess the people who live here don't have shoes either. They must be poor."

The central street widened as they got into the area where the houses were. All of them were modest, made of brick, and decorated with two curious symbols. One was an axe with two curved blades, the other a concave shape with a rectangular base underneath a U-shape, the upstrokes of which formed two swoopy horns.

"Have you ever seen anything like this?" Benyamin asked his sister.

"No. Maybe it's a resistance holdout. If so, we'll be safe here."

A door creaked open. "You may enter," came a voice from within.

"Who are you?" Hanna asked, nervous.

"My name is Gida. That is all I can say now. Come in, it will be best if you enter at once."

Although the speaker's voice sounded female, the pitch was nonetheless low. They could have sworn a cow mooed at the same time that Gida spoke. Gulping, they moved toward the door. It was pitch black inside, the darkness concealing Gida.

"Gida, is there anyone else in your house? Any German soldiers?"

"Of course not. We hate them up here. You are safe if you come into my home."

"So you're alone?"

"My family is in here too."

"We need to be hidden from the Nazis."

"Naturally. We're all loyal in here. The Germans are our enemies."

Exhausted as they were, they didn't ask any more questions. The house was so dark inside that they still couldn't see Gida as they entered and the door swung shut behind them. That wasn't too surprising, as lighting a candle could draw attention. Hanna wondered if someone else on the street was a collaborator from whom Gida had to hide her activities. It wasn't unlikely.

"Come this way. There is a spare room with two beds in it, ready for a time such as this."

Now, behind a closed door and curtained windows, Gida did light a candle, and Hanna and Benyamin were surprised by how tall she was. The height of an average man, Gida wore some kind of headdress – not that they could see it very well – that brought the top of her head even higher. The ceiling was higher up than they had expected from the house's exterior. But they didn't want to ask more questions or even notice anything else. Hanna simply thanked her for the safe place to stay. Gida showed them to a room with two empty beds. They stepped in and closed the door. Sleep soon found them.

Dawn came, and they awoke to see that the pictures hanging on the walls all showed people with cow heads, like the Minotaur of ancient legends they had learned in school but a whole society of them. It was the only thing that prepared them for what they saw when they opened the door into the hall.

"Good morning!" said a minotaur standing in the hallway. With the body of an ordinary person – the hands and bare feet looked normal enough, if somewhat hairy – their host had the head of a cow!

"Gida?" asked Hanna.

"I'm Gida's mother, Noama" the minotaur replied. Her voice sounded like a mix between a cow mooing and a more typical old lady voice. She was dressed in clothing that wouldn't have looked out of place in Iraklion, although her black headscarf covered what they now saw was a pair of horns. "You will come to breakfast, I hope?"

"Yes," they replied, too hungry to consider skipping another meal.

"Was that real?" Hanna muttered to Benyamin after Noama had walked away.

"Yes. Do you think we're safe here? The Minotaur was supposed to eat people."

"If they were going to eat us, we'd be dead already. I'm sure we're safer here than among the Germans."

"True. I wonder what kind of food they're going to serve us."

At the table in the kitchen sat an entire family of minotaurs. A woman (a cow?) whom they assumed was Gida sat between two children (calves?). Between two empty place settings on the other side sat a man (bull?) whom they assumed was Gida's husband. Hanna and Benyamin felt a bit awkward as they took the empty seats.

"How did you sleep?" asked Gida, her voice still sounding like a moo. Now that they could get a good look at her, the height and the shape of her headdress made sense. Gida was about the height of an average man if you measured to the top of her head without the horns. The bull who sat between Hanna and Benyamin was even taller.

"We slept well," said Hanna, trying not to stare, "and we thank you for your hospitality."

Gida smiled, the facial expression coming across despite the great difference in her features. "I'm glad. You've no doubt had a difficult past few days."

"Very," said Hanna. "First the Nazis put out a decree that all Jewish residents of Iraklion needed to assemble in the town squares. We feared the worst. They made us do calisthenics for a few hours, just to get us embarrassed and tired, and then they started seizing people. There weren't enough Germans to grab everyone, so a lot of people fled. That was the last time we saw our parents. I don't think they got away. They told us to get as far from the sea as possible."

"We've been on the run ever since and have nowhere to go now" said Benyamin.

"You need not go anywhere," said Gida, "for you are in a place of refuge."

Her husband snorted. "I don't know about that. We took a vow not to help humans."

As if to drive home the difference between minotaurs and humans, the bull tossed an entire apple into his mouth and chewed it. He didn't even spit out the seeds!

"So," said Benyamin hesitantly, "are you not, then? I mean, are you not people? Human, I mean."

"Oh," said Gida, "we're people, but not human. I suppose we are human in a sense if one goes back far enough, but a different sort of humans. We're not so different inside. Four stomachs, unlike your one, but the rest of our anatomy is the same below the head."

"And we can intermarry with humans," added her daughter, who was about the same height as Benyamin. He didn't miss the big-eyed look she was giving him.

"Anyway," continued Gida, "my brother was saying that the adults of our village have taken a vow not to help humans. Technically…"

"I'm sorry," said Hanna, "your brother? I thought…"

"This is my brother, Phazoul. And my daughter Suma and son Kaston."

"Then your husband is not at home?"

"We don't do that among our people. Suma and Kaston's father lives with his sister and her children. My and Phazoul's father lived with his sisters and their progeny all his life. Minotaurs are matrilineal, like the humans of Crete long ago."

Hanna and Benyamin tried to imagine what that would be like. They couldn't picture their family without their father. Their parents were always together, their father doing everything their mother told him. He made it look it was always his idea.

"As I was saying," Gida continued, "my brother thinks we should not get too involved in the affairs of humans. I agree, there is a point beyond which we should not be helping humans too much. But we also took a vow to Hathor that we will defend our territory against foreign invaders, a vow that has bound our village for over two thousand years."

"And I am the leader of the village," added Noama proudly. "Under my roof, you are protected."

"I think we might have been followed by the Nazis." Benyamin still looked worried.

"They've come near our village five times this month," said Gida, "and every time we've chased them away. We take our vow to Hathor seriously. Nobody invades Zoukali. The Romans tried to conquer us back when they took Crete. We still have a few old legionary shields as souvenirs. The Ottomans were smarter. They never even tried to subdue us."

"Still, we've invited trouble upon you. I'm sorry for that." Hanna wasn't reassured either.

"None of that, now. It's their fault and theirs alone. We allowed you to come here. In fact, we've been watching you since yesterday morning and we're glad you found us." Noama was that sort of old lady with whom one simply does not disagree.

Silence fell across the table, broken by Phazoul scarfing down another apple whole.

"You mentioned Hathor. Wasn't she an Egyptian goddess? I would have thought minotaurs would follow the Greek gods." Hanna had learned about the Greek and Egyptian deities in school, back before the war began. They had lived in Salonika, on the mainland, until Hanna was twelve and Benyamin ten. Then five years ago they had moved to Crete, the largest island in the country, hoping it would be safer if Greece was invaded by Germany. The invasion had happened, and the island hadn't been safe.

"Crete isn't really part of Greece historically," said Noama. "The first people who made this island great came from Africa. Mostly from Egypt, including our folk. Did you notice that many of the Egyptian gods have animal heads? That's because long ago in Egypt, there were other races of people who had heads like birds and beasts, at least compared to your species. We worship Hathor, not just as an Egyptian goddess but a minotaur goddess."

"That makes sense," said Hanna, realizing that the cow-headed deity was indeed a minotaur.

"I see you've finished breakfast. We should get moving. There's a better place than this house for you to go. We'll have a meeting in the village square next."

At that same moment, four Germans on horseback rode up the hill to the village. Limited resources meant that motor vehicles weren't available for the patrols sent to the mountains. Their orders were to find any Jews who had escaped the roundups in the cities of the coast. So far, Rudolph, Johannes, Fritz, and Sophie had found no one. They were beginning to get frustrated.

"Two young Jews passed this way yesterday," the old farmer down the road had said, but that wasn't a lot to go on.

"It's still worth pursuing them," said Rudolph, the oldest and unofficial leader of the group.

"It's a wild goose chase by now," said Fritz.

"They must be found. Our survival as a race depends on every one of them being dealt with appropriately," Rudolph insisted.

The others shrugged and looked at each other. None of them dared admit it aloud, but to them, rounding up Jews was just another mundane job. They didn't care either way about Hitler or his politics. There was a war going on, their country was in it, and they had to take part in the war effort somehow. That was all it meant to Johannes, Fritz, and Sophie.

As they rode to the crest of a hill, a booming voice emanated from behind a tree.

"Who dares bring horses to the land of the cows?"

The Germans laughed. Rudolph and Johannes dismounted, drawing their guns. How dare some villager challenge them on land occupied by the Third Reich?

Time to teach these Undermenschen a lesson.

"Here is the village square," said Noama, "where we have community meetings."

Hanna and Benyamin looked around. The square, down the street from Noama's house, looked very different from the town square in Iraklion. Blocks of stone surrounded the relatively small open space, arranged like benches in a stadium. Minotaurs sat all around them. They watched as one snarfed down an entire corncob, including the part humans wouldn't eat. At the front of the square, which Noama now made for, stood a block of stone carved in the same shape they had seen decorating Noama's home: a U-shape with two distinct horns atop a rectangular base.

Noama stood in front of the horn sculpture and raised a double axe high above her head. Hanna and Benyamin hadn't seen where she'd got the axe, but as soon as she held it up all the minotaurs stopped talking. They recognized the double axe; this image had been found all over the site of Knossos, a short way east of their home. Hanna realized she had seen the U-shaped design too, in school; an archaeologist at Knossos had dubbed it the "Horns of Consecration."

There looked to be about a dozen families in the village, to judge by the number of houses along its single street, and they guessed more or less everyone in the town was here. They stood in the center of the square as all the Minotaurs stared at them.

"I say we send them onward," said a cow-woman seated to their left. "Humans bring us nothing but trouble."

"We can offer them shelter without breaking our vow," retorted a bull-man to their right. "Hathor will not judge us for showing hospitality."

"Zador is right," said Gida. "They come to us asking no help but the chance to live. That is in keeping with our people's values. We can resist the invaders, who are far more evil than those we have fought in days past, by sheltering those whom they persecute. That will fulfill our vow, not break it."

Just then, sounds of gunfire rang out.

"To the watch post!" someone yelled.

"Take my hand!" shouted Suma, Gida's teenage daughter. She reached for Benyamin's hand, but he hesitated. Hanna took Suma's hand instead, and Benyamin took hers. They followed Suma down an alley between two of the houses, leading away from the village in a different direction than the one they'd come. The alley turned into a footpath leading up the hill, and before long the footpath led to a door in the side of the mountain.

"What's in there?" Benyamin asked.

"A safer place," said Suma. "The labyrinth."

Down the hillside from the Minotaur village, Rudolph and Johannes, guns drawn, walked toward the source of the voice they had heard. Sophie and Fritz stayed on their horses, scanning the surrounding area.

"Nervous?" Fritz asked Sophie, teasingly.

"Nope. I'd much rather be out here than sitting in an office sending telegrams." She'd been able to avoid that assignment, unlike most women in the auxiliary forces who were down in Iraklion away from the excitement.

What happened next qualified as more than excitement, however. Three arrows flew at them from the shrubbery and from behind a thick tree. One stuck in the saddle of Fritz's horse, another sliced through Rudolph's left ear, and the third grazed Sophie's shoulder. Then their enemy switched from range to a direct attack. A monster – a man with the head of a giant bull – charged out from behind the thick tree and beheaded Johannes with a single swing of a tremendous double-bladed axe. Sophie gasped as she swung her gun toward the beast. She and Fritz and Rudolph all opened fire, and the creature fell to its knees. Another of the same sort fell from the shrubs next to the tree, hit by a bullet that hadn't been aimed at him. A third creature appeared in the shrubbery and dragged the second one out of sight. Fritz steered his horse closer to the first monster.

"Wait," said Rudolph, clutching his bleeding ear, "we need him alive for questioning."

"What is it…I mean he?" Fritz didn't seem any more prepared for this than Sophie had been.

"He's a minotaur," said Rudolph, "a resident of one of the nearby villages. I didn't think we'd encounter any, but they warned me that some of these live in the mountains. I should have mentioned that to you before we left town."

"Should have mentioned that mostly to him," said Fritz sarcastically, pointing to Johannes' body.

A bellowing noise came from behind him. All four of the horses reared and took off, throwing Fritz and Sophie to the ground in a tangle of limbs. They pulled themselves to their feet to discover a dozen more minotaurs standing in a half-circle around them. Sophie reached for her gun, but a female minotaur threw a lasso around her neck and seized her, lifting her by the throat into the air with both hands. Another minotaur woman aimed a blade at her abdomen. Rudolph and Fritz reluctantly dropped their guns.

"It's safe," said Suma, "and I never took the vow to stay out of human affairs. I'm not a full adult yet, so I'm allowed to help you any way you need."

"That's reassuring. I didn't understand what the vow was about."

"Well, some Minotaurs, like my Uncle Phazoul, think we should stay out of all conflicts between humans. The vow to Hathor technically just says we don't seek to influence human affairs other than keeping our lands safe from human conquerors."

"How does the labyrinth work?" asked Hanna.

"Well," said Suma, "first we just walk down this tunnel until we get to the first door."

They were inside the mountain now. Suma had pulled the door shut behind them, but it wasn't totally dark; small windows just above head level (for a minotaur) let in periodic light that was enough to see by. The passageway curved slightly to the right – they had gone to the left after entering the door – and made its way gradually, rather than straightaway, into the interior rock.

"Was this a larger cave at first?" asked Benyamin. "The wall on the right side looks like masonry, not carving."

"You are correct," replied Suma. "We built this place hundreds of years ago. It was a cave before; now it's a series of spirals. There's one way into the center, the same way out. It's not a *maze* like you might think. Look, we're at the first door."

The passageway turned at a right angle to the left; Hanna and Benyamin were momentarily surprised there was any room to the left for more tunnels but realized they must have gone far enough into the mountain. The door ahead of them was a sheet of metal with a series of concentric circular dials in the middle. No handle or hinges were visible.

"How do we open it?" asked Hanna.

"This one's easy enough," said Suma. "See the engraving of Osiris on the top panel?" She produced a torch – the electric kind – and shined its light on the top of the door. Sure enough, there was a carved depiction of a scene from Egyptian mythology. "We use the dials to tell the story of Osiris. I've been through here enough times that I can do it, but you should take a look."

Suma turned the outer dial until a picture showing Osiris and Isis' wedding, the first event in the story, stood atop the circle. Hanna and Benyamin now noticed a small triangular protrusion right above that spot, as if to indicate that this was the place to which the pictures needed to line up. Suma then spun the second dial to show Set standing next to Osiris inside a wooden chest, then the third to show Osiris cut into several pieces.

"Can I do the last one?" Hanna asked.

"Sure," said Suma.

Hanna looked at the center dial and found pictures of Set, Isis, Anubis, Hathor, and Horus. Horus had had the most to do with putting the mutilated Osiris back together, so she picked the engraving of Horus and spun it to the top of the circle. Something clicked, and the door swung open away from them.

Suma beamed. "Very good. You know your stories."

"I know *your* stories. I wonder how much you know of mine."

"Well, our people both came out of Egypt once upon a time. I know that much."

That's an interesting point, thought Hanna, who hadn't made that connection until now.

The passageway continued in another circular arc, which turned a corner and then followed along the other side of an interior wall. Turn after turn now had them thoroughly disoriented. Benyamin began to look scared.

"It's alright, Ben. The minotaur is on our side."

"I'm on nobody's *side*," corrected Suma, "but all the same I don't want you two to be in danger. I like you."

"But didn't your people eat us back in the day?" asked Benyamin.

Suma laughed. "Nope. The Athenians had to send captives every ten years to Knossos to be *given* to the minotaurs, but we didn't eat them. We needed them for, well, other purposes."

"What would those be?" Hanna wondered.

"Breeding," said Suma bluntly. "Minotaurs and humans can reproduce easily enough. Minotaur blood is thicker than human blood, so the offspring normally looks just like a full Minotaur. Occasionally a hybrid looks human. Those go out among humans as spies who report back on what is happening in the wider world. Although we have to shave their fur first."

"But I thought you were supposed to stay away from humans?" asked Ben, surprised.

"We're not supposed to interfere," Suma corrected him. "Making sure we know what dangers lurk in the outside world is quite different. We've been having children with humans for thousands of years, ever since we saw what happened to one of the Pharaoh dynasties when they married their siblings to keep the bloodline pure. We Minotaurs believe in keeping our bloodline diverse."

"So you have human ancestry?"

"My grandmother's father was a human. In fact, it's been enough generations since then that it's my turn to take a human mate too."

"Oh. I guess that will be a while?" Benyamin tried not to think about where this was going.

"It might be, but now that one's arrived…"

That was exactly what Benyamin was afraid of. Hanna tried, unsuccessfully, not to giggle.

"Oh, look, we're at the second door," said Benyamin, trying to change the subject.

"Another combination lock?" asked Hanna.

"Yes, this time with numbers. No mythology required this time."

"Is that all that defends this place?"

"There's another guardian down here, in the innermost circle."

This time, there was a keypad with digits 0-9 arranged in two rows of five. On the wall to their right, a half-circle of black and white circles had been painted on the wall. The black ones were slightly larger. To their left stood another half-circle of short stone pillars with white and black stones embossed in the tops. A different digit was written at the bottom of each pillar.

"Shoot, I always forget this one," said Suma, sounding embarrassed. "I don't go down here by myself, you see. I'm always with an adult."

"I notice it uses modern numerals," Ben pointed out.

"Yes," said Suma, "we've adapted to the human world in some ways. This way of writing numbers makes more sense than what the ancients used. Which doesn't tell us which ones we need now."

"Well," said Hanna, "I would guess that somehow the painting on the right tells us which pillars we need, and those tell us which numbers to push."

"Yes," Suma agreed. "I can't remember if it's the white or black stones we need."

"Does anything bad happen if we get it wrong?"

"Yes."

"Oh. Well, I think it's the black stones, because they're painted bigger. And it's probably the order…yes, there's a little arrow pointing which way to go." Hanna was gaining confidence that she was on the right track. "So we start at the end marked four, then go around the circle clockwise. What's the next black stone?"

"Seven" replied Benyamin.

"Then eight," said Suma.

"Okay, there's five total, so we need two more."

"Wait," said Benyamin, "what happens if we get it wrong?"

"I don't know," replied Suma. "Every time I've been here, whoever I'm with – usually my mother – just punches five digits in and it opens. But I've been told each door has a trap."

"Great. I thought this place was supposed to be safe."

"Ben, they wouldn't bring us here if it wasn't."

"How do you know that? We've been here how long, twelve hours? Why do you trust them?"

"Please do trust us," said Suma. "We're not monsters."

Hanna sighed. "So what would be the last two digits?"

"One and nine," said Suma. Stones two, three, five, six, and zero were white.

Hanna gritted her teeth and punched 4, 7, 8, 1, 9 on the keypad. Suma ducked and motioned for them to do the same. The door swung open. Suma exhaled deeply.

"I was afraid I was going to get you two killed instead of helping you. The rest, I can remember."

Gida snarled and hurled the Nazi woman at the two men, knocking all three of them flat on the ground. "Get lost!" she snapped.

Instead, one of the men, who had blood coming from his ear, whipped out a pair of grenades from inside his jacket. "If I toss even one of these," he shouted defiantly, "it will explode and kill you all!" The minotaurs froze, giving the other two surviving Germans just enough time to grab the guns they had dropped on the ground and aim them at three of the minotaurs. The minotaur villagers all aimed their axes at them, ready to swing.

"You monsters have lost!" shouted Rudolph, holding out one of the grenades and threatening to pull the pin. "When our glorious Reich is done with the Jews and Gypsies and other degenerate races, abominations like your kind will be next!"

"Don't take the bait," Gida warned the minotaurs next to her, hoping nobody would be enraged enough to charge. She didn't want to lose anyone. Two of her neighbors picked up Godan, the wounded sentry who had killed the other German, and helped carry him back to the village square. He'd live, but that left them with ten to three instead of twelve to three. With no guns, every advantage mattered. Gida wished the folk of Zoukali had engaged with the modern world a bit more and stockpiled guns instead of relying on the traditional arms of yesteryear. *Too late for that now*, she thought glumly. If they survived this encounter, she would see to it that they updated their arsenal.

"We charge them now," said Phazoul into her ear. "They won't have time to shoot us all before they all die."

"I don't want them to shoot anyone else!"

"They're hiding Jews," said Sophie to Rudolph and Fritz, not knowing if any of the Minotaurs could hear her. "I'm certain of it. Otherwise, they wouldn't have attacked us."

Rudolph and Fritz nodded.

"We demand to see your leader!" yelled Rudolph.

"How do you know she's not here?" replied Gida.

"Take us into your village, and we won't shoot."

"Surround them," said Gida to her forces. They had the numbers to form a circle around the Nazis as they walked into the village square, keeping axe blades trained upon them. Fritz quickly grabbed a satchel that had fallen from Rudolph's horse and slung it over his shoulder.

Noama was waiting for them in front of the Horns of Consecration, still holding the ceremonial axe. "Welcome to our humble town. What brings three soldiers of the Reich to a place like this?"

"Don't play games with me, old cow. Where are the Jews you're hiding?" Rudolph had his gun trained on Noama, despite Phazoul's attempts to shield his mother.

Noama smiled. "There are no Jews here. No humans live in this village at all. You can search all the houses; there are no Jews in any of them."

"You're not telling the whole story. The last mistake you'll ever make, degenerate monster." Rudolph pulled the pin out of a grenade.

Phazoul swung his axe and hit Rudolph's outstretched arm near the elbow. A full blow would have severed the limb completely; as it was, Rudolph's arm dangled limp, broken and useless. Fritz and Sophie fired wildly, but the minotaurs they were aiming at were too fast and the bullets pinged off the walls of buildings. Minotaurs grabbed all three

Nazis in bear hugs and squeezed them until Sophie and Fritz dropped their guns and fell on the ground, gasping for breath. Realizing from Rudolph's words what the grenade would do, someone seized it and threw it away from everyone. The grenade hit the Horns of Consecration and disintegrated the stone monument.

"You'll never catch the two children who were here this morning," Noama sneered at the Nazis, looking at them the way one looks at a particularly disgusting bug.

Fritz looked panicked at the sight of a dozen angry minotaurs closing in, but Sophie's eyes followed the alley that led to the path into the mountains and settled on the outline of a doorway in the hillside. "They must have gone that way!" she shouted, diving under a large bull minotaur and running at top speed. Fritz hastily followed, finding a way between two minotaurs. A panicked Rudolph, horrified by the thought of being taken alive by the minotaurs, ran after them, cradling his broken arm.

"Stay here," said Phazoul. "We fulfilled our vow. I wounded one invader and Godan killed another. We don't interfere with the affairs of humans!"

"They brought the fight here. They wounded two of our people, and if they aren't stopped they'll bring more with more weapons. They'll kill us all!"

Phazoul scowled. "I guess you're right."

"Suma is with the human teens," said Noama. "We protect our family above all else."

Gida and Phazoul nodded and took off in pursuit of the Nazis.

Hanna, Benyamin, and Suma crossed through two more puzzle doors but began to hear the sounds of pursuers entering the labyrinth. Not accounting for the walls, they were probably fairly close. Benyamin wondered if the Nazis could simply smash their way through a wall, cutting down on the distance they were from their quarry.

Fritz and Sophie knew the Osiris legend from school and passed the first door. At the second door, Fritz guessed that the white stones were the ones being emphasized, and typed 2, 3, 5, 6, 0 on the keypad. A pair of stone blocks shot out of the darkness to either side of his head, squishing it and instantly killing him. Sophie screamed, the distant sound giving Hanna and Benyamin a little hope. However, she quickly realized, as Hanna had earlier, that the black stones were bigger on the diagram for emphasis, and typed 4, 7, 8, 1, 9 on the keypad. She ducked just to be safe. The door swung open, and she ran through. Suma, Hanna, and Benyamin hadn't shut the third door properly in their haste, and Sophie ran through it unchallenged. Rudolph, his running speed unaffected by his arm wound, caught up with her, having stepped through all three doors that she'd deliberately left open. Sophie came up to the fourth door, figured out the correct sequence for six buttons with shapes on them, and entered. As Rudolph reached for the door, he accidentally pulled it shut and was left on the wrong side.

Suma charged Sophie as soon as the door swung shut. Although not yet full-grown, as a minotaur heifer she was the same size as a human adult. They wrestled on the floor, evenly matched, until Hanna knocked Sophie out cold with a knee to the face. They left the blonde Nazi where she lay, focusing their attention on the last door. Suma remembered the code, a significant date in minotaur history, and it swung open to reveal a large chamber.

They had not suspected that such a large cave could exist within the mountain, not when so much space had been built into a twisting labyrinth of passageways. The ceiling soared far above, a few windows in it admitting enough light to show the space around them. The chamber was higher than it was wide or long. Its floor looked suspiciously flat, as if the minotaurs had chiseled and sculpted it.

What most caught their attention, however, was the hundred-foot-tall statue at the room's center. It looked like metal, not stone, unusual for a statue of that size. The male figure wore a breastplate, shin guards, and a helmet as well as a short "skirt" and a long cape, sculpted to look like it was flowing in the wind. The face had a beard and shoulder-length "hair". In his right hand was a short sword, while his left hand held nothing.

"The other guardian of whom I spoke," said Suma.

"It's a statue."

"How is a statue going to help us? Do we hide in it?"

"Not a statue," Suma replied. "This is Talos, the Old Man of Crete." She strolled up to Talos's right ankle and spun a few circular gears.

The ceiling opened, revealing itself to be a pair of huge doors in the mountainside above them. One of the doors had a notch cut out of it, the other a tab that fit into it. Talos began to move. He took a step forward with his huge right foot and bent down to look at Suma,

Hanna, and Benyamin with eyes that looked alive. The eyes locked on Suma and quickly scanned back and forth between her and her human companions. As if satisfied that they were guests of the minotaurs, Talos looked past them to the open door.

Sophie, having regained consciousness, dashed through it and pulled a radio out of the satchel Fritz had been carrying. Through the open door above them, the radio got enough of a signal to make a call for backup. She cursed herself for not calling for backup much sooner.

Hanna and Benyamin didn't understand the words Sophie spoke in German, but they could hear a voice responding on the other end. The sound of a distant airplane came through the huge gateway. But so did light that revealed a staircase leading up.

Before they could make for it, and before Talos had identified Sophie as a threat, Rudolph burst through the doorway from the labyrinth. Gida and Phazoul followed in hot pursuit. Sophie raised her radio again. Benyamin dove at her and grabbed the radio, throwing it on the ground and breaking something. Sophie backhanded him across the face and sent him sprawling. Gida seized Rudolph by the neck, but Sophie grabbed Hanna the same way and held her gun to her head.

Not caring what happened to Rudolph, Sophie dragged the Jewish girl up the stairs. She wasn't crazy enough to pull the trigger yet, needing a live hostage, but as soon as the plane found her position the minotaurs would be eliminated.

What she didn't count on was Talos. As she climbed up the stairs, Sophie passed Talos' eye level, fully awakening the metal giant who had been waiting for a live threat. He reached out his left hand toward her. Sophie screamed and released her hold on Hanna, making for the opening and stepping out onto a narrow ledge just outside the hangar door. She and Talos both looked down to see Gida shove Rudolph to his knees. Just before Phazoul's axe swung and beheaded him, Rudolph locked eyes with Sophie. Talos swung his head back up to look Sophie straight in the eye, and his turned red.

Everyone present realized Talos had identified Sophie as an active threat, his priority to eliminate.

"Talos will always take the side of the minotaurs and hunt our enemies," Suma whispered to Benyamin.

Sophie fired her gun three times in the air, attracting the attention of the pilot she had radioed earlier. Realizing that the German fighter was headed straight toward them, Hanna jumped onto the ledge with

Sophie and punched the Nazi woman in the face. Sophie swung her gun at Hanna's chest and pulled the trigger. An empty click wiped the triumphant grin off her face.

"Looks like you're out of bullets, *makhasheyfe!*" Hanna punched again, furious at what was happening to her people, knowing that Sophie's pretty face that hid the ugliness of a soul willing to cooperate with evil. Sophie staggered backward, starting to fall down the stairs, but caught herself and readied herself for another blow.

Phazoul seized her arm before it could move forward. Behind him, Gida, Benyamin, and Suma emerged from the stairs. But they weren't all that came out of the cavern. Talos' head, then shoulders, then torso loomed into view as a pedestal rose until his feet were level with the ground outside. They were higher up on the mountain than the labyrinth door, but still well below the peak. The hangar doors followed the slope, closer to horizontal than vertical, so there was room to stand on the outside.

"That's a Messerschmitt Bf-109," said Benyamin as the plane turned its course from them, "the most dangerous of the German planes."

"What's he doing?" asked Gida.

"Going to attack the village," said Hanna, realizing the pilot was preparing to strafe the minotaurs' homes in the reprisal she feared would come. A second later, she noticed her brother was holding Rudolph's gun, dropped when Phazoul killed him.

The pilot never followed through on the threat. He was flying low enough that Talos, lunging with surprising agility from his pedestal, swung his sword and sliced the plane's left wing completely off. The plane careened out of the sky, and Talos seized it in two hands. He was powerful enough to totally halt its momentum. Hanna, Benyamin, and the Minotaurs watched in awe as Talos tore the right wing off the plane and ripped the fuselage in half. The terrified German pilot fell only a short distance before Talos caught him and sent him hurtling through the air to an ignominious death. Talos stabbed the broken wreckage of the plane into the mountainside as a monument.

"Go," said Gida to Sophie, "run back to Iraklion with a message. Tell your Fuhrer that minotaurs will never bow before him."

Relieved to be alive, Sophie turned and fled down the mountainside, making for the distant road she had ridden up that morning. Back to messenger duty after all. She'd tell the truth, but knew it was useless trying to explain what really had happened to her superiors. Nobody would believe her.

No, thought Hanna. *Can't let that happen.* Yanking the gun out of Benyamin's hand, she shot the last Nazi twice before she could get out of range.

"I had to," she explained. "I can't risk more of them coming after you, after you helped us."

Gida nodded, realizing the risk she had been taking allowing any survivors.

Suma gently took Benyamin's hand, and he gulped and blushed; her earlier suggestion hadn't been a joke. Talos looked in the general direction of Iraklion and let out a defiant bellow from his enormous metal lungs, the minotaurs proudly joining in.

Excerpt from a letter from the Protector General of the Sway:

War is hell. One should not need to state that there are monsters in every war ever fought. In fact, war can be the perfect place for the non-human variety to hide among their human brethren.

Shifting Iwo Jima

Melora Johnson

Two men in swim shorts and flippers and carrying waterproof bags, rose out of the water then stripped off their air tanks and anchored them in the rocks below the buffeting waves. One of the bags held an SCR-300 radio.

It was February 17, 1945, in the North Pacific islands. In the distance, on the southeastern side of Iwo Jima, Japanese guns fired repeatedly to repel the reconnaissance teams of the UDT, Underwater Demolition Teams, and U.S. ships returned fire, providing cover for the mission.

With far less support, and along a more circuitous path, the two men—Jim McClure and Daniel Thompson—had separated from the team and made their way underwater along the shore.

Moving quickly, McClure led the way into a cave that opened just above the waterline. It was little more than a fissure and the men had to inch sideways for several feet before it widened enough to let them move normally. Inside, there was just enough room for them to sit down, side by side. It was far too small a cave for the Japanese soldiers to use it for any significant operation. Here they would wait for nightfall.

Thompson sat next to McClure, praying that no one would stumble upon them, though he knew that the other man had chosen the spot well. Surely no one would be checking such a small fissure, it barely qualified as a cave.

The ground beneath him radiated heat to an uncomfortable degree. The smell of sulfur was acrid, stinging his nostrils. *Hope to God I don't sneeze at the wrong moment.* "This must be what Hell feels like," he said under his breath.

The U.S. Forces had been bombarding the island for nine months and there wasn't much left on the surface, but the Japanese were entrenched. They had evacuated all the islanders. It was purely a military installation now, a landing pad in the hop to attack allied positions and a line of defense for Japan itself.

"Naw," McClure said in a conversational tone. "This isn't Hell. I've been there, though I don't remember most of it."

Thompson tensed, his body straining as he listened for footsteps that would tell him they were about to be pounced on by a Jap with a knife, or simply shot where they sat. He tried to look over at the other man but all he could see was a bit of his profile from a sliver of light that filtered in through their air tube. Was the guy nuts? Did he want them to get found? He didn't respond, hoping that would shut the other man up. It didn't.

"I was fourteen," McClure said. "I was in the kitchen of my parent's house in Nebraska when . . ."

Thompson interrupted. "Should we be talking?" Thompson phrased it as a question because he was just the radioman. At an appointed check-in time, he would encode the information McClure gave him and transmit it to the waiting receiver who would decode it. When they completed their mission they would receive instructions on being extracted. Their information might well be vital to the success of any landing force. Thompson had been chosen out of the Navajo Code Talkers for his diving experience.

They were so close that he could hear the moisture as McClure's lips parted in a smile. "Relax, there's no one nearby. Trust me, I'd know."

Thompson was skeptical but he had been ordered to do whatever McClure told him to do, and a story might take his mind off the anxiety of the situation. His grandfather had kept him entertained with stories all the time when he was young, in the traditional way of instructing Navajo children.

McClure continued, "Like I said, I was in the kitchen and I could see the window. The rain and wind seemed to turn sideways. It rushed by faster and faster until the house shuddered continuously under the assault. I was old enough to know that meant a tornado. I was petrified;

no one else was home. There was no way I could make it to the storm cellar entrance outside so I dropped to the floor and crawled to the stairway at the center of the house. It was a small, enclosed area so I thought I'd huddle in there. I managed to get the door open but the house was torn up, and I could feel it was being carried into the funnel cloud. I tried to pray but I couldn't remember the words. Then I blacked out."

Thompson was silent. He'd known a man who was attacked by a bear once, but he hadn't come out of it unscathed. That man had lost an eye and one of his arms was now useless. The man next to him had seemed better than fine when they met, he was a walking model of the perfect Navy man. Loath as he was to talk, Thompson had to know how the other man had survived the force of nature. "What happened?"

"I woke up in a meadow a half-mile from where I'd been. Parts of the house were missing but it was solidly built. The ceiling had dropped down on top of the stairway and I was kind of boxed in. The door wouldn't budge. I couldn't get out. It was two days before they found me. Well, they found the house, they didn't expect to find me alive."

"The Great Spirit kept you safe," Thompson said. "There must be a purpose to your life."

"I guess. Maybe," McClure said into the hot and dark confinement of their hole in the sand. "Maybe this is it."

Thompson had also endured a near miss, but his had been with an unnatural phenomenon, a skinwalker. Over the years he had watched the events play out in his memory over and over again, as if observed from outside his body.

As a boy of twelve years, he had spent a great deal of time with his grandparents, while his father worked and his mother tended to his younger siblings. One day he had been approaching his grandmother's hogan outside the Navajo village at dusk. She was a wise medicine woman, revered. She and his grandfather lived a little apart from the others.

The boy heard her scream inside. He ran forward but before he got there, a large wolf came out of the shelter. He saw it run to a gulch then stop. As he watched, it changed form with a series of wet cracks. After a minute or a two, a man stood where the wolf had been. It continued away from the Hogan back toward the village.

The boy went to check on his grandmother but it was too late, her throat was a bloody mess. She was dead. The boy ran back to the village for help but when he told his story, his father assumed that he was combining the tales his grandfather had told him with the horror of a wolf attack. Grandfather had believed him, though.

McClure spoke again, drawing Thompson out of his brooding memories. "Where you from?"

Thompson sighed. Talking seemed like a really bad idea. They weren't going to make it out of here alive, he accepted that likelihood, but he'd rather accomplish something worthwhile before he died, save at least some of the lives of his fellow Americans that would likely be lost in this war.

"I'm from the United States of America," Thompson replied under his breath.

McClure barked a laugh that sounded more like a fox to the Navajo's ears. He glanced toward the other man in the darkness of their hiding space but could see nothing more than the last time. "Me too."

There was silence for several minutes then McClure tried again. "You got a girl back home?"

A mental picture of Sarah Yazzie filled Thompson's mind and he smiled involuntarily. She was beautiful, everything about her soft and womanly, graceful. His eyes began to water. *Must be the sulfur.* He cleared his throat. "Yeah."

"So do I," McClure said. "Millie. She's something else. Carves the name of every one of the enlisted guys and girls from our town on a laundry peg and prays for 'em each time she puts laundry out to dry, like her doing that will protect 'em. I don't know, but I don't expect I'll ever see her again. That's okay, long as what we're doing keeps her safe."

Thompson sighed. The ground was too darn warm beneath him. He shifted uncomfortably then opened his mouth to reply but a hand clamped down on his arm. "Someone coming," McClure breathed out.

Thompson froze. He couldn't hear anything for several minutes but Jim's hand stayed on his arm and he strained his senses to listen. How the hell could the other man, a *baligaana*, a white man, to boot, hear someone moving around up there? He was beginning to doubt it when he heard a faint crunch and then another, then another, as someone in boots walked by the opening to their hiding hole mere feet away.

Thompson felt the urge to hold his breath but knew that was ridiculous.

Finally, after several more minutes, McClure removed his hand and shifted a bit. "I need to grab some shut-eye while the sun is high.

Gonna be a busy night."

Thompson didn't reply, and before long he heard the deep rhythmic breathing of his companion. *Guess I've got first watch, not that I can watch anything. First listen?*

Thompson woke to a stirring beside him. It was the growing energy of a man about to get up. *Heat must have made me doze off.*

"Must be dark now. Time to head for a better position."

The two men stood and stamped their legs to get some blood flowing again then made their way out. McClure started up the beach, his eyes scanning the surrounding terrain as his feet sank in almost to his ankles. The strange black particles of volcano dirt beneath their feet shifted even more than sand, making forward progress difficult. He quickly grabbed his flippers, scraped off his feet, and put them back on, to spread his weight out over the surface, like snowshoes.

Thompson had been admonished several times during the mission briefing to do exactly as McClure did, so he quickly followed suit. They grabbed their gear and proceeded up the beach.

McClure picked a spot and pulled out a thin but sturdy fabric,. The two men used small collapsible shovels to scoop out a place big enough to hide, the detritus going on top of the fine material. In a matter of minutes, they had pulled the material over the depression they had created, staked the edge to hold it taught, and covered the stakes. Then they shoved their gear in and crawled in after it. It was hardly big enough to qualify as a foxhole, but it would do. They placed a cylinder at the entrance to allow air in. Finally, they could take a moment to rest. It didn't last long.

McClure turned on his flashlight for a minute and pulled out a T-shirt and lightweight pants from his pack to put on. "Well, that's enough of lying around, I'm off to do my job. Can't say how long it will take. Stay low. I'll be back with updates every so often."

Thompson twitched in surprise. The other man was just taking off and leaving him there. He had known that was how it would work, but a little shot of fear still surged through him. They were on an island surrounded by Japanese soldiers after all. He'd be a fool not to be scared.

As if in answer to his unspoken protest, McClure said, "You'll be fine, I got work to do."

The man must be nuts, maybe that was why he was here and

thought he could accomplish this impossible task. Thompson sighed. "You're crazy, just like those banzai Japs."

There was silence for a moment.

Thompson tensed. *Probably shouldn't call a crazy man crazy.*

Finally, McClure replied. "I don't think they're crazy. They're willing to do whatever it takes to protect their friends and family. We just differ in our tactics, and the way of life we want for them."

Thompson grunted noncommittally.

The edge of the fabric shifted and Thompson saw moonlight shine on the red hair of his companion briefly as the other man wriggled out. McClure was short and wiry, with a swimmer's physique. Thompson had no idea how the other man was supposed to complete recon of an island this size on his own, but nobody had asked for his opinion. He was just the radio guy.

The fabric lowered and Thompson began his lonely vigil. He started by getting out his T-shirt and pants, though he wasn't sure he really wanted them in the stifling confines of their underground refuge.

Thompson didn't know how long it was before he heard feet outside again. His heart beat faster. He reached for the knife and the compact flashlight he'd brought with him.

The fabric lifted as McClure's voice said, "It's me," and he slid into their hiding spot.

"How did it go?" Thompson asked as McClure settled in.

"I've finished the recon of the northeast quadrant of the island. I can't quite figure it out. There's something off here. I'll tell you what I've found before I go back so you have the information . . . in case I get into trouble."

Thompson didn't like the sound of that but his feelings about it wouldn't change any outcome. "How did you cover that much land so quickly?" Thompson asked, incredulous.

McClure gave a short bark of a laugh. "It's what I was sent here for. Now listen up."

"Okay."

"As we knew, it's a volcanic island with large amounts of sulfur so it's rough and rocky ground, deep gorges, high ridges. There's little vegetation, just rocks, boulders, and scrub growth.

"It's crawling with Japanese soldiers. They've added pillboxes, bunkers, and gun positions.

"Coastal defense guns are protected by concrete, there are also mutually supporting automatic weapons. Antiaircraft guns in pits. Mortar pits are sunk into the ground like wells and covered with concrete lids. Tanks are dug in with only the turret exposed. I've found tunnel entrances but I can't say exactly how far the tunnels go.

"There's a blockhouse containing radio equipment above ground, about 150 feet long by 70 feet wide.

If they were to radio that information out now, there was every chance the transmission would be intercepted and they would be found, so Thompson did his best to repeat what the other man said and commit it to memory.

McClure heaved a sigh. "Okay. Enough lying around. I've got to get back out there."

He wriggled toward the opening and out into the night, leaving Thompson to his thoughts. At first, he just repeated to himself what McClure had told him, to help him remember. But then his mind came back to the unanswered question – *how on earth is McClure covering so much ground in such a short period of time? Is he some kind of superman? Faster than a speeding bullet? No, that's just a character in a comic book. What man can do what he's doing?* It didn't make sense.

He took a deep breath and shifted uncomfortably. It was so bloody hot and the fumes were pervasive. He almost envied McClure the mission for the sheer chance at fresher air.

Something was moving around outside. Thompson froze. There was a snuffling like a wild animal then a sneeze like a dog. Could any animals live on this barren volcanic island? What if the Japanese had brought dogs over? Or if the Germans had joined them and brought those Shepherd dogs over to hunt down the enemy? *Crap!*

Thompson searched the ground carefully with his fingers for his flashlight and his knife. Before he could put his hand to them a series of wet cracks and a grunt stopped him from moving. *What the hell was that?*

The edge of the fabric flipped up as he found his flashlight and he frantically pushed the switch. Light flooded the small space and he saw Jim McClure, his teeth bared, red glinting on his face. McClure threw an arm up to shield his eyes. "Turn that out!"

Thompson did as he was told but he went still, trying to process what he had seen. Was that blood on Jim? And there was a tattoo on his arm. A wolf? No. A fox. What the hell? The man himself had looked strangely animal-like.

McClure moved into the small space and closed the fabric over them. Thompson smelled a definite tang of fresh blood. "You hurt?"

"No, I'm fine."

But there was blood. Had he come in contact with the enemy? Wasn't he supposed to be avoiding them, at all costs, to keep their mission secret?

Thompson licked his lips, his senses straining against the dark, his heart still pounding in his chest. "Did you run into any Japs out there?"

McClure grunted. "One."

"You kill him?"

"Nah."

"Why not?"

"If people stop reporting in, they're going to know something is up, that someone is here. We don't want them realizing that until we're well away if we can help it."

"What if he tells someone you're here?"

"He doesn't know what hit him."

Thompson breathed a little easier. "You hit him from behind or something?"

"No," McClure said, with an edge to his voice.

Thompson searched for an explanation. "Throw your knife?"

"No."

Thompson noticed the other man still didn't volunteer anything.

"I'll boil down what I found for you," McClure said, lying back with one arm thrown over his eyes wearily. He took a deep breath and sighed then began, describing the two airfields he had skirted and the third that was under construction. "Not much different from before. There are field fortifications, pillboxes, and covered artillery positions everywhere you turn."

Even as McClure related information Thompson knew he had to remember, his mind kept coming back to the sight of McClure in the light of his flashlight. He had seemed more animalistic than human. Was that how he was covering so much ground so quickly? Was there something . . . different about him?

"I need to head back out and recon the southwest quadrant now,"

McClure said wearily.

"You sound like you need some rest," Thompson suggested.

McClure chuckled. "No rest for the wicked." He crawled back out of their shelter.

Something Thompson had overheard echoed in his head now. He'd been getting settled in on the U.S.S. Blessman when a couple of the guys had met in the corridor outside the doorway to his billet and hailed each other like long-lost buddies.

"Did you go through Northeast Platte Junction? In Nebraska?"

"Sure did. Weren't they the best?"

"Even had a birthday cake for me!"

"Say, did you see Jim McClure?"

"From UDT training? No! Is he here?"

"Yeah, but, it's funny . . . didn't he have blond hair?"

"Sure! White blond!"

"Well, he doesn't now, it's red."

"Huh." Silence stretched. "You sure it's him?"

"Pert near sure."

"Well, they pulled him out of the final training on Maui for something. Maybe it was a secret mission where he had to have his hair dyed."

"That must be it."

The two men had moved on down the hallway then and Thompson hadn't heard anymore, but he had thought it strange because Jim McClure definitely had red hair. Red as a fox.

Stories began to drift through Thompson's mind, things his grandfather had told him, tales of the *yee naaldlooshii*, skinwalkers, former shaman who had done terrible things to become even more powerful. *No rest for the wicked.*

Could McClure possibly be a skinwalker, like the one he had seen as a boy? He had tried to put those thoughts out of his head and, as his father wished, become a modern man, but his grandmother's death haunted him. Now he thought back to the stories his grandfather had told him.

Skinwalkers had started out as men, shamans who had taken on the task of caring for the tribe, their spiritual well-being. Maybe they had been power-hungry and evil from the start or maybe they took a wrong turn somewhere. Perhaps being so powerful had gone to their head and infected their heart with a desire for more. That was why the skinwalker had gone after his grandmother, jealousy of her powerful medicine.

The evil witches had taken the wrong path, a dark path that no one could retrieve them from. They took part in a ceremony that changed them from something human to something subhuman. They killed one of their own family and ate the flesh. In the ceremony, they became much stronger and faster, inhuman. They would then have the power to turn into one or more animals and have an enhanced version of that animal's skills.

This was ridiculous, though! McClure was a white man, not a Navajo shaman. *But do the white men have something equivalent to the Navajo skinwalker?*

McClure displayed the characteristics of the fox, the red hair, and even had a tattoo of the animal. He might have a pelt of one somewhere. He could have the additional skills of a fox, the keen sense of smell, the wily skills of the predator, and the night vision.

But why would he have enlisted in the army? Skinwalkers were only interested in their own well-being and what would benefit them. Maybe McClure hadn't enlisted, maybe he had been conscripted. Or maybe he had his own reasons for what he was doing. Could a skinwalker be concerned enough with preserving his homeland to keep things the way they were by working for the greater good?

McClure arrived back after an interval. The heat and fumes had made Thompson feel vaguely sick, like he was floating in an oven. His mind swerved back and forth between going over everything McClure had told him and considering how to relay it in code, and thinking about what he knew of Jim. Could this friendly man really be some kind of monster? Monsters often hid in men.

Thompson tried to pay attention as McClure related what he had found. "There's some kind of tunnel system here, but I don't know how far it goes. I think there are a lot more Japanese soldiers here than we thought. I need to figure it out!"

"Tunnels, huh?"

"Yeah."

"How far do you think they go?"

"I don't know, I didn't dare go too far in one because they're narrow and there's no way I could hide if someone saw me. But it seemed to go on for a good ways. Some of the things I've heard and seen make more sense now. These tunnels could go all over the island."

Thompson couldn't quite picture it. "How could they dig such a tunnel system in the time they've been here?"

McClure sighed. "I dunno, maybe they were just expanding on something that was already here. Families lived here, maybe they built them to escape from the sun or bad storms."

Even as he listened, Thompson's mind was working on its own track. "Hey, uh, Jim, you got family back home?"

"Sure."

"Mother? Father? Siblings?"

"Mother and father. I had a brother and a sister, but my brother died. Sis married and moved to Iowa."

How did he die? Thompson wanted to ask but the words stuck in his throat. A skinwalker went through a ritual where he killed someone else in order to get his powers. Often a family member.

"How'd you, uh, get that fox tattoo on your arm?" Thompson asked, hoping he didn't sound as nervous to McClure as he did to himself.

"Weekend leave, in Hawaii, during some special training."

Thompson drew in a breath to ask another question but McClure cut him off.

"Sorry, no offense, but I really need to rest before I head out again. I know I'm missing something here, and I need to figure out what it is. It could make a big difference to our forces."

"Oh, sure, yeah."

Thompson closed his mouth and settled back onto tenterhooks, listening to the breathing of his companion and contemplating the situation as his hand lay on his knife. He wouldn't be resting until McClure left the safety of their foxhole again.

Skinwalkers were dangerous. They could turn on you at any moment. *Will I make it back to the ship alive? And if I bring the skinwalker, will it help us or destroy us before the battle even begins?*

After a time, McClure stirred again.

While McClure had napped, Thompson had come to a decision. He would follow McClure when he left on the next leg of reconnaissance. He had to know for sure if McClure was one of the evil witches.

As soon as McClure was out of the fox hole, Thompson began counting to ten. When he was done, he quietly crawled out of the shelter and followed the other man. As he opened the flap, the relief of being in the open air was bracing. For all that it was a North Seas night, there was a breeze and the built-up heat of the volcanic island radiating into the shelter had slowly been roasting the man alive. Now he breathed more easily and looked around for some sign of Jim.

Out of the confines of the hole, Thompson began to feel more sane, and a little foolish. How could McClure, a white man, be an evil witch? Maybe he should just get some air, then go back into their shelter.

There, thirty yards ahead and off to the right, the other man had paused and was taking off his clothes. *What is he doing?* The moonlight was patchy on the overcast night but he could see McClure fold his clothes and drop them in a hole at his feet then cover it with volcanic ash.

Was he going to run around the island doing reconnaissance naked? That seemed to be the case.

But as he stood there, Thompson saw his worst fear realized and he gulped air. A series of wet cracks carried through the night, slightly muffled. *I've heard that sound before.*

The form of the other man seemed to bend over on itself, growing lower, closer to the ground. though it didn't appear to be moving away. A cloud passed in front of the moon and when the light came back, an unusually large fox stood in the spot where Thompson had last seen his comrade in arms.

A shudder rippled through his body, alarm making him tremble. He had been right, Jim McClure was a skinwalker, an evil witch. He reached for his sidearm, then remembered they were surrounded by Japanese soldiers. If he shot, whether he killed the monster or not, he would die there too.

Should he go after him? Try to ambush him? Call the ship and tell them what was going on? Find out whether to try to bring him back? Would they believe him or think that the sulfurous fumes and heat had gotten to him? He could wait until he got back to the ship and try to convince his superiors of what he now knew to be the truth.

The problem was that skinwalkers were powerful. If he let McClure get back to the ship, he could wipe out half the ship's population before they confined him, if they even could. He might even damage the ship in the intervening time. Plus, Thompson was a Navajo. As much as they needed him for the code talking program, would they believe him over one of their fellow white troops? At best they might think him deluded by his tribal legends. At worst they might think he was crazy and needed to be confined himself.

No, he had to handle this here. But what chance did he have against a skinwalker?

Or he could radio the ship and tell them McClure had not returned from reconnaissance. That he needed to be picked up. Try to get off the island before McClure knew he was missing. Yes, but he needed to buy himself time.

Hurriedly, he scrambled back into the shelter and gathered what little he had brought with him, including the radio. He would find a safe place to call the ship, nearer the shore where they could pick him up.

Thompson scrambled back out and headed down the slope toward the shore. Without his partner's heightened senses, he didn't make it forty feet before his foot landed on a spot that sunk and clicked.

McClure heard the explosion and turned in his fox form, his nose going up to sniff the air. Was there some kind of native animal that had accidentally set off a land mine? Birds weren't big enough and he could sense no other animal out there. He loped back toward his shelter to check. As he neared the hidden spot, he picked up the strong scent of his fellow American. *Thompson.* What had he been doing out of the shelter? McClure smelled something else. *Fear.* Had the code talker been found by a Jap?

McClure picked his way carefully but quickly, scenting blood on the wind. The clouds continued to pass across the face of the moon, alternately plunging the landscape into darkness then lighting it up again. It didn't take long to find Thompson, the smell of blood strong.

He lay some twenty feet away from a crater in the sand where a landmine had clearly gone off. A groan told McClure that Thompson was still alive. One of his legs seemed badly damaged. There was no way to know what other injuries there might be, internally. McClure needed to shift and get him out of there fast, before Japanese soldiers arrived to check on what had set the landmine off.

McClure swiftly put his mind to the shift back into his human body. It was not without some pain, but he was used to it by now and it was momentary. He seldom threw up anymore. He pushed the change, urgency filling his mind, increasing the speed of the change, and therefore the pain searing along his synapses as bones elongated, filling swelling flesh.

With a gasp, McClure filled his lungs and shuddered, stretched his muscles, and with a series of wet crunches, everything popped into place. He hated running around naked but there wasn't time to retrieve his clothes at the moment. He took in the scene, bleached by the silver moonlight, through different eyes now. The radio was nearby. It seemed to be in one piece, but would it work? He slung it over a shoulder along with Thompson's pack then turned to scoop the unconscious man up.

There was no time to do anything for him there, McClure had to get him somewhere safe first. But the man would be leaving a trail of blood from the wound in his leg. He tore off Thompson's shirt and wrapped it around the leg, to stem the crimson tide.

McClure loped back to their shelter. After all but stuffing Thompson inside, McClure changed into his fox form and trotted back along their path, sweeping out the footprints with his tail.

He hoped Thompson was still alive when he got back to their shelter. What had the man been doing down by the water with the radio? Had the unrelenting heat radiating up from the ground gotten to him? He hadn't been out of the space the way McClure had, after all. Or was it some kind of overwhelming fear from staying alone in the small space on the enemy-held island? He hoped Thompson would be able to tell him at some point.

Just as he was finishing up, he heard a couple of Japanese soldiers who must have been dispatched to check on the explosion. He hurriedly finished nosing the site and sweeping with his tail to cover the blood.

McClure raced back to his clothes then shifted and carefully made his way to their shelter, not sure the other man would be alive, or if he would ever make it out of the shelter again. It might well be his grave. *Not if I can do anything about it.* He had left his brother behind on the shore of Normandy, but he wouldn't leave Thompson behind. If nothing else, he would get his body home so his family could bury him.

He squirmed into the space and found his flashlight to check the other man over. The first thing he needed to do was staunch the blood flow from the leg. He didn't have much to work with. He'd been given emergency medical training, along with all his other training, but the small field bag they'd each carried held a minimal emergency medical kit. He played the light over the man's leg. There was no doubt it was going to have to be amputated if he did survive. He pulled out the tourniquet and fitted it around Thompson's leg, firmly but not too tight.

He turned the flashlight to Thompson's face. The younger man was still breathing.

He checked the radio. It was wrecked, parts rattling loose. There was no way he could call for help or a pickup. What were his options? He could try to get to a radio, but he didn't think he would be able to get a message out to one of the ships. Certainly not in code. His best bet was getting him to one of the boats he had found in a cave on the water's edge up the beach. There were two boats. He suspected they had belonged to locals. Perhaps they had hidden them there to keep the soldiers from taking possession of them. He could wrap Thompson in the fabric they'd used to hide their shelter, then get him to the boat and try to make it to a rendezvous with the ships.

It would be a bit of a haul, especially on his own, and the shore here was no friend to anyone, but it was their best shot without the radio. He would have to make it work.

"Wha…?"

McClure turned to Thompson and lifted the light so that it illuminated the space a bit. "Hey, bud, glad you're still with me there. What were you thinking?"

"You, you're a . . . skinwalker!" Thompson panted, frantically shrinking back away from McClure, his hands seeking purchase to drag himself back, though there was nowhere to go.

McClure put a hand out. "Hey, hey, take it easy. What the hell is a skinwalker?"

"Skinwalker. Evil witch. Killed your brother to become . . . skinwalker. Evil." Thompson's breath came in irregular gasps, his back arching.

McClure shook his head wearily as he realized what the other man must have seen, him changing into a fox. "I'm no skinwalker, Thompson. I'm a werefox, created by the U.S. military to help win this war."

Thompson gasped again as McClure wrapped a bandage around his leg. "Were – fox? You . . . killed your brother."

McClure swore under his breath. "I did not. He was on the beach at Normandy." He swallowed. "We both were."

Thompson was silent for a minute except for his labored breathing. "You're were . . . fox? How?"

Jim's eyes flicked to Thompson's face then back to where he was working on the damaged leg. "I was a seaman, landing party on the beach at Normandy. Then my brother died, and they asked for volunteers for a special mission, extra dangerous, and I volunteered. They sent me to Florida for special training. Those of us who made it through that leg of training went to Honolulu to finish. Then they needed someone for a highly classified project. They said they were going to do something to trigger my genes, make me stronger, faster. They didn't tell me until after, they were hoping to create a werewolf. Instead, they got a werefox. Something about latent genes. Probably my great-grandmother, a Chinese bride from California during the gold rush."

Thompson gasped. "What happened? My leg feels like something tried to gnaw it off."

"You stepped on a landmine, but you're okay. I'm gonna get you back to the ship," McClure told him, sounding more confident than he really was. "I just need to get some more supplies to stabilize you then we'll get you to the boat. But listen, when we get back, you gotta forget about what I am. It's a top-secret program, they won't like you knowing. You understand?"

When Thompson didn't respond, McClure looked over at him and raising his eyebrows. "Understand?"

Thompson nodded once, curtly. "What 'bout . . . callin' for help?" he asked.

McClure checked his leg again. The bleeding had slowed considerably, whether because of swelling or because of the tourniquet, he didn't know. "No good, the radio was heavily damaged in the explosion. Plus, I could operate it in a pinch but I wouldn't know the code. We don't want the enemy knowing we're here on the island until we're gone or we'll never make it off."

There was no response. McClure checked Thompson's breathing and pulse. Both were still marching along. He hated to leave him alone in the condition, but he needed to find something to sedate Thompson or the pain might make him scream his head off when McClure moved him to a boat, which would bring the enemy down on them.

"Hang in there, bud. I'll be back for you as fast as I can."

Without the need to hide what he was from Thompson anymore, McClure quickly stripped and shifted into his fox form. Pushing the entrance flap aside with his muzzle, he left the den and headed for the nearest hidden tunnel entrance. He suspected the tunnels were the best place for him to find any medication for Thompson.

There was no way he was going to get Thompson down to the water by helping him limp along. The man was more out of it than with it. He was going to have to carry him.

Or he could leave Thompson behind. It was an option.

But it wasn't one that he could entertain. The moment that he tried to, his brother's face rose in his mind's eye. Either they would both get out or they would both die there.

So, he would clear the fabric off and roll him in that to help stabilize him. It would hurt - there was no way around that. But if he got him out to one of the ships, he would at least have a chance.

The obstacles? Well, it was almost morning. They would have to wait for nightfall to get him down to the shore without the enemy seeing them. Maybe the fabric would be more useful to drape them in the dark, it could camouflage them to get down to the boat. Then he had to get Thompson into the boat and off the coast without getting dashed against any rocks in the rough waters around the island. It might take superhuman strength to do it on his own. He could then drape the boat in the material to camouflage them somewhat. The enemy might cast a blind eye over it if it didn't look like something specific, just a dark patch in the moonlight.

Then they would have to travel out to one of the ships without being shelled by the Japanese or by their own people thinking they were the enemy. The Allied forces wouldn't be expecting them back without radioing in first for a pick-up.

There was a landing strip, that was how the Japanese were bringing men and supplies in and out, but he didn't know how to fly. That was one thing he'd not been taught.

McClure trotted down the tunnels, turning this way and that. They seemed to go on forever. As he had done before, when he came upon a single soldier, he darted back, in the shadows, to find another cross tunnel. Either they didn't see him because of the lack of light or were too surprised to do anything about it.

Then it happened. He came to an intersection with two soldiers in front of him. He turned but there were two more behind him. The four Japanese soldiers had him cornered in this intersection, up against a wall. He might be able to dart between them, but they were talking. They had trained him in the language and culture while he was undergoing conditioning after his gene therapy. His Japanese was not the best but he could parse out their meaning if he concentrated.

The one with the belt of a thousand stitches, meant to protect him from bullets, looked at the fox that was McClure warily. "How . . . fox

. . . island? Huge! Is real? Is ghost? Perhaps . . . spirit of ancestors . . .?"

Another man wearing a headband glared at him then shrugged his shoulders. ". . . ancestors, of course . . . real fox! You . . . superstitions. He . . . fox . . . dog . . . wolf . . . islanders . . . pet . . . left behind . . . evacuated."

A third man frowned. ". . . possible, but . . . see before?"

The fourth man waved an arm and McClure ducked instinctively. ". . . many tunnels, caves . . . hidden."

The second man scowled. ". . . enemy infect . . . disease…plague, fleas!"

All the men took a step back at this, but the second man raised his shovel as if to strike him. ". . . kill it."

The first man darted forward, holding his arms up. ". . . sick? You . . . anger ancestors . . . surrounded by enemy ships."

The second man grumbled but lowered his arms.

The first man pulled something from a pouch at his belt, unwrapped it, and tossed it to the fox. "Ancestor, welcome . . . nourish you . . ."

McClure sniffed. It was clearly food, he delicately ate it. It had some kind of dried fish in it.

The four men parted to let him pass, and the fox continued on his way.

He needed to find more bandages and medication. That was his first priority. Then get Thompson to the boat and off the island, back to the U.S.S. Blessman.

He sniffed his way through the tunnels, careful to avoid any more humans. Going into a small chamber, he could smell that it was where someone spent a fair amount of time. There were medals and a teapot. It was a small space, but not as small as some others. Clearly, someone of standing lived here. He nosed around and found a medicine box.

With wet cracks, McClure shifted into human form and quickly picked through the medications until he found the kanji for morphine and wrapped the medication into fabric that could be used as bandages. In less than two minutes, he had what he needed prepared and shifted back then picked it up in his mouth and began making his way out of the tunnels.

The Japanese had a system of tunnels that was far more vast than the allied forces had ever suspected. He couldn't begin to estimate how many people were under there. He needed to get this information back to command, but for right now, he had to get the medication to Thompson.

McClure hunkered down with Thompson, checking on him periodically, providing medication when needed, and aerating their space frequently throughout the day, in between resting to conserve his energy.

Now it was growing dark and time to move. McClure positioned himself near the entrance of their lair and listened hard, tuning in with every bit of the heightened fox senses still at his disposal while human, particularly the keen hearing. He needed every second he could get. He didn't hear anyone remotely nearby, so he exited the shelter and stood, looking around.

Slow is smooth, smooth is fast. He moved around the shelter in a crouch, brushing the volcanic sand away from the darts that held the fabric in place, then pulling them out. With one movement, he dumped most of the sand off the fabric then tossed it across, revealing Thompson and allowing the air to circulate.

He pulled the rest then buried the radio and anything else they would not be taking with them. There was no point, as long as he could hide it sufficiently. He gathered their minimal supplies. He picked Thompson up, putting him over his shoulder in the slack position to carry then arranged the fabric, over his head, and down his back, like a cape, so it hid them both, as they moved.

Down at the shore, he set Thompson into the bottom of the boat and pushed it into the water then jumped in. He used oars until they were away from the shore, pulling hard - focused on rejoining his fellow troops and bringing them the information they needed.

About a mile out, he lowered the motor into the water and pulled the cord to bring it to life. It roared. McClure heaved a sigh of relief.

He could just see the U.S. ships in the waning light. Distance was tricky under the circumstances, but he estimated twelve nautical miles. There was nothing for it but to set his sights and strive. Straining his muscles to steer the boat in the right direction through the choppy waters, he prayed his comrades wouldn't mistake them for Japanese and blast them out of the ocean.

As they approached, a boat was sent out to meet them.

"Identify yourselves!" a man called from the boat.

"Jim McClure, Lieutenant, Underwater Demolition Team. With Navajo Code Talker Daniel Thompson, private first class. He's been hurt, badly, by a land mine."

"Begging your pardon, sir, but how the hell did he trip on a land mine in the middle of the ocean?"

"We were on the island, special recon."

Silence followed for a minute. McClure assumed they were conferring amongst themselves.

"Okay, sir, follow me, and we'll get him seen to."

"Affirmative."

McClure felt like slumping in relief and denning up for a week to sleep but he did as directed. Once onboard the ship, he could report in then wash and eat and sleep. Maybe not for a week, but a few hours at least. Thompson would no longer be his responsibility.

McClure had just set foot on the U.S.S. *Blessman* and was watching the men carefully bring Thompson aboard when planes flew overhead. As he watched, there was a flash of light and the big ship rocked beneath him, throwing him against the hull and he fell to the deck. He couldn't seem to make his body obey any commands.

As his vision clouded in, the ship guns returned fire, and the sound of the plane engine changed to a whine as smoke began to pour from it. It descended into the ocean, striking with an explosion. McClure saw the light and then everything went black.

McClure opened his eyes to find himself laying in a hospital berth. He reached a hand up to touch the bandages wrapped around his head and a passing nurse called for a doctor then grabbed his hand and tucked it back down by his side. "Welcome back," she said with a smile.

His mouth felt too dry to reply but a doctor was suddenly over him shining a light in his eyes and asking him questions. It turned out he had been unresponsive and was no longer on the *Blessman*. McClure's head still swam.

"Thompson?" he asked weekly. "How is he? I took care of him in the field and brought him back."

Her gaze flicked to the bed then back to McClure, clearly trying to decide how much he had the right to know and how much he should know. "He's stable. They had to amputate his leg. He's comfortable, for now. But, he hasn't woken up either."

Shit. "I need to report what I found over there, on the island," he said, struggling to move, but his body was too weak.

The nurse smiled down at him reassuringly. "Don't worry, they'll be down to talk to you directly, they've been asking after you daily." She turned and left.

McClure relaxed a little. Daily? How long had he been out?

The nurse was right. It wasn't long at all before McClure found himself found himself honored with a visit from a scowling Commander Jergensen himself. "What's this about a special UDT recon on the island itself?"

McClure couldn't stand, couldn't really even salute but he attempted to answer clearly. "Sir. It was a special mission under Commander Hanlon himself, of the Underwater Demo Teams. I reported directly to him."

"I see. We sent word to Commander Hanlon. Recon on that island was a suicide mission, son. Why did they send you? How did you even survive it?"

Who would, who could, do it? Only a shifter. "Just lucky, I guess, sir."

Jergensen didn't look satisfied by that but gave it a pass. "What can you tell me about the conditions on the island?"

McClure took a moment to think, hesitating to speak. He disliked reporting to someone other than his CO since his project was a top-secret one. This man did not have the clearance necessary to know about his mission. He would report some information, but nothing that would give away his special abilities.

"Sir, as we knew, it's a volcanic island with large amounts of sulfur. Mount Suribachi is at the South end of the island. The best beaches are at the southwestern and southeastern shores.

"The northern two-thirds are rough and rocky ground, interspaced with deep gorges and high ridges. There's a nauseating smell of rotten eggs permeating the air and sulfur deposits release a vapor. It's a stark landscape - gray, black, and brown. There's little if any vegetation, just rocks, boulders, and scrub growth with a few trails winding across Mount Suribachi. Caves honeycomb the island."

"Son, you're wasting my time, this isn't anything we don't already know!"

McClure sucked in his cheeks. He knew he didn't have permission to tell Commander Hanlon about his mission, and the Commander should know better than to ask. "Sir, begging your pardon, sir...."

Luckily, a private hurried in at that moment and saluted. He held a mobile radio. "Sir, Commander Hanlon on the radio for you, sir."

Jergensen took the radio. "Go ahead, Commander."

Hanlon wasted no time in getting right to the point. "Please report on the status of Lieutenant McClure."

Jergensen looked at McClure. "I was just talking to him, Commander."

"Are you debriefing my man, Commander Jergensen?"

Jergensen arched an eyebrow, frowning. "I am taking information from Lieutenant McClure to go along with what the other underwater demolition teams found for the next briefing. We're in a hell of a fight over on that island, we need everything we can get."

"You are not cleared to take this man's debriefing, Commander. I'm going to have to ask you to desist," Hanlon said stiffly.

Commander Jergensen drew himself up, his face going red. He looked as if he were about to blow his stack but then he looked over at McClure again briefly and gave a nod. "I'll have him wait for you, but I expect to hear every detail. Over and out." He handed the radio back to the private.

With a blank face, he turned to McClure. "Alright, son, you've got a reprieve until your commander arrives."

"But sir, how long will that be? They need this information now."

Jergensen looked down at him and sighed. "Son, though I heartily want to hear what you know, and see if there is anything at all that we can use, the truth is I doubt there's anything you can tell them that they have learned in the last month on that island."

McClure's eyes narrowed. "Month, sir?"

Jergensen nodded. "That's right, you've been out of commission for a month solid." He stood up. "Now, we've all got work to do." The commander's tone softened. "Look, follow your doctor's orders and you'll heal up fine then we can get you back on active duty."

"Yes, sir."

Jergensen nodded, looking less than crisp in his uniform, and turned to leave.

The nurse came back with more fluids. This time she even had a clear broth. "Let's see if we can get some nourishment in you. We need to build you back up."

His heart grew heavy and his thoughts were a tangle of briars. Memories of his brother kept cropping up, as he had been when they were boys playing together, and that last day on the beach at Normandy. He wondered how Thompson was being treated, whether he'd make it. He'd done what he could for him.

Just eating wore him out, but he only napped for a little bit before he was woken by the big, blustery red-headed Commander Hanlon himself.

McClure tried to sit up but Hanlon waved him down. He sat on the edge of the bed and looked around. They were alone. "Give me your report, son."

"Sir, the island is crawling with enemy forces. What we see on the surface is only a fraction of what's there. They've enlarged caves and added tunnels, hundreds of pillboxes, blockhouses, bunkers, and artillery positions.

Hanlon nodded sadly. "We know that, now."

McClure searched his mind for anything that would be of use, with the growing conviction that he had failed in his mission. "There are antiaircraft guns in pits. Mortar pits are sunk into the ground like wells and covered with concrete lids. Tanks are dug in with only the turret exposed. A blockhouse contained radio equipment . . . ."

Hanlon just kept nodding as if none of this was news to him.

"I saw soldiers wearing white samurai headbands and the Sennim bari, cotton bands around the waist with one thousand stitches to ward off enemy bullets."

McClure went over everything he had discovered, detailing the recon mission, leaving nothing out. Then he got to the most important finding of the mission. "There are extensive tunnel systems - thousands of feet of passageways and multiple entrances. I found one natural cavern, but the Japanese have dug and enlarged everything. They're like ants under there, sir. There's no way to overestimate what's in there."

He sagged on the bed, exhausted from just talking.

Hanlon nodded. "Okay, Lieutenant. Your service is beyond exemplary. I only wish we had gotten the information about the tunnel system in time, but we've discovered most of this information over the past weeks."

The commander rubbed a hand over his face and sighed. "I'm

sorry, Jim, when you're fit to travel, they're putting you on ice, literally, sending you up to Alaska. It's been decided by the head of the OTA himself that if anyone found out about you, it would have a detrimental effect on morale."

"No, please, sir! I can still be of use to my team. I—"

He put a hand on McClure's shoulder. "You will be of use, son, just not here and now."

"But, my team?"

Hanlon looked down. "Son, almost half the team died in that explosion, and if the rest saw you shift, well."

"I wouldn't let that happen, sir," he pleaded.

Hanlon eyed him. "Can you state, absolutely and categorically, that under duress you wouldn't shift?"

Mcclure's opened and closed, once, twice, before he could speak. "That hasn't happened in quite some time."

"I'm sorry, Jim, it's been decided. In the meantime, get some rest and nourishment so you can get back to work. It just won't be here."

"What about Thompson, sir?"

"He could wake up anytime, but . . . ." Hanlon shook his head then stood and put his hat on. "Are you positive that Thompson has no idea about your abilities?"

McClure opened his mouth to answer the question honestly but found himself denying it. "No, sir. No clue." It was the least he could do for Thompson after he had botched the job so badly that he was being put out to pasture. Who knew if Thompson would even recover?

McClure watched his commander walk away then closed his eyes. He had thought he was going to be a hero, but they had decided he was a monster, just as Thompson had accused. Was he? Right now, even he didn't know.

From the private journal of Director Balaoo, Directorate of Altérité Security:

Keeping France safe has damned my soul so many times over that even I have lost count. Much of my damnation came due to my nurturing and protecting a body-stealing spirit of evil which also is my most effective field agent. Many times over, France would have been destroyed or again ground beneath the heel of a tyrant where is not for the machinations of The Phantom.

Other nations do likewise in employing those of great evil serve their needs because they, like I, know that one unpleasant truth can only be ignored at great peril. There are times when the only thing that can defeat great evil is another great evil.

I laugh to think how the world owes its existence to France's hidden evil, if only to staunch my tears.

Fallout

Thomas Karwacki

The light emanating from the multiple chandeliers and wall sconces that surrounded the ornate grand staircase of the Palais Garnier dimmed and brightened several times, alerting the operagoers that they had five minutes to take their seats. The throng of well-dressed Parisians streamed onto the main floor or mounted the wide staircase to their private boxes. The crowd was in a festive mood; the wine had flowed freely in the Ninth *Arrondissment* that evening, and the opera being performed, Verdi's *Otello*, had been performed here regularly through the 50s and was extremely popular. The sold-out crowd quickly filed into their seats. The lights dimmed one last time and the opening strains of the overture filled the opera hall.

Half-way around the u-shaped balcony from the stage, in a private box, a single individual sat, wrapped in shadow. The man wore a beautifully fitted tuxedo and had a wide-brimmed fedora pulled down low over his eyes. He was of medium build, with a lean, angular face. His right cheek was a mass of scar tissue. From his vantage point at the top of the hall he scanned the crowd. He appeared to be less interested in the opera than in searching for someone on the floor. At last his gaze settled on a man seated on the aisle left of house. This man looked slightly out of place amidst the finery surrounding him, his suit cheap and out of style. A tight, evil grin crossed the face of the gentleman in the box, bunching the scar tissue along his jaw.

The man with the scarred face raised his opera glasses to his eyes and followed the shabby figure as he left the gallery floor. He scanned the lower balcony levels, knowing his target would reappear in one of them. He finally spotted the man entering a private box on the middle level. The person sitting alone in this box had a typical Eastern European look to him-gaunt and lanky, with hair buzzed short. The man from the floor settled in next to him and looked out on the performance. The gentleman in the tuxedo raised a small radio receiver to his ear and listened.

"Are you familiar with Verdi?" The person in the box asked in a thick Russian accent.

"I have a passing acquaintance," replied the new man, whose name was Fabron. This was obviously the previously agreed-upon sign and countersign. Once the men had confirmed their identities to each other, the gentleman knew he was free to act.

As Jose Luccioni, the opera's tenor, took the stage the scarred man rose from his seat. "Thank God," he muttered to himself, "at least I don't have to sit through that damn Corsican plodding his way through this again." He quickly headed out the back door of the private box. A spiral staircase descended into the darkness beyond. He fairly ran down the stairs, eventually going much lower than the floor of the opera. Finally, the stairs ended at a solid wooden door. He knocked once and quickly entered.

Within was a brightly lit stone chamber. One wall was dominated by a large organ. Opposite a manikin stood, dressed in an out-of-date tuxedo with a short black cape, wide-brimmed black hat, a stylish walking cane and a white half-mask covering the right side of the face. Against the back wall of the room was a large metal pod with several hoses running over and out of it.

"Renard!" called the man in a loud voice.

Through a door in the back wall came a tall person in a butler's uniform. He had large shoulders and stood with a wide, forward-leaning stance, as though ready to spring in any direction. Jet black eyes stared out over a thick, well-shaped beard. Renard had the look of a street ruffian. His mannerisms, however, were formal and cultured.

"Yes, *Monsieur* Phantom?"

"The Communist is on the move. Ready the chamber."

Renard nodded and moved to the large pod at the back of the room. He flipped a toggle switch and the end of the pod slid up, revealing a padded seat within. The Phantom, meanwhile, had already discarded his hat and coat, and now quickly stripped off his formal white shirt. He settled himself onto the chair and leaned back while Renard wrapped a band of sensors around his chest and expertly inserted an IV into his arm. The Phantom reached up to pull a mask connected to hoses over his face, and gave Renard a thumbs up, letting him know he was ready for the chamber to be sealed.

As the door swung close and oxygen flooded the mask, the Phantom closed his eyes and reached out with his special ability, seeking the essence of the Communist amongst all the lives nearby. This is what made him so useful to the *Directorate de Altérité Securite*; as a spirit without a permanent body, he could pour his essence into the body of anyone he had touched in the last hour. It was simply a matter of imprinting himself with the target's DNA. Of course, this was…less than kind to the target.

The Phantom had made a point of "accidentally" brushing up against the Communist in the crowd right before the opera doors opened. To his heightened senses, the target's DNA stood out like a neon sign. With his current body secure in the life-support pod, he let his spirit surge out, leaping through the darkness and contacting the Communist's spirit. The Communist, whose real name was Remy Fabron, was not much of a target for French Intelligence. He was rather a sad figure, full of rage over his personal failures in life and eager to blame them on the system rather than on his own lack of talent and ambition. However, he was part of a communist cell operating in Paris and had managed to contact a Russian intelligence officer. Therefore, Director Balaoó had charged the Phantom with infiltrating the meeting and finding out the plans of the conspirators.

He let his spirit surge forward, taking control of Fabron's body. He felt the rush of having five senses again as he settled into his new form. He also smiled cruelly to himself as he heard, as if listening to a far-off echo, the scream of Fabron's spirit as it was ripped from its own body, never to return. It was a haunted, tortured scream that the Phantom was well familiar with.

The Phantom turned Fabron's head to the right, intending to ask a question. He found the Russian operative already staring at him. The man had a look of satisfaction on his face.

"Ah, there you are, Monsieur Phantom," the agent said. "I was expecting you."

The Phantom was slightly taken aback yet intrigued. It had been a long time since something so unexpected happened to him. He was also unsure of how this Russian cur had unmasked him so easily.

"Well, well, most curious. You have me at a disadvantage, sir."

The Russian agent gave a small smile. "My name is of no importance. I am here merely to pass on a message from the Commissar. It is he who set up this assignation, knowing you would come to investigate."

The Phantom mulled this over for a moment. This situation was getting stranger and stranger. "Who is this Commissar of yours, and what is his message?"

"The message is simple. Our operatives have learned of a plot to try to take control of a French nuclear weapon, which they will use against the Soviet state."

The Phantom stared at the little Stalinist messenger boy, waiting for the punchline. He began to laugh. "This is your message? What nonsense is this?"

The Russian shrugged. "It is not a joke. It is a desperate attempt to destabilize the political situation in Europe, yet our Commissar feels that there is a chance that they could succeed. Clearly, we do not wish this to happen, which is why I was sent to contact you. As to the identity of the Commissar," and here the Russian gave the Phantom a haughty, disdainful look, "he said you would remember him best by the wound he gave you at the Battle of Kursk."

The Phantom froze, anger and hate flowing in equal parts through his soul. He stood quickly, glowering down at this impudent dog. "So did this pig Commissar of yours have any more information to give, or did he just send you with this ridiculous story to anger me?"

"He said for you to 'come have tea with him, on the beautiful blue

Danube.'" The Russian agent shrugged. "Shall I tell him to expect you?"

The Phantom grunted. "Yes, tell the swine I shall meet him there." He looked out towards the stage, where Luccioni was at full squawk. He thought for a moment, then a huge grin crossed his face. He turned back to the Russian. "Of course," he said with a laugh in his voice, "it may be some time before you get to give him my message." As a look of bemused non-comprehension crossed the Russian's face, the Phantom threw his own body up against the balcony railing.

"No!" He yelled as loud as he could, "what are you doing?! NOOO!!!"

The Phantom then turned and threw himself over the side. He left the Communist's body before it slammed into the floor below. He therefore missed the shouts and screaming as people looked from the mangled corpse up to the box it had fallen from, seeing the ashen face of the Russian provocateur staring down at them.

The Phantom settled back to his original body, chuckling quietly to himself over the prank he had played on the Russian agent. His medical canister hissed as the door swung open, showing not the expected Renard, but Flopsy staring down at him. Flopsy stood about 5' 6" tall and was dressed in a peasant dress. She had pelt brown hair pulled back into a ponytail, a small button nose and a rather plain face. Her most striking features, however, were her ears, which were so long that they tucked back into her hair. She helped remove the PICC line from his arm, then handed him his shirt as he stood up.

"*Bonsoir*, Flopsy." The Phantom stretched before sliding his shirt on, then looked down at Flopsy in amusement. "I expected Renard to still be here." He let the question hang in the air, unasked.

"He will be back, Monsieur Phantom." Flopsy had a soft alto voice. She swiftly straightened the chamber and reset it for its next use as the Phantom finished dressing. "He just went to check on dinner."

The Phantom raised an eyebrow at this. "Yours, or his?"

Flopsy straightened and looked the Phantom in the face. She didn't bother to hide the dislike in her expression. "Both of ours. He's making a stew."

At this the Phantom began to laugh in earnest. "So, this is what a *loup-garou* and a *lapin-garou* have for dinner? Stew?" He shook his head, still chuckling. "Honestly, the two of you are proper comic opera. Now, if you would be so kind as to go take over the stew making and send Renard to me. I have some arrangements to make."

Flopsy nodded and turned, driving quickly towards the door. "Hop to it, Flopsy!" Her reply was a growl of anger, as she stepped through the doorway and slammed the heavy wooden door.

The Phantom shook his head, still smiling. He strolled over to the manikin and remove the wide-brimmed hat, settling it onto his own head before taking the cane in his hand. He checked his appearance in the large mirror next to the manikin, straightening his tie and running his fingers lightly over the scars on his cheek. His gaze rose to an oil painting hanging above in an ornate frame. It showed the likeness of a beautiful young woman, with long, light brown hair. The artist had captured her sitting in front of a harpsichord and wearing a flowing violet dress. The Phantom stop smiling as he stared at the painting. His expression became rueful. He had paid a small fortune to get his hands on this oil painting. Olympia would not have wanted him to have it. She had not wanted him at all. But this did not deter him.

"Someday, *Cheri*. Someday…"

Someone cleared their throat behind him. The Phantom turned to find Renard had entered the room. Renard nodded towards the manikin. "You only don that hat when you're going to see the Director."

"Yes, it seems that matters have become more urgent than I had expected. I will be leaving for headquarters immediately. Please call and let them know that I'm coming, then ready my travel bag; I'll probably be leaving very quickly once I return."

Renard nodded in acknowledgment. "I will see to it immediately." He began to turn away, then stopped and looked back at the Phantom. "Monsieur, I would appreciate it if you would stop baiting Flopsy. I am thankful that you give us work and a home, but I would prefer that you two would get along better."

The Phantom shook his head. "Ah, Renard, I value your assistance. Your services have been useful over the years. That is why I had no problems with you moving Flopsy in. But do not expect me to placate your pet rabbit just to ease your marital troubles. Now, see to my wishes." With that, the Phantom brushed by Renard and headed through a small door to the left. Down three stone steps, and he was at the edge of the canal which is part of the system which ran under the city. Back in the 1930s, the *Directorate de Altérité Securite* had bored tunnels from the subterranean lake that sat under the opera house, connecting it to their headquarters, as well as a few other government buildings. This gave the DAT agents the ability to travel around Paris undetected. This had proven quite useful during the Occupation in the 40s. A small wooden boat stood waiting there for him. He climbed aboard and started the outboard motor. The trim vessel quickly puttered off into the dark.

The Phantom climbed the wrought iron circular staircase and stepped through the archway that led into the reception area on the bottom floor of DAT headquarters. The marble walls held portraits of the former directors and other notables who had served the *Directorate de Altérité Securite*. The DAT had public offices at street level, but the offices of the senior staff, including the Director, were in the subterranean levels. The Phantom strode over the deep red carpet to the curved reception desk. He greeted the junior agent on duty there. "Good evening. I called ahead. Is the Director in his office?"

Just as the blond-haired agent was about to answer, the elevator doors on the opposite side of the lobby opened. A 7-foot-tall silverback gorilla wearing a tuxedo and top hat stepped out. He strode briskly towards the two men at the desk. "Good evening, Marcus." The gorilla nodded politely to the agent. He looked towards the Phantom and rumbled, "In my office." He strode towards the door marked 'Florian Hugo Balaoó, Director.'

The Phantom followed Balaoó into the spacious office. Dark oak furnishings were offset by light green wallpaper and tasteful wall hangings. An antique phonograph stood in the corner next to a small wet bar. A large desk covered in papers dominated the room. The Phantom settled himself into one of the armchairs facing the desk, as Balaoó hung his cloak and top hat on the coat rack and settled into his reinforced office chair. He regarded the Phantom for a moment from under shaggy brows.

Florian Hugo Balaoó was a direct descendent of the original Balaoó, who had been created by a mad scientist. After escaping his creator, Balaoó fell in with a street gang, using his strength and ability to communicate with other animals to assist in their crimes. After he was apprehended by the French authorities, he reformed and began assisting French intelligence. Several of his descendants have followed him into this line of work. Florian was the third Balaoó to hold the title of director of the DAT.

The Phantom gave Balaoó a knowing smile. "Tough night, Chief?"

Balaoó gave an impatient snort. "I've spent the last hour arranging for the release of a Russian agent who was arrested for the murder of a communist sympathizer. Thank you for that."

"You're welcome. You SHOULD be thankful, I probably saved you from some boring board meeting."

"What you saved me from," Balaoó growled, "was a much-anticipated dinner with my wife. Josienne is not very happy with you right now. I would avoid her at the next office party."

"I don't go to parties." The Phantom leaned forward in his chair. "Before that Cossack was taken away by the *gendarmerie*, he gave me some startling information. It seems our Soviet friends have credible information about a plot to steal a French nuclear weapon and use it against Russia in an attempt to start a wide-scale nuclear exchange."

The Phantom sat silent for a moment, watching Balaoó process this information. The well-dressed go brilla leaned back in his massive chair, eyes closed and rubbing his chin. Without opening his eyes, he inquired, "Do you think they are telling the truth?"

"It is possible. There are groups out there that would love to see the East and West annihilate each other. The Chinese or Koreans, the Deep Ones, even the Sway would seize the opportunity to become the world's premier power."

Balaoó nodded, sitting back up and leaning elbows on his desk. "Did they offer any proof of their claim?"

The Phantom bared teeth in a grimace. "Their Commissar wishes to meet with me in Vienna." Balaoó raised an eyebrow at this. The Phantom nodded. "Yes, it's him. The bastard is good at disappearing, but he always turns up again, and it is never a good sign when he does."

"Nevertheless, you'll go there and meet with him. If there's any truth to the story, we need all the information we can get. This is too important for personalities to get in the way, understood?"

The Phantom nodded. "Understood. As much as it galls me to admit it, you're right." He stood and gathered his hat and cane. "I'll collect my things and set out. Do we still have the private clinic in Vienna where Renard can take two of my bodies?"

Balaoó nodded an assent. He had a photographic memory and didn't have to go check. "The Döbling Clinic. I'll make the arrangements. Any particular bodies you want them to bring?"

The Phantom settled his fedora on his head, tilting it at a rakish angle. "I'd like him to bring the expendable ones." He gave Balaoó a wide, cheerful grin. "But then, that describes any of them, doesn't it?"

With that, he turned on his heel and strode out the door.

The Vienna State Opera House glowed like a radiant jewel against the deep black of the night sky. Towering over the street below, the building was a study in archways and Neo-Renaissance décor. The Phantom stepped out of his cab and approached the grand building. Five bronze statues, representing heroism, tragedy, fantasy, comedy, and love, stared down at him from their archways over the entrance. The Phantom glanced at them as he rounded the two fountains which guarded the building and entered the foyer. He swept up the grand staircase to the first floor, passed the Schwind Foyer and entered the Tea Room.

A small grouping of tables sat in the room where Emperor Franz Joseph had once enjoyed his tea. Only one was presently occupied; a tall man with long dark hair sat at it with his back to the door, reading the newspaper. The Phantom approached and seated himself across from the man.

The man completely ignored the Phantom as he continued to read his paper. He had a mustache and long beard. His hair was parted in the middle and tied in a ponytail. He wore a black shirt with a Roman collar under an old-fashioned double-breasted long coat. He stirred his teacup then took a slow sip, then returned to his paper without once acknowledging the Phantom's presence.

A waiter stepped up to the Phantom's side. "*Was möchten Sie, mein Heir?*"

The man answered the waiter before the Phantom could. "He will have a double espresso." The Phantom nodded confirmation of this order to the waiter who hustled away.

The Phantom decided he wasn't in the mood to play games. "So, I travel over 1000 km to meet with the KGB's vaunted Commissar Rasputin to discuss matters of utmost urgency, and here he sits reading the gossip column and drinking his effeminate herbal tea."

Rasputin calmly turned the page. "Hello, Erik. How is that talking baboon of yours?"

"Balaoó is fine. He asked me to send you his regards and thanks. The incompetents you keep promoting have made his job that much easier."

As the waiter returned and placed a coffee setting in front of the Phantom, Rasputin folded his paper and set it aside. His piercing blue eyes met the Phantom's gaze for the first time. "And yet, these incompetents have discovered a plot against your country that you French imbeciles had no knowledge of."

"So you have asserted. Would you like to share some of the details of this so-called plot?"

Rasputin picked up his teacup. "In due time." He took a measured sip. "Ah, chamomile and mint. Come, finish your cup of burnt mud and then we'll retire to my private box. We can discuss your problems while we enjoy the ballet."

The Phantom shook his head ruefully. "Ballet. A perfect artform for you Bolsheviks. Weak and inferior." He swallowed his espresso in one long gulp, set the cup down and stood. "Well, Grigori Yefimovich, shall we go watch the dance?"

Rasputin looked up at him with a slight sneer on his face. "Yes, the dance. There is always a dance. The question is, who gets to lead?" He finished his tea and rose. At six and a half feet, his lean form towered over the Phantom. "Follow me."

Rasputin led the way up the grand staircase to a private box directly opposite the stage. The gallery seats two floors below were filling rapidly as they took their places. After a few minutes, the rows of lights running along the balconies of the gigantic oval room were dimmed and the curtain rose. The orchestra struck up the introduction to Swan Lake.

The Phantom observed the dance for a few minutes then turned to Rasputin. "Well now, this is fun and all, but I believe we have business to discuss. What information do you have for me?"

Rasputin continued to gaze contentedly at the ballet. "You should be enjoying this. The role of Siegfried is being played by George Balanchine. He was born and trained in Russia before his family fled to France. He is now the ballet master at the Ballets Russes." Rasputin set back in his chair and crossed his legs. "Our intelligence section has been following up leads on a new group of seditionists. Usually these groups fall along ethnic lines, but we found this new group is made of minor government functionaries from several Soviet states. So far, we found cells in Estonia, Latvia, the Ukraine, and Georgia." Rasputin finally turned to look at the Phantom. "There could be many explanations for this, but I did notice one consistent theme between these locations."

The Phantom pondered this for a moment. "The one thing that stands out is that each has multiple harbors on either the Caspian or Baltic Sea." He inhaled sharply. "Does this mean…?"

Rasputin nodded. "The Deep Ones. They seem to be recruiting surface dwellers in advance of a *pusht* against the Soviet state. We have interrogated a few of these turncoats, and they've confirmed that the Deep Ones are attempting to gain control of one of your nuclear weapons. They plan on launching it against Moscow, knowing that an attack on our capital would cause our leaders to launch against their NATO targets. The resulting destruction would allow them to step into the power vacuum and become the dominant force on the planet."

"But why France?" The Phantom demanded. "Why not an American or British weapon?"

Rasputin shrugged. "We are not exactly sure. It may be that, since your weapons are not under the direct control of NATO, they feel that they will be easier to compromise. There is also some indication that the surface agent they've hired to assist them may have chosen your nation as a target."

The Phantom's stomach roiled with frustration. His espresso was not mixing well with the information he had been given. "So not only are we dealing with a hostile force from under the sea, but we also have an unknown mercenary with God knows what powers in the mix." He cocked an eye at Rasputin. "Did your interrogations give you an idea of where their target may be?"

Rasputin pulled a folded map from a pocket inside his coat. "We do not believe that they are interested in any of your aircraft or sea-launched systems. Their target will be one of your more powerful S2 ballistic missiles at your site here in Saint Christol Albion. We are not sure exactly when they plan to move, but it will be soon." Rasputin put the map back in his pocket. "We should proceed there as quickly as possible."

The Phantom sniggered. "We? You actually think I'm going to allow you to stroll into our most secure missile base?" The Phantom wiped at his brow. He seemed to be getting hotter in the box. "No, we will handle it from here, thank you."

Rasputin watched the dancers on stage for a moment. "You will need my help. Once we arrive at the silos, I will be able to sense the rogue agent. We will not have to spend hours searching the entire base. Besides, this plot threatens my country as well as yours. I will not allow these beasts to draw us into a war not of our choosing."

"I need help from no one. Go back to your scrying and nostrums, Grigori Yefimovich. I'm sure you'll be aware once I've succeeded in stopping the Deep Ones." The Phantom stood to leave, and pain shot through his abdomen. He doubled over, gasping.

Rasputin began to laugh. It was high-pitched and unsettling. "Same old Erik. I knew you would refuse help. I had your espresso poisoned so you would have to use an alternate body to return to your comrades. By the time you are back with them, my offer of assistance will have reached Balaoó, and he will have accepted." Rasputin began to laugh again, then paused. His features twisted in confusion, then he vomited all over himself.

The Phantom managed to summon a laugh, although his muscles were trembling with the pain coursing through him. "I guess it's a good thing I poisoned your tea as well then. Great minds think alike, don't they Comrade?"

Rasputin wiped vomit from his beard. "You imbecile, you know I can't be killed by poison. This gains you nothing."

"It gains me a little time to get out of here. I also get the pleasure of seeing you wallowing in your own filth on my way out. *Dasvidaniya, mudak!*"

With that, the Phantom staggered out of the box and down the staircase. He didn't care if he left a body here in the Opera House for Rasputin to explain, but he wanted to get outside to make his escape easier. The pain was beginning to become overwhelming as he quickly exited through the front doors and headed for an alley. As he ran, he pulled a small box from an inner pocket of his overcoat. Once in the alley, he slumped to the ground. Panting, he opened the wooden box. Inside was a large cockroach. The Phantom always kept one or two on his person for just such an emergency. As the searing pain in his gut reached up towards his heart, he sent his consciousness surging into the roach. It took him a few moments longer to adjust when he used a non-human host, but this was not the first time he had done so, and he was soon scooting towards an open drain, hoping to get to a new body before Rasputin recovered from his poisoning.

The Phantom sat up on the gurney where his new host had been lying and let Renard remove the intubation tube running down his throat. He impatiently tore the IV lines from his arms. "Get me some clothes," he demanded as soon as he could speak. The voice was raspy from disuse. He looked around the sterile white of the hospital ward for a mirror. Renard handed him a looking glass before turning to fetch his clothing. The Phantom looked over his choice; a corporal from *La Légion Etrangére* who had been court-martialed for crimes in Algeria and sentenced to death. The Phantom smiled cruelly; this one had scars already. He rose and began to quickly don the officer's uniform that Renard had laid out next to the bed.

Renard cleared his throat. "Monsieur Balaoó called and said you will be meeting Rasputin and a squad of special agents at the police station in Saint Christol Albion. You will have papers giving you clearance to enter the base, but there will be no way of knowing if the enemy has already infiltrated." He handed the Phantom a travel satchel. "Your plane leaves as soon as we can get you there."

The Phantom checked the contents of the satchel. Identification, a MAB Model D pistol with three clips, two M26 hand grenades, money, and a new cockroach box. He closed and slung the bag, then followed Renard towards the door. "Right. Let's go stop a war." He laughed harshly. "And see how that bastard Rasputin liked his tea."

The corporal leading the security detachment brought the jeep to a halt at the front gate of the missile base. A transport truck carrying the detachment pulled up behind. The Phantom and Rasputin, both dressed as colonels, led the way up to the waiting gate guards, who gave crisp salutes to the "officers." The sergeant in charge stepped forward.

"Good evening, Colonels. May I help you?"

The Phantom handed the sergeant his orders allowing him access to the base. "Good evening. We have received intelligence that someone will be trying to breach your perimeter security. We are here to reinforce your garrison and search for the infiltrator."

The sergeant looked over the papers and handed them back. "Of course, Colonel, but I can assure you there has been no breach of security so far."

"You are wrong." They all turned to look at Rasputin, who stood with his head bowed, a frown of concentration on his face. "They are on the base. Over there." He pointed to a solid block building a quarter mile away.

The sergeant shook his head. "That is the entrance to launch control. No one can enter there without authorization." Even as he spoke these words, all present heard a distant scream, followed by two pistol shots.

The Phantom and Rasputin turned and sprinted back to the jeep. The Phantom called over his shoulder, "Sergeant! Alert your men!

I'll take my squad straight there!" He jumped in the front seat as the corporal accelerated through the gate.

The jeep raced up to the concrete bunker that was the entrance to the control room. The heavy steel doors that led inside were each several inches thick. They had been wrenched open, seemingly by hand. The mangled corpse of a guard lay just inside the doorway.

The corporal waved two of his men forward. They quickly cleared the entryway, MAS-36 rifles at the ready. They then led the way down the interior corridor, the Phantom and Rasputin right behind them. Four more troopers followed them, while the corporal took the rest of the squad to clear the area around the bunker.

The corridor quickly led to a stairwell headed to the subterranean control levels. The team proceeded cautiously and made it down two levels before sudden gunfire from below caused them to stop and seek cover behind the stone handrail. One agent stood to return fire, but was immediately hit and fell, sliding down to the next landing.

The Phantom cursed. "We need to keep moving." He looked at Rasputin. "Any ideas, *Comrade?*"

Rasputin nodded. "Just one." He took a grenade from his pocket, pulled its pin, and tossed it over the railing. A moment later the grenade detonated with a roar that seemed three times too loud in the enclosed stairwell. Ears ringing, The Phantom led the way down the final set of stairs. At the bottom, three corpses were sprawled, flayed by shrapnel. They were man-sized, but were green and scaly, with webbed fingers and toes, and gills on the sides of their bullet-shaped heads. On the left was a metal door that had blown in from the force of the grenade's explosion. Shouting could be heard from within.

The squad ran through the doorway. The room was covered in gore. Blood and organs covered the instrument panels. Two eviscerated corpses lay strewn across the floor. In the middle of the room, two more of the Deep Ones held an Air Force captain between them. He had a swollen eye and his sidearm had been stripped from him. Standing before him was a woman in a black turtleneck and fatigue pants. She stood about 5'7" and had a muscular build. Her long brown hair was pulled back in a ponytail that still showed off a streak of platinum blonde running back from her temple. Her skin was waxy and had an unhealthy greyish tinge. Her blue eyes were wide and wild, blazing with insanity.

The woman had a lieutenant kneeling in front of her. Her left hand was sunk into his shoulder deep enough for blood to ooze around her fingers. Her right hand held a wickedly curved blade against his throat. "Give me the launch codes!" the woman screamed at the captain's swollen face. "Give them to me, or I'll gut you next!" Swift as lightning, she opened the lieutenant's throat from ear to ear. Tossing the still twitching corpse aside, she advanced on the captain, blade raised.

The Phantom recognized the woman as Eve Frankenstein. The former wife of Adam Frankenstein, she had been murdered and brought back to life by the same process that Victor Frankenstein used to animate his creation. Over the years, she had drifted away from Adam and become a mercenary, jumping in and out of bed with whatever faction caught her attention at the moment.

"Eve!" the Phantom cried out. "It's over! We have the base secured. Give up and you may get out of here in one piece."

Eve spun on them, screaming in defiance. She caught sight of Rasputin and hate distorted her aristocratic features. "You!" she raged, "I figured I might run into you, Erik, you sniveling coward, but I never expected you to let this neutered freak follow you here! You're really rutting with dogs now." With that, Eve whipped her arm up, flinging the knife at Rasputin. He dodged aside, but she used this distraction to pull a pistol with her other hand. The Deep Ones raised their rifles and began shooting. Two of the agents fell immediately, while the others dove for cover and returned fire. The Phantom shot one of the fish men in the chest, then turned on Eve. She grabbed the captain and to use him as a human shield. The last DAT agent caught a round from the second Deep One and fell. The fish man hissed in triumph, before a head shot from Rasputin sent him flying. Erik kept his sites on Eve. She had fired her pistol dry, and her grip on the captain kept her from reloading. She was looking around wildly, obviously considering her options.

"Stay back!" she cried out. "You will let me leave here, or I will rip this man's face off."

"He has the launch codes. If you kill him, your mission is over."

Eve laughed maniacally. "Who cares about the mission? It's just an excuse to make more bodies. Look how lovely they are!" She looked around the room, obviously enjoying the carnage. "But I know you've always been a squeamish little bitch, so let me walk out of here and I'll leave your little boy here alive."

The captain was half choked by her grip on his uniform. He stared pleadingly at the Phantom. "Colonel, please..." he gasped, tears running down his damaged face.

The Phantom hesitated a moment, then faced the young officer. "*Je suis désolé, Monsieur.*" He fired, striking the captain in the chest. As the man slumped, he fired twice more, this time at Eve's now exposed torso. She screamed in pain and fury and flung the captain's limp body at the two men, one-handed. As they dodged aside, she ran through the doors leading to the missile silo. They quickly ran after her.

A long concrete tunnel ran straight to the nearest silo. The walls were painted green and covered in conduits. Both the Phantom and Rasputin fired their pistols at Eve as they ran, striking her in the back. She screamed and stumbled into the wall. Looking up, she saw a high-capacity power line and pulled it down to her. She peeled the insulation back and grabbed the exposed copper. Eve screamed again, this time in ecstasy. She writhed in an almost sensual manner. Her wounds stopped bleeding instantly. The overhead lights blinked out as the breakers tripped. Eve spun and sprinted even faster, pulling ahead as she reached the steel access door to the silo. She grabbed the wheel in the middle of the submarine-style door, spun the mechanism to open, then ripped the foot-thick door off its hinges and flung it down the hall. The men leaped over the ruined door and followed her out onto the catwalk that surrounded the missile.

They stood at the warhead level of the fifty-foot-tall S2 missile. This particular missile had obviously been in a maintenance cycle. Several access panels stood open at different levels, left that way by the technicians when the emergency began. Halfway around the catwalk, Eve stood in a combat stance.

The Phantom stopped in front of her, pistol raised. "That's enough, Eve. It's over."

Rasputin spoke from just behind the Phantom. "Yes, it is." His pistol fired twice. White hot pain lanced through the Phantom's back. He fell to the catwalk, his legs unable to move.

Eve laughed as she walked back to stand next to Rasputin. "That's right! You walked right into our trap, you gutless slug! I guess I have to pay up on our 'wager'." She leered at Rasputin, rubbing against him.

"Later." Rasputin pushed her aside and stepped closer to the Phantom, kicking his pistol over the side of the catwalk. "Yes, Erik. Eve and I are working together. Our agents convinced a group of the Deep Ones that following our plan would allow them to extend their influence on the surface. They thought we were following the plan I fed to you. But now, we can detonate the missile right here, destroying a large part of France's *Force de frappe*. In addition, we get to eliminate you, the constant thorn in our side. There is no one else here for you to perform your unholy trickery on." Rasputin smiled. "Don't worry. I'm sure Balaoó will give you a lovely eulogy."

The whole time he was speaking, the Phantom had been reaching out, seeking another body to jump to. Alas, Rasputin was right; no one else remained in range. His anger fought with the pain radiating from the bullet wounds in his back. He looked around, then realized that he was only feet from the open access panel in the side of the warhead. A wave of agony washed over him, and he rolled over onto his stomach, whimpering.

Eve giggled again. "Let me gut him. I owe him some pain. Let me do it, please!"

"He's mine." Rasputin pushed her aside and walked up to the Phantom. "Come now, you dog. Sit up and face your end like a man." Rasputin put his foot under the Phantom and flipped him over. As he rolled, his hands came into view. The left was holding a small retaining pin. The right was holding the grenade it had recently been attached to. Rasputin stepped back in shock. The Phantom managed a laugh.

"Grigori Yefimovich, you talk too damned much." With his remaining strength, the Phantom pitched the grenade at the open access panel. It rang off the metal frame and bounced into the warhead. A moment later the detonation sent chunks of shrapnel flying through the electronics and protective casings inside the warhead. The Geiger counters attached to the walls at several levels of the silo almost immediately began to go off. Seconds later, the scream of a siren sounded in every room of the entire base.

Rasputin screamed in frustration. "You ass! You've ruined everything!"

"Yes, I have." The Phantom continued to chuckle. "You'll be lucky to get out of here in time. Even you cannot survive gamma radiation sickness. By the time you get outside, the base will be on full lockdown. No more playing with warheads for you."

Rasputin looked at the wrecked warhead, then back at the Phantom. "At least we have rid ourselves of you, *bol' v zadnitse*. Goodbye, Erik." Rasputin grabbed Eve's hand and ran out the door.

The Phantom lay his head back on the floor. His vision was beginning to dim. As the alarms continued to wail, he reached into his pocket and removed the cockroach box he had put there. He slid it open and held the small insect up in front of his face.

"Let's see how radiation resistant you truly are, my friend." He closed his eyes and let his consciousness drift away.

Slowly sensation returned. First there was sound, a hollow, booming echo that eventually resolved into the beep of medical equipment. He could feel smooth cotton sheets under his hands. Eventually he blinked his eyes open and was able to focus on the figures around his bed.

"Well, I must admit I'm impressed. We weren't sure what effect the radiation would have on your ability to jump." Balaoó seemed out of place without his usual jacket and pince-nez. The issue fatigues he wore made him seem even larger somehow. He stepped back from the Phantom's bed to let a nurse adjust an IV line. "You're lucky Renard realized who you actually were when that roach climbed up his leg. We got you to a body just in time."

The Phantom sat up slowly. He couldn't remember the last time it took him so long to adjust to a body. He must have been fairly far gone when he transferred himself. He cleared his throat, then addressed Balaoó. "Rasputin? Eve?"

Balaoó gave an exhalation of displeasure. "Gone. They were able to slip away in the chaos. On the plus side, the base personnel were able to lift the silo doors back into place and seal the silo temporarily. This kept the entire base from becoming uninhabitable. I understand that an American contingent from the OTA is coming with some top-secret Martian technology that they are hoping will help damp down the radiation." Balaoó frowned at the Phantom. "This of course doesn't help the casualties from the attack and those who were exposed trying to close off the silo. Do you know how many men we lost, or will lose?"

The Phantom waved this away. "Collateral damage. I stopped Rasputin from killing a thousand times that number. Now stop babbling and give me a looking glass."

Renard stepped forward with the mirror. Balaoó shook his head and turned to leave. "I'll expect you back on duty as soon as the doctor clears you."

The Phantom grunted an assent as he examined his new face. Dark hair, angular, Saturnine features. It seemed he would be tall when he could stand again. Not bad, thought Erik. Only one thing was lacking. "Renard. Knife."

Renard pulled a folding knife from his pocket and handed it to the Phantom. "It is rather dull."

"Good." The Phantom studied the face a moment longer, then began to drag the point of the knife down his right cheek in jagged lines. He smiled with pleasure as the blood began to stain his hospital gown.

Excerpt from Hidden Geography, the Sway training manual:

There are places where ancient creatures live on thanks to a conspiracy of nature and other forces. Do not believe those who tell you that the reptiles that ruled the Earth for millions of years are extinct. For proof one only need travel to a secret plateu hidden in the Amazon. Of course, the return trip is less than assured, especially since an enemy survivor of the first two Wars of the Worlds has taken up residence there.

The Martian and The Lost World

G.H. Monroe

Shadows of fear darkened the faces of the sweat-soaked Permindex employees gathered in the middle of their logging camp. They were there to cut trees from the heart of the Brazilian rain forest. However, no one was working yet on this morning. They'd been awaiting the arrival of the men in the small parade of jeeps that was rolling to a stop in the oasis of open ground at the center of Camp Cepeda. The perimeter was ringed by simply constructed cabins in a sea of humid, green jungle.

At the moment, all harvesting had come to a halt for the third time in the last seven weeks because of the disappearance of several workers. The count was now up to four.

A green tree boa flicked its tongue and watched from above as the four jeeps, painted in jungle camouflage, eased to a stop. It was clear that the occupants were military. The leader, who got out of the front passenger seat of the lead vehicle, was a barrel-chested man with a proud bearing, a side arm, and seven soldiers in his wake.

Gen. Javier Beltran spoke English, but he did so with the stilted precision of someone for whom English was not a native language.

"Mr. Risen, Mr. Jack Risen," he extended a hand to the shortish, thirty-something man who had stepped forward to greet him, "I thought that you were some sort of petroleum engineer or something. What in the world are you doing in a logging camp in the middle of the Brazilian rain forest?"

Risen shook hands and spoke with an accent that could have been Russian, or German, or a mix of the two. "General Beltran. Good to see you again. My education is indeed in petroleum geology, but we at Permindex have our irons in many fires around the world. I'm more of ... shall we say ... a facilitator, a Jack of all trades."

They shared a short, disingenuous laugh at Risen's pun, and Beltran got back to business. "I understand that you have had some difficulties?"

"Yes," said Risen, the acting site leader, "two more of our employees have come up missing. My men are uneasy."

"Surely you can appreciate the irony. *You*, Jack Risen of all people, being uneasy because people are disappearing."

It was either Beltran's chuckle, or his reply, but something caused Risen's smile to straighten out. Though unhappy that Beltran would make such a remark in front of others, Risen said nothing, allowing an uncomfortable silence to grow between them. Beltran didn't seem bothered. In fact, he seemed less interested in the conversation than he was in the huge cliff that rose high out of the jungle no more than a football field ahead of them. He looked up at the rock formation through the tiny openings in the canopy as he spoke.

"The jungle has eyes, ears, teeth, and claws. She is hungry, my friend. Have you taken precautions to keep the smell of your food from the noses of the hungry jaguars?"

"Yes!" Risen said abruptly. "Look, my company has paid a handsome honorarium to President Goulart, and we would like some security assistance."

Beltran's widening smile held more menace than the surrounding jungle. "Mr. Risen, your tribute to President Goulart has gained you access to this site and nothing more. *You* are responsible for your own safety. Your friends were probably taken by a jaguar, and the Brazilian Army is not in the animal control business. But ... since we are here, we will do you the courtesy of having a look around. Now what can you tell me about your missing people?"

Risen shot Beltran a look, but he answered Beltran's question. "The most recent two are Tony Martinez, he's an archaeologist, and Gavin Harvey, who's a heavy equipment operator, he drives and maintains the big machines we use to harvest and move the trees. Before them, there were two forestry engineers-Mick Duty and Vic Dawkins."

The soldier behind Beltran took notes in a small notepad as Beltran continued his inquiry. "And where were they last seen?"

"Follow me. I'll show you."

Beltran gestured with his head for two of his soldiers to follow him. Although the path that had been carved out by the huge tires of the heavy equipment was ten to twelve feet wide, it had quickly been reclaimed by the jungle. The four men, sweating profusely and swatting at a swarm of biting insects, swam down the path, through dense undergrowth with leaves the size and shape of tennis rackets. The clamorous calls of frightened black howler monkeys above them pierced the sweltering jungle air loudly enough to be heard miles away. As the men came to a clearing in the undergrowth where three large trees had been felled and removed, the roar of a jaguar, which was very close, startled all of them, except for Beltran.

That unsettling grin spread across his face again. "See, just like I told you. There is our suspect, Mr. Risen."

Risen ignored Beltran and pointed ahead of them, in the direction of the towering cliff face as he spoke. "Martinez and Harvey went down this path. They went out scouting. It was late in the day, two days ago, and they were marking the next trees they wanted to harvest. I told them it was late and they should wait until morning, but Martinez was eager. He'd seen some sort of tree that he thought looked prehistoric and was in a hurry to take photos and scrapings."

"Well, you heard the roar of the jaguar. She's close, and we are on her menu. You have local security people for this little ... expedition, don't you?"

"We brought a security man, he has weapons and his bullets fly just as straight as the bullets of your locals."

"If you think one security man is enough, Mr. Risen, you are very naïve? Also, the locals know the jungle. You need people who know the jungle."

Risen chaffed at this remark. He was anything but naïve, maybe cocky and overconfident, but *not* naïve. It was his *job* to never be outmaneuvered.

"We *attempted* to hire locals. They weren't interested. Every time we tried to bring some of them on, they were okay until we showed them where we wanted to go. Then they passed. All of them said the same thing ... 'Curupuri.'"

Beltran's sneer flickered off for a fraction of a second, and Risen didn't miss it. "Oh?" Beltran said, and quickly pasted the bravado back onto his face.

"What?" Risen demanded. "What did I say that bothered you?"

"I am not bothered," Beltran said, unconvincingly, "Curupuri, it is a silly superstition that the natives have. It's their word for the spirit of the jungle, something terrible, something malevolent, something to be avoided. None can describe its shape or nature, but it is a word of terror among the natives."

"What I just saw on your face tells me you might not think it's so silly."

"Just get yourself some local security people."

"I told you, they have no interest in being in our camp."

"Then I guess you are not offering enough money."

After this terse exchange, the men spoke genially as Beltran toured the places in camp that had any significance regarding the missing men. Beltran pulled Risen aside.

"Mr. Risen, may we speak candidly for a moment?"

"Certainly General, what can I do for you?"

"Well ... I'm just wondering what an important United States Intelligence officer like you is doing here, in the middle of a Brazilian rain forest."

Risen took a step back and looked Beltran up and down, as if evaluating him. "Gen. Beltran, I'm not sure I know what you mean! I work for Permindex and –"

"Mr. Risen, I know who you are and I know what Permindex is. It is a cover for the Agency, the CIA, and you are a legend. Quite frankly, I'm surprised and a little bit insulted that you thought you would not be recognized here."

Risen smiled. "Well, If I *were* what you say I am, I could tell you, but then I'd have to kill you." the sardonic smile flickered to something very dark for an instant, then returned. "But for now, let's just speak in hypotheticals. Your country has air defenses, like every other country. And I imagine those air defense systems have RADAR facilities. I further speculate that if Brazilian authorities picked up strange RADAR signals in a strategically important area, they might be curious, they might want to know what was going on there. I don't imagine U.S. Intelligence is any less curious."

Beltran's face told Risen that he'd accepted this explanation. Everything that Risen had suggested *was* true, but none of it was the main reason for his presence at Camp Cepeda. *That* was classified.

The passage of six days proved Beltran to be correct, at least partially correct. Nate Leonard, the short, wiry man in charge of site security, had convinced Risen to call Permindex Headquarters. Risen successfully lobbied for a bit more money in the budget. While Risen couldn't offer enough money to get *most* of the locals to join the camp, seven of them *did* have their price.

In Camp, some of the men passed around newspapers from the states that had been included with the shipment of additional weapons. There was banter about the recently completed 1963 World Series, in which the Los Angeles Dodgers had prevailed over the New York Yankees. Some were talking about the closing of Alcatraz Prison in the spring of that year. Others just milled about, waiting for the site meeting to begin. Risen had called the meeting to introduce the new local security men, and the new security protocols that came down from corporate.

"Hey, Pratt," Owen Casey said, "did you see where your Yankees took it on the chin?"

"Normally, I'd tell you to go screw yourself, but I'm not so worried about baseball right now. How can you be so calm with all these guys vanishing?"

"Meh, they're just idiots who wandered off into the jungle and got lost. I've seen it on these harvesting expeditions before. Once you're lost out there, there's a lot of bad stuff that can put an end to you; jaguars, poisonous spiders, bushmasters –"

"Wait, wait, bush-what?"

"Bushmasters, huge poisonous snakes," Casey said. "One of the longest poisonous snakes on the planet. Damned things get as big as twelve feet."

Brian Pratt began to lose his color at the word, 'snake', and the more Casey spoke, the more pallid Pratt became.

"Wait, why the hell didn't anybody tell me about these Godforsaken things?"

"If they had told you about them, would you have signed on?"

"Hell no!"

"Well there you go, Pratt. That's why nobody told you." While he enjoyed making Pratt lose his water, Casey thought it was time to change the subject. "What was Martinez's job here anyway?"

"Archaeologist," said Pratt, now intently scanning the ground around his feet.

"An archaeologist? Why the hell did we bring an archaeologist on a harvest?"

"Jesus Christ, I don't know, Casey," Pratt said, his eyes still scanning the ground. "Go bother someone else."

When the meeting began, Risen read a letter from corporate that addressed the lost men, and offered the normal, BS condolences that they offer when misfortune befalls one of the nameless, faceless cogs in the corporate machine. Nate Leonard spoke next. As head of site security, his objective was to provide a stronger sense of safety among the employees. To this end, he showed everyone the fancy new weapons that had been shipped in. Some of the new guns were powerful enough to bring down an elephant, which was odd, because the largest thing they should have to deal with was a jaguar or an anaconda. Leonard then introduced each of the seven locals who had signed on to the security detail, as if everyone wouldn't forget their names in five minutes.

The last order of business was the only part of the meeting that felt like anything other than propaganda.

"We have implemented some new security protocols," Leonard said, "One, no one is to leave camp alone. If you leave camp, you will do so in groups, at least two at a time, but preferably more. Two, whenever you go into the Frontier-" What the loggers called new areas of the jungle. "... you are to be accompanied by an armed member of our security team. Three, if you leave camp, record your departure and return in the log that will now be kept in the security cabin. Are we clear on these rules?"

After an unenthusiastic, but affirmative reply from the employees, the meeting was closed, and everyone turned in to listen nervously to the eerie sounds of the Amazon jungle at night.

In the subsequent days, everyone tried their best to get back to something close to business as usual.

Owen Casey, who'd tormented Pratt on the night of the big meeting, was the first to disregard the new safety rules. He wanted to get a head start on planning for the next day's cuts and wasn't sure about how close to the big rock face they'd be able to get. They weren't much more than a hundred yards from the vertical face of the formstion, and he was curious about what the terrain would look like as they got up close to it. To this point, the jungle hadn't gotten any less dense, and a hundred yards in this impenetrable jungle might as well have been a hundred miles.

The security rules were clear. It was late in the day and beneath the jungle canopy, darkness did *not* come gradually. Hank Madlock, Casey's partner, was gathering his supplies and getting ready to head back to camp when Casey suggested that they do some quick scouting for the next day's work. Madlock scratched his red beard, contemplating Casey's suggestion before he passed on it, pointing out that the new rules called for a security escort. Casey, however, was an engaging fellow, and it didn't take much for him to talk Madlock into going another seventy feet in ... just to have a quick look.

"Damn," Casey said, as he used his machete to chop his way through the dense jungle undergrowth, "this shit is thick."

"Yeah," Madlock said, "maybe this was a bad idea. You want to call it a day and head on back?"

"Nah!" said Casey, a fireplug of a man with a brush cut, and a tattoo of his granddaughter on his thick forearm. He pointed to two wide tree trunks twenty feet ahead of them, "See those two big trees up there? Let's just work our way up to them and see if the ground is going to be solid enough to get your harvester in there."

Madlock, now several feet back from Casey, was reluctant, but he agreed.

Casey saw it first. Initially, he thought it was the glow of the last fingers of sunlight, snaking down through the canopy to the jungle floor. But as he got closer he saw that this strange, luminescent glow actually emanated *upward* from the jungle floor. Three more whacks with his machete cleared the way for Casey to see the source of the glow. It was coming from some sort of ... rocks. They were strange oval pearl-colored rocks. They ranged from egg-sized to softball-sized, and they were set in a very smooth, very gently curving line.

"Holy shit!" Casey said in a near whisper.

"Yeah," Madlock agreed, "what the hell are they?"

"I don't know." Instinctively, Casey squatted down to get a closer look.

He tried to pick one of them up but dropped it with a yelp. The stones were hot to the touch, as if they'd been in an oven.

There was a noise to the right, and they both jerked their heads up. It wasn't a small noise, not like the rustling of a monkey swinging through the treetops. It was more like something crashing through the undergrowth somewhere ahead and to the right.

"Let's go back!" Madlock said, almost pleading.

"Look," Casey said, "see how the jungle isn't as dense behind this line of rocks. It's almost like ... a path."

Madlock was still looking in the direction of the noise. "Casey, let's go back."

A howler monkey screamed, and they both jumped. Another crashing noise came from ahead and to the right, but closer this time. Madlock pleaded again. "Come on man, let's go back while we still can."

Casey's heart was pounding in his throat too, but he wasn't *about* to let his fear show.

"Alright, alright. But we came this far, let's just go the last few feet to those trees. Then we'll get out of here. Okay?" But Madlock was shaking his head, the look on his face didn't just say 'No' ... it said, 'Hell no!' "Alright, alright" Casey said, "you just stay here and watch my back. Okay? It's only another five or six feet. I'll check the rest of the way myself, then we'll go back, okay?"

Madlock's eyes said 'No', but he nodded. There was another crash, closer, maybe fifty feet right. Three howler monkeys yelped and scampered away through the treetops above. Casey's bladder was close to betraying him, but he patted the air in front of him in a calming gesture.

"Relax! Just relax. I'll be in and out in five minutes and we'll be on our way. Alright?"

"J-j-just hurry," Madlock said, on the edge of tears as Casey slowly advanced, vanishing into the dense jungle.

Casey was no more than two minutes out of sight when there was a roar. It began like a half-second of elephant trumpeting and lowered into the rumbling roar of a crocodile. There was another crashing sound, something barging through the jungle undergrowth. Too close! It was too close and it was moving fast!

What he heard next made his stomach fall. "Help me! Help me! Aaaaaiiiiiiieeeeeee!"

Casey's high-pitched scream, and the sound of breaking bones cut through Madlock's soul. The jungle foliage thrashed about in front of him and he pissed himself. As he turned to run, something flew through the air and thunked down in the undergrowth between him and the line of glowing stones. He parted some large leaves in front of him, and saw a human arm, attached to a chunk of bloody shoulder, still in shredded pieces of Casey's shirt.

Madlock screamed, and instinctively started to turn back. First, he saw nothing but leaves, then a flash of brownish, leathery skin. For an instant, there was pain, a flicker of blue sky. He pushed against something solid, leathery. With his next breath, Madlock inhaled the hot rancid breath of the beast that was now upon him. The horrific inside of the creature's mouth was his last mortal sight.

His headless body dropped to the jungle floor.

At least one of the new security guidelines worked well. Casey and Madlock were discovered to be missing in little more than ninety minutes. They'd signed out in the logbook, entering their planned work location, and the time they left camp. When it was noted that they hadn't signed back in, Nate Leonard mustered a search team, consisting of himself and six of his native security men. They knew from the logbook entry to begin their search in sector Bravo-Four.

Even with flashlights, the unsettling darkness of the jungle at night is a darkness like no other. The dense canopy blocked almost all celestial light and there were no cities or towns nearby to throw off any light. This was a full, enshrouding darkness. They went to sector Bravo-Four, where the big harvester stood, dormant, and swept their flashlight beams from left to right, along the face of the jungle undergrowth until they saw a clue. It was a slight crease in the wall of foliage where Casey and Madlock had gone in. When they went closer and inspected the area with their lights, it was obvious that some plants had been cut with machetes.

Leonard bent over to get a closer look at the chopped plants. "This is it. No doubt about it. This is where they went in."

He stood up and motioned the front two natives to go in. Their eyes grew wide and they both stepped backwards. One of them pointed at Leonard and motioned for *him* to go in, while the other shook his head vigorously. It was clear that Leonard wasn't crazy about going in first either, but using the barrel of his rifle, he parted the plants and reluctantly took the first step into the undergrowth.

A bird cawed and he jumped, but he regrouped and took another step. His heart pounded as he took another tentative step and the bravest of the natives took a step to follow him in. A howler monkey screamed what sounded very much like a warning.

A jaguar roared somewhere off to the right and the rearmost native threw down his rifle and ran back toward camp.

"At least he left the gun," Leonard joked to no one in particular.

No one laughed. No one even smirked.

Leonard nudged a few more plants aside and moved several steps forward. His jaw dropped when he saw the glow of the line of smooth, oval stones. He wiped the perspiration from his forehead, knelt down, and touched one of the stones. The sweat on his finger sizzled and he flinched. He cursed and put his finger in his mouth. He lowered himself to hands and knees for as close a look as he could get, even smelling it. Leonard was so enthralled with these stones that he hadn't noticed what the natives were looking at, several feet to the right - ... until he looked back at them and saw their faces.

A foot or so inside the line of stones, and several feet behind Leonard, there was a single footprint. From heel to toe, the three-toed print was at least a foot and a half in length, and came to a point at each toe, indicating that its owner was in possession of some rather formidable claws.

"What do you think it is?" asked José, one of three natives in camp who spoke English.

"I know what it looks like," Leonard said with a concerned look, "but I don't even want to say what I'm thinking."

"Morte com chifres," came an answer in Portuguese, from one of the other natives.

He looked quizzically at José, who answered his unspoken question. "Death with horns."

Leonard thought for a moment, then gulped hard.

It can't be!

He had tracked something with such a print once before. He'd accepted that job strictly for the money, and he wasn't surprised that they never found any creature. But he remembered the job because of what his client, Justin Warner, told him they were hunting. He'd been certain that Warner was insane, but his tens of billions of dollars were quite lucid. Photographs of very similar footprints had been given to him as part of the hunt package, along with several sketches of Warner's intended quarry, a friggin' dinosaur. Warner's hunt had ended exactly as Leonard knew it would. Some eccentric rich guy had shelled out nearly two million dollars to run around his newly purchased island, chasing a creature that no longer existed.

But this time, the footprints were right here in front of him. Could this be real?

He answered his own question with a near imperceptible shake of his head. *No. That's insane.*

He stood up, and started forward, crossing the line of glowing stones. He'd gone a few feet when he noticed that his men hadn't followed.

He waved then forward. "Come on, let's keep moving. We have two lost men to find."

But when he looked back, the natives were fervently shaking their heads, no. Two of them said something to José in Portuguese, and left, taking one gun, and one flashlight.

"They say they will leave your gun and your light at your camp."

The search party now had only two flashlights, one of which had a dying beam, so they decided that discretion was the better part of valor and returned to camp.

Even though everyone in camp already knew that two more men were missing by the time Jack Risen started the next day's meeting, he opened the meeting by telling them that Casey and Madlock had vanished. Risen used the five minute meeting to emphasize that the two men had contributed to their own fate by failing to follow the safety protocols that had been announced the night before. They went into a previously unexplored tract of forest without the protection of an armed escort.

While this was probably a very effective way to ensure that everyone else in camp would take the security protocols seriously, what he failed to mention was that two more of the natives providing security had left camp. The security force was now down to Nate Leonard and five *very* nervous natives. There might not be enough security people in camp anymore, to facilitate such fidelity to these guidelines.

When Risen pulled Leonard aside after the meeting, Leonard could see the concern in his eyes.

"Nate, do you have a minute?"

"Sure," Leonard said, leading Risen off to the side where they were less likely to be overheard. "What's on your mind?"

"Are we going to have to shut this operation down?"

"I don't know, sir. I guess that's going to be your call. That's sort of above my pay grade."

The impact of the missing men was dissipating like the fog that is burned off the rain forest each morning. One by one, the passage of the next eight workdays burned the fear away. Workdays were gradually returning to normal.

Plans had been changed. The area where Casey and Madlock went missing had been ignored for logging since then, and today would be the first time anyone returned to Bravo-Four. Joe Steyer, Owen Casey's replacement, and Stan Kunkle were venturing into sector Bravo-Four. Steyer and Kunkle however, had the good judgment to radio Nate Leonard and request an escort from site security.

"This late in the day? Is this something that has to get done today?" Leonard asked, "All of my armed guys are tied up on other assignments right now."

"Just following security protocols, sir," Steyer said, "and that *is* Bravo-Four, you know, where those last two guys vanished."

"Well, I can go with you, Joe, but I don't have anyone else availa ..." just then Leonard saw Jack Risen, who he knew to be something of a bad-ass, come out of the communication cabin. "Just a minute Joe, I may have found someone to go with us." He called out to Risen. "Hey Jack ... Jack ... I have to escort a couple of guys into Bravo-Four. You wanna walk point? I'll cover our backs?"

Leonard and Risen were out to the border of Bravo-Four in less than ten minutes and Steyer explained to them what he wanted to do. Much like Casey and Madlock, Steyer and Kunkle were planning to move their work closer to the plateau. Leonard nodded and they all started their trek.

Risen walked out front, rifle slung over his left shoulder, and a machete in his right hand. He hacked away at the thick undergrowth and led the others deeper into the frontier. Leonard guarded the back, trying to keep up with the men in front of him while maintaining his watch to make sure nothing crept up behind them.

Leonard's head was on a swivel. His ears picked up every jungle sound, from the howler monkeys swinging tree to tree in the canopy, to the margays, which are the smallest rain forest felines, who were beginning their nightly hunt for various small animals. The first hint of the coming darkness was the gradual cessation of the daytime chorus of birds, the whistles of tamarins, and the rhythmic cadence of cicadas as these creatures found their way to roost.

Then came the brief period of silence that arrives at the same time every evening in the rain forest. For the four men, this was probably the most unsettling time. The silence wouldn't last long though. Soon the first katydids would begin calling, and the amazing buzz, whistles, cacks, trills, snores and croaks of the different types of frogs would emanate from the dense vegetation.

As it was very near the same time of day that Casey and Madlock had vanished, the soft glow radiating from the forest floor offered the same optical illusion the missing men had seen. Like Casey had days earlier, Risen thought he was seeing one of the last fingers of sunlight reaching into the jungle, and he too moved forward. Without turning, he threw a hand up behind him, signaling the others to stop. He unslung his rifle from his shoulder, laid it and his machete on the ground, moved some plants, and knelt.

"What the Hell ..." he said.

"What? What? What do you see?" Steyer asked, urgently.

"Not sure." Risen touched one of the glowing stones and recoiled, "Son of bitch!"

"What? Damn it. What is it?"

Risen retrieved his rifle and machete from the ground, stood back up, and stepped over the line of glowing stones. "It's nothing. We should keep moving. Daylight's almost gone."

The others followed him, but their eyes stayed on the line of glowing rocks, which they'd carefully stepped over.

"Just a bunch of stones, huh?" Steyer said. He and the others were still looking back with concern as they advanced farther into the jungle. But their concern would be directed elsewhere soon enough.

Ten feet farther in, they got to the two trees that Casey wanted to mark for cutting when he and Madlock vanished. Steyer noted that the ground had been sturdy on the way in and the trees were suitable for harvesting. Risen wandered a little deeper into the thicket and Steyer stepped forward to mark the trees. Steyer's mind wasn't fully on the tree that he was now marking for future harvest. He was still thinking about that peculiar line of glowing stones.

He'd have been better served to have been paying attention to his surroundings.

After marking the tree with an 'X' at knee level, Steyer tilted his head back and let his gaze slowly meander up the tree. He'd visually climbed about fifteen feet when his jaw fell, and his heart slammed into his throat. He knew what he was looking at, but he couldn't make sense of it. These creatures didn't exist outside of science textbooks and the imaginations of young boys. The others hadn't noticed the beast, or Steyer's reaction to it yet. Risen had wandered some ten feet ahead of him, and the other two had turned around to watch their back side more closely.

The sixteen-foot tall dinosaur standing behind the tree had the face of a snub-nosed alligator with a pair of four-inch horns, and it stared at Risen with a terrifying, toothy smile. Every few moments it twitched its head left or right, in bird-like fashion, to keep track of the other three men.

When Kunkle turned around to say something to Steyer, it started the chain reaction that led to total chaos.

He saw Steyer frozen in an upward stare and followed his partner's gaze upward until he also saw the brindle-striped, olive green and brown monstrosity. When he saw the beast, Kunkle let out a shrill scream. That made the allosaurus twitch its head to the left to focus on Kunkle, who saw this, and took off running back toward the glowing stones. He didn't stand a chance. The enormous reptile was on him in two giant strides.

When he heard Kunkle's blood-curdling screams, Risen whirled around, dropping his rifle in the process. He'd turned just in time to see the big dinosaur throw back its head, flex the thick muscles of its throat, and gulp down Kunkle's wildly kicking legs. One of his feet was severed and fell to the ground. As this was happening, Steyer stumbled backwards, onto the other side of the glowing rocks, and turned to run. But he tripped over a root, fell, and hit his head on a large rock.

"Shoot it! Shoot it!" Leonard screamed, as he leveled his own gun at the thing.

His first shot hit the beast high on the right side of its chest and didn't seem to bother it at all. The only effect it appeared to have was to draw its attention to Leonard. His second, and final shot flew off wildly into the jungle canopy.

Oh dear God, was the last thing to go through his mind before he too, became part of the evening meal.

Risen was more fortunate. The beast was between him and the path back to camp, but the foliage was dense. He flattened onto his belly and slowly eased backward into the undergrowth. It seemed to work. With short, avian twitches of its head, the allosaurus looked all about but didn't see him. He continued to creep backward with no particular plan in mind other than putting as much distance as possible between himself and the reptilian nightmare. He was shocked when he hit something solid. He hadn't realized that they'd been that close to the face of the plateau.

Just then he heard something crashing towards him through the forest, almost certainly the giant dinosaur, and it was close, extremely close. Risen jumped to his feet and looked all around. Ahead of him was a darkening rain forest with a giant, hungry reptile, and behind him, nothing but a sheer rock face. Whatever was coming his way was coming fast. He looked left, then right. That was when he saw it, a crevice in the rock. It might be big enough for him to squeeze into, and it might not. But what other option did he have?

As the prehistoric nightmare roared and snapped at the outside of the crevice, the hot breath of the dinosaur, putrid with the shredded remains of recent prey, blew into the crevice like some unholy blast furnace. With every chomp of its massive jaws, its blood-soaked, three-inch teeth clicked and gnashed mere inches from Risen's head. After several minutes that felt more like an hour, the roaring and ravening went quiet, but all was not silent. There was a sound, like the high-pitched residue of a xylophone strike. Risen didn't come out right away. In fact, he might never have come out, if not for what happened next.

"It is safe to come out now." The voice was low, robotic, and not loud. "It is safe to come out now." Unconvinced, Risen stuck his left land out of the crevice. He could function without a left hand, not well, but he could function. "Yes," the voice said, louder now. "I am speaking to you."

Heart pounding, Risen poked his head out of the crevice, and his jaw dropped. The dinosaur stood there, upright on its powerful legs, its tiny arms bent like those of a begging dog. Its hideous red eyes were locked on him, but it didn't budge. There was something between them, shaped like a metallic black fire hydrant, but much bigger, about eight feet high. It was wider around than an eight foot fire hydrant would be and had a row of blinking white lights stretching horizontally around its girth, two-thirds of the way up from the ground. Instead of the three water valves that a hydrant would have on the sides, there were two retractable arms with claw-like grabbers, one on each side. In the front, there appeared to be a retractable weapon of some sort. Instead of a nut on top, there was a glass-like cap from which a rotating beam of light projected. Since he didn't see anything that looked like a person around, Risen wasn't sure where the voice had come from until the robotic thing spoke again.

A rectangular panel about the size of a playing card flashed yellow light for every syllable it spoke. "Are you injured?"

"Uh ... no," Risen managed, looking back and forth between this odd being and the prehistoric monster behind him. "I'm okay, but ... Kunkle and Leonard ... the other two men ..."

"I have transported what remains of the other humans to my medical facility. They are being rebuilt."

"Medical facility? Re ... built?" Risen asked, venturing from the crevice.

"Correct ... or do you humans call it repaired?"

Risen gawked at the talking robot-thing as he crawled out from the crevice. "But ... they were ... torn apart."

"Affirmative. They violated the boundary, you all did. I find it surprising that you survived."

"Boundary? What boundary?"

"Did you not see the glowing stones? They keep the beasts contained. I felt that if I was going to take them off the upper level and put them here on your level, I should contain them. I have learned that it is not prudent to disrupt the ecological balance of the planets I visit."

Risen nodded towards the dinosaur. "Why isn't that thing eating me now?"

"I have implanted a behavior control device in its brain. It does as I ask." When the robot thing approached him, Risen realized that it was mounted on tank-like tracks which were its means of transportation. It helped him get up with its side arms, then aimed the front, weapon-like arm at him. The end of it lit up as it scanned up and down his body. "You appear to be in good health."

Jack took a step back. "No thanks to your monster."

"It is not my creature. I found it here while I was looking for a safe place on Earth after the war. I modified behavior control devices my people had built to use on humans and on one another so I could live here in peace with these beasts."

"Wait. You said Kunkle and Leonard are being ... re-built?"

"Affirmative."

"How is that possible? I saw them eaten."

"Our Marian technology is a bit more advanced than what you are familiar with. I merely require a small piece of a being's remains to rebuild them. I have been toying with the idea of repopulating my people, but I cannot be certain they will not disappoint me again. But you are concerned about your companions. As I said, I can rebuild them. Would you like to see?"

At the mention of Martian technology, it came back to Risen. He knew there'd been a reason this thing had tickled the underside of his memory. He'd read the briefings on Martians from the 1918 and 1938 invasions of Earth. He recalled photos of the slimy, octopus-like creatures with bulbous heads whose folded flesh resembled that of human brains. The vile beings living in those armored fortresses were roughly the size human infants, each with a single over-sized eye and a lethal beak. The mere thought of them turned Risen's stomach. By now his mind was so torn from the present that he had no answer.

Risen couldn't speak, but, mouth agape, he nodded. Almost immediately, a tingling sensation began at the top of his head and crawled down his entire body. He felt woozy, as if he was about to pass out.

The next instant he was stable again, but he wasn't in the rain forest anymore. He was inside, and it wasn't sweltering. It was cool and comfortable. It was also dark. The armored Martian and he stood, facing one another, in a circle of light about thirty feet in diameter. Looking all around, Risen could see blinking lights of various colors in the darkness beyond the circle. There were also clicks, beeps, hums, and whirring sounds in the darkness.

"Can I provide you with nutrition or liquid refreshment?"

This came from behind him, and Risen spun around. The Martian had moved, it was now behind him.

"Water would be nice." A square of floor slid open, allowing a table with a glass, and a pitcher of ice water to slowly rise up right beside him. Risen poured himself a glass of water, took a sip, and looked around. "Thank you but, uhm ... where are my guys?"

He looked down at the water and took another sip. *Damn! That's the best water I've ever had.*

A wider beam of white light descended from the ceiling in the darkness some thirty feet to the left. The beam illuminated two large, clear tubes, each fifteen feet tall and four feet in diameter. The tubes were full of a clear liquid, in which a naked Stan Kunkle and a naked Nate Leonard floated.

"Their bodies are fully repaired," the Martian said. "however their memories and all of the information that was stored in their minds, that's a bit more complicated."

"You mean they're zombies?" Risen took another sip of water, subconsciously relaxing thanks to the ideal temperatures, refreshing water, and the dark, calm setting.

"Zombie?"

"It's a word we use for a body that's alive, but without a working mind."

"Yes. According to your definition, that is correct, they are ... zombies. It appears that brain data might be irretrievable, as it has been with my own people."

"What about the others?" Risen asked.

"Others? There were others?"

"Yes. How is it you were aware enough of *our* attack to save me, but you don't even know about the others?"

"Do you have a title by which you wish to be called?"

Risen took another drink of water and refilled the glass. "Title? You mean a name?"

"Affirmative ... a name."

"Jack. I'm Jack."

"Jack, I do not monitor what these creatures do in their daily lives," he motioned back toward the dinosaur without looking at it. "Number three here, eats what he wishes to every day. I do not focus on what that might be. The only reason I was aware of your attack, was that number three's blood pressure rose sharply. You appeared to be frustrating him."

"Well I apologize for upsetting your homicidal lizard, but I wasn't quite ready to become dinner."

"I find no fault with your survival instinct. You asked why I did not know your colleagues had been attacked. I was merely answering your question. How many?"

"What?"

"How many of your colleagues were attacked?"

"Six, counting them," Risen said, pointing to Kunkle and Leonard.

"I will scan the area for fragments of the others. These beasts are untidy eaters and tend to leave scraps."

Risen considered this, stroking his chin between thumb and index finger. "So you're saying that you can rebuild an entire person based on the scraps of them left by one of these things?"

"Affirmative. I require only a few cells from one of your bodies to rebuild it. Six rebuilds will tax my resources, but I will do my best."

"So ... I cut myself on some thorny plants while I was hiding from number three there. Are you saying if you take some blood from that cut, you can build another me?"

"Not exactly. I can build a physical near duplicate of you. But it is not another you. Consider it to be like your copying machines. They make copies that are very similar, but close inspection reveals differences."

"How long does this take?"

"Between two and three of your days. But for you, in here, it will feel like much less time. Humans experience time differently in here." With a shake of his head, Risen mouthed the word 'wow' and the Martian continued. "If you wait one moment, I can give you a demonstration."

"O-okay."

"As I stated earlier, this procedure is extremely taxing on my resources. I can rebuild approximately six humans before I have to renew my resources, which is a long process. So your people must take care to avoid any further casualties."

"I understand."

"Also, this is a kindness. In return, I would expect you to respect my privacy, and refrain from making my presence widely known. I am a refugee, my presence here must be kept secret."

"I can promise that. But by my count, this would only be five men. I might ask you to rebuild *one* more person for me."

"Agreed."

A screen that looked like a huge, flat, television hanging from the darkness of the ceiling to Risen's left, lit up, and showed what appeared to be film footage of the area of sector Bravo-One where Martinez had been working when *he* disappeared. The image appeared to be taken by a camera hovering fifty feet in the air. The picture on the screen changed from color to dull shades of gray and panned back and forth until it came across a very bright speck on the image. As the view zoomed in closer, the bright speck grew and its focus narrowed in on about ten square feet of foliage. The brightly lit spots were clear now. They were stains of some sort on plant leaves. Suddenly, a beam of light from above encircled the stained area and became bright, so bright that it created a blinding glare that filled the entire screen. When the beam receded, there was a circular hole in the foliage where the stained leaves had been. A bank of lights came on to Risen's right and began flashing and flickering wildly. Within what seemed like minutes, a third liquid-filled tube was illuminated next to Kunkle's tube. Inside was a naked Tony Martinez.

Risen gawked in slack-jawed amazement.

Four mornings later, in Camp Cepeda, the workers milled about in a confused, panicked cluster. Some were making a plan to try to find Risen and/or any of the other missing men, others were tending to the catatonic Joe Steyer, who'd staggered back into camp several days before. The rest were talking among themselves about how they were going to get the hell out of there. A wave of quiet swept across the clamor as, one by one, they saw Jack Risen lead a parade of five naked forestry workers into Camp Cepeda. The alien had been unable to find remains of Mick Duty, the sixth man, but the other five were there.

As the Martian had warned, time wasn't reckoned the same in the Martian's lair as in the surrounding jungle. So while Risen had been gone hours by his reckoning, no one at Camp Cepeda he seen him in days.

"Oh my God," one of the crowd said, "it's Risen and he's brought back five of the missing men."

"Mr. Risen, are you alright?" another asked, as they crowded around the returnees.

"Somebody get these men some clothes ..." Risen said, pushing through the crowd, "and some food!"

Jamison Holtz, second in command at Camp Cepeda, pushed his way to the front and took hold of Risen's arm. "Jack, what the hell happened?"

Risen motioned for the five to follow him, gently pulled free of

Holtz's grasp, and strode toward the medical cabin with Holtz hurrying to stay by his side.

"Holtz, you wouldn't believe me if I told you. Can you get these guys into medical and take care of them?"

"Sure Jack, what's going on?"

"I'll tell you later. Right now I have to go into the communication cabin. Listen, these guys are in shock or something like it. You're not gonna get much out of them. They don't remember shit, and they're not talking. So cut 'em some slack, okay?"

"Whatever you say, Jack."

Risen peeled off towards the communications cabin and motioned for two of the native security men to come with him. As they walked, he gave them instructions in surprisingly good Portuguese. They were to guard the perimeter of the communications cabin, no one was to enter, or even come within ten feet of the cabin. The two armed men nodded and took up their positions as Risen went inside and locked the door. He went to a small safe, whirled the dial in one direction, then the other, each time slowing to the desired number. Finally, he threw the door open and pulled out a metal box, connected by a coiled cord to a telephone handset that was strapped to the top. He freed the handset, opened the box from which he pulled out a cord, plugged it into the communication generator, threw some toggle switches, and pushed a series of buttons. He waited about a minute, put the receiver to his ear, and dialed three numbers. He spoke loudly as if on a bad line.

"Hello? Peters? This is Risen. No, I don't want CIA, put me through to Colonel Fletcher Prouty in Cent-Com would you? This is high priority."

"Yes, yes, this is critical and I'm on the sat-phone. Wake him up, and do it now!"

Risen tapped his foot and drummed his fingers on the desk. While he waited, he kept looking out the windows to be sure no one was outside listening. After several minutes, a groggy Colonel Prouty picked up.

"This is Prouty."

"Colonel Prouty, this is Jack Risen."

"Jack, where are you?"

"I'm in Brazil."

"Brazil? What the hell are you doing there?"

"Do you remember that internal problem I was telling you about? The rogue element we have at JM/Wave in Miami?"

"Yeah, I've been working on that, are you sure this thing is on for the twenty-second?"

"Yes Sir, Colonel Prouty, we got that on solid intel."

"I don't know what we can do about it. We can't warn Secret Service, McCone, Hoover, or Johnson. We don't know who's in on it, or how deep it goes. "

"Well listen, I'm down here, checking out some Intel we had on Jean Souetre."

"The Corsican hit man?"

"Yeah. If someone big is scheduled to be hit, you want to know where Souetre is."

"That's for sure!"

"We had information that the CIA ogres were hiding him out in the Amazon with this forestry crew. My orders were to find him and neutralize him."

"Is he there?"

"No, but forget all that. I have a solution to the whole problem."

"You do?"

"Yeah, but you have to trust me. Can you get in touch with his doctor?"

Prouty sat up straighter in his bed. "Number one's doctor?"

"Yes sir."

"His doctor is always wherever *he* is. I can probably get to him within the hour."

Outside, Holtz approached the cabin and was stopped by one of the guards Risen had posted.

"Entrada proibida!"

Holtz didn't speak Portuguese, but the way the guard raised his gun, he could certainly figure out what 'Entrada proibida' meant. Holtz showed the man his badge, but the only result *that* got was for Miguel to rack a round into the chamber, the universal gesture for, 'this conversation is over!' Holtz understood and backed slowly away from the cabin.

"Yes Colonel, get it here as quickly as possible, and make sure the pilot knows he is to stay until he has his return cargo."

"I'm going to ride down there with him," Prouty said, "just to make sure nothing goes wrong. Give me those coordinates one more time?"

"Yes sir Colonel Prouty, latitude, minus 4.528721605294037, longitude, minus 63.27167284527589."

"Reading back, latitude, minus 4.5287216052940 37, longitude, minus 63.27167284527589."

"Correct."

"Have a landing site clear for us in seven hours ... and Risen ..."

"Yes sir?"

"... this better work."

Exactly seven hours later, a man-made wind swirled, cooling Camp Cepeda as the gleaming Black Huey Helicopter with no call numbers touched down in front of a crowd of gawking forestry workers. Risen ran out to the craft before the blades came to rest, and saluted the tall, thin man wearing camo fatigues and sunglasses.

"Good afternoon, Colonel"

"Good afternoon, Jack."

Without another word, the man handed Risen a small metal box and the two men walked into the communications cabin, which was under armed guard again.

Risen emerged within minutes, now carrying a duffel bag. "I'll see you in two or three days, Colonel Prouty," and with that, he disappeared into the jungle on the dead run.

Three days later, with a crowd of men looking on, Risen led a six-foot-tall man out of the forest by the hand. This man was wearing fatigues and had a blanket over his head.

When Risen led the man into the communications cabin, a grizzled Colonel Prouty sat up in his chair and put his coffee down.

"Now remember Colonel, this is just a copy. He's had a basic interaction program, but he has none of the memories, scars, or knowledge of the original."

Prouty nodded, "Okay."

With that, Risen checked the gaps between shades and window frames, then walked back over to the covered man and removed the blanket.

Prouty gasped.

Risen grinned. "Do you believe me now?"

"Oh my God, he's a dead ringer!"

The dead ringer remained silent. "Does he have the Boston accent?"

Risen nodded. "He has the accent, but not much else. Again, he just has that basic interaction program. But then, we don't need him to do very much do we?"

Prouty couldn't suppress a smile as he picked up his coffee. "No, I guess we don't. But I do wish we could take one of the dupes back to HQ, to reverse engineer him."

"Take Kunkle. None of them are any good to us. They have no memory of how to do their jobs. We sent the doubles back to their families to avoid lawsuits. Just told them something in the jungle scared them and left them this way. Kunkle has no family to send him back to, we've been stuck babysitting him. He's all yours."

Two days later, at two-forty-five in the afternoon La Paz time, the men were hurriedly called to the center of camp where Jack Risen addressed them.

"Men, I was in the communications cabin and just received some bad news from the states. About fifteen minutes ago in Dallas, Texas, the president of the United States was shot and killed. I'm calling it the end of work for today, and no work tomorrow either."

There was a buzz in the crowd as most mourned, and a few, who were political opposites, rejoiced. Risen, oddly unemotional, retreated to the communications cabin where he put in another call to Prouty.

"Hello, Colonel, please tell me that you got our duplicate placed in time."

"Yes sir, Jack. The victim was your dupe. Kennedy is safe and sound. The dupe was missing some scars, so we had to put a stop to the autopsy in Texas, but Kennedy's safe."

"Now, he can't just stroll back into the White House. Colonel Prouty, I work with these guys, as soon as they know something went wrong, they'll try again, and they *won't* fail. They do this sort of thing for a living."

"Don't worry," Prouty said, "Lyndon is probably on Air Force One taking the oath as we speak. Kennedy will be a shadow president from now on. We've moved him to an undisclosed location. You're a hero, Jack. No one can ever *know* you're a hero, but you're a hero nonetheless."

Risen put away the sat-phone, got a bottle of Scotch from the back of the bottom desk drawer, added a hit to his coffee, and took a sip. He kicked his feet up on the desk, leaned back in his chair, put his hands behind his head, and smiled.

A Time, A Place, and A Purpose
Glossary of Terms

ARVN – Army of the Republic of South Vietnam.

ATSB - Advanced Tactical Support Base – small, forward operational base usually manned by about a dozen U.S. Navy and about fifty South Vietnamese Navy riverine personnel.

Black Ponies – Attack (Light) Squadron FOUR - Flew fixed-wing twin boom, twin turboprop driven aircraft with 2-man crew, armed with four M60 machineguns and pods of zuni rockets.

Coxswain – Navy crewman at the controls of a boat.

Dufflebag – Electronic device capable of detecting movement of personnel remotely and at a distance by sensing body temperature.

FASU – Fleet Air Support Unit – provided repair, maintenance and logistical support for aviation squadrons.

Hootch – sleeping quarters for about a dozen personnel, made of wooden framework, plywood, screening, and corrugated metal roof, a bit larger than a one-car garage.

ISB – Intermediate Support Base – base of operation where some repair and refitting of patrol craft was possible, stores of food, fuel, and munitions were available, and from which one or a few helicopters could provide air support.

LSB – Logistics Support Base – manned by hundreds of personnel, provided heavy maintenance and repair and logistical support for squadrons of patrol boats and aircraft.

MACV – Military Assistance Command Vietnam – Headquarters for all U.S. military operations in Vietnam, located in Saigon.

NAB – Naval Amphibious Base – Home port and training center

for SEAL, NAG, and other amphibious naval units, located in the U.S.

NAG – Naval Advisory Group – small units of special U.S. Naval personnel who advised and operated closely with the South Vietnamese Navy riverine forces.

NVA – North Vietnamese Army.

PBR – Patrol Boat Riverine – 30 foot, fiberglass hulled boat with 4-man crew, armed with one twin 50-cal. machinegun turret forward and one M60 machinegun mounted on each side.

SEAL – U.S. Naval Special Warfare Group - elite, special forces operating on SEa, Air and Land, performing unconventional operations in small, detached units of up to a dozen personnel.

Seawolves – Helicopter Attack (Light) Squadron THREE - Flew single-rotor UH1 (Huey) helicopters, manned by 4-man crew, armed with one M60 machinegun at each side door and a forward mounted, maneuverable minigun.

SERE school – Survival, Evasion, Resistance, and Escape training; part of the special training required for SEAL and NAG personnel.

Skimmer Boat – 14 foot, flat bottom, blunt bow boat, armed with one M60 machine gun mounted forward on a pedestal, a helm midship, and an outboard engine at the stern.

Excerpt from a letter from the Protector General of the Sway:

As I've said before, war is hell. War between monsters makes it such that even the devil grows pale.

A Time, a Place, and a Purpose

Dave Muffley

S EAL Team ONE, Detachment GOLF, had just one more mission to complete before rotating out of Logistic Support Base Binh Thuy, Vietnam and back to their homeport of Naval Amphibious Base (NAB) Little Creek near Virginia Beach. That is, unless another Seawolf helicopter or a Black Pony aircraft got shot down, and the SEALs needed to go out and look for survivors.

That's the kind of missions they did, mostly, during this six-month rotation. Both the Seawolves and the Black Ponies had lost a few birds. Unless the war ended, Team ONE would be back in-country again to relieve Team TWO after six months, in July '72. By this time, SEAL Team TWO was preparing to depart their homeport of NAB Coronado on North Island in San Diego Bay.

While most U.S. military personnel in Vietnam served in-country for a one-year to-the-day tour and were then replaced individually, members of the U.S. Naval Special Warfare Group, commonly known as SEALs, were rotated in and out of country together as a team on a six-month basis. As the name SEAL implies, they operate on Sea, Air, and Land, doing the type of tasks that would be too dangerous for others. These three environments in which they are highly trained to operate are well symbolized by the Trident emblem they proudly wear on their chests.

One of the accomplishments of Team ONE's past six-month rotation was the turning of a Viet Cong soldier into a confidential informant. Ever since the day they'd surprised and captured him on a trail in the U-Minh Forest, interrogated him back at Binh Thuy, then decided to trust him and turn him loose again on the same trail, they'd been rendezvousing with him at the same spot periodically to gather intel.

Team ONE's last chore was to clear the overgrown foliage choking an old canal so it could be dredged out, thereby opening a shortcut from one tributary of the Mekong River to another in the delta region.

Some engineers in an office up in Saigon, in their infinite wisdom, had devised a plan for accomplishing that daunting task. The next morning, Detachment GOLF would find out if it worked. It would, however, take more than their own few men treading water and crawling through mud to guide a long, floating two-inch diameter fire hose filled with plastic explosives into the overgrown canal. They needed about a dozen men in the river and canal to push the hose along, while others unrolled it from a spool on the back of a patrol boat – river (PBR). Another PBR stood by as well, with all hands—four South Vietnamese Navy sailors and one American advisor—manning their guns to keep watch over those involved in the operation.

Lieutenant Commander Calvin Lawrence entered the SEAL's hootch and interrupted the men playing cards. "Petty Officer Gomez, are you up for accompanying us in the morning?"

"Looking forward to it, sir. I know someone else who's also available to help, if that's alright."

"Who's that? Is he a good swimmer?"

"Lieutenant Shane MacTire. He's a great swimmer. Swam across San Diego Bay same as you guys."

"How did he do that? He's not a SEAL."

"He's Naval Advisory Group, so he completed the whole SERE school. He didn't have to do the swim training part, but he got the instructors to let him do the swim from Coronado to the 25th Street liberty launch dock with the SEAL trainees, just to show he could."

"Very well, see if he's available, and tell him we're mustering here at 0800."

Treading water along the bend of the firehose, Julian Gomez laughed as he commented to the next man on the hose, "Hey Lieutenant, you swim pretty well, for a – you know – an officer. Are you doing the doggie paddle?"

"That's enough of that, Gomez." Shane MacTire replied. He said it loud enough for others to know that he wouldn't be disrespected, then flashed a quick smile at his friend. Some men near the end of the hose close to the PBR were already climbing aboard, as the hose was now completely off the reel with its trailing end making its way to the mouth of the canal as the men treading water in the river carefully passed it along.

When the hose end reached Julian, then Shane, they both started swimming toward the boat. Chief John Martin and another man remained at the confluence of the river and canal to finish hooking up the detonator, while those farther into the canal crawled out through the muck.

In a few minutes, with those last men all aboard, Lieutenant Commander Lawrence gave the order for both boats to make way to a safe distance upstream. Then, with both PBR crews and their twelve passengers watching the small opening on the riverbank, he tripped the detonator.

Instantly, all vision of the bank was blurred, along with the jungle and sky above. All Shane saw through the sunglasses he wore constantly during the day was a vast, brownish fuzziness from the surface of the water up into the overcast sky. His other senses reacted to the impact of a deafening "crack" and a concussion of air that hurt his ears and thudded against his chest. He noticed an increase in the foul smell he'd sensed since they first approached the canal.

The sky seemed to fall as sheets of water, mud, and palm tree fronds pummeled them from above. They clearly hadn't backed off upstream far enough. After a minute that seemed like ten, it was safe for both boats to approach slowly and survey the damage–or, hopefully, improvement. What they found, among the dead fish and debris, was that they could not determine if they'd accomplished more harm than good and certainly couldn't enter the canal until the mess was cleared away.

Lieutenant Commander Lawrence announced, "Well, we did our part. It'll be up to the River Rats to come and clear out what we knocked loose. Let's head back to Binh Thuy." Turning and looking up at the taller man, he asked, "Lieutenant, will you join us for our little Christmas celebration in Charlie's Den tonight?

"Charlie's Den, sir?" Shane inquired.

"Oh, that's what we call the hootch we converted into the officer's club. I don't believe I've ever seen you there. It's behind the mess hall."

"Very well, sir, I'll be there."

"Just bring a thirst. I owe you a few for your help today."

Everyone on the boats seemed happy with what they'd done. But someone, or rather some*thing*, watching from the river's edge nearby wasn't happy at all.

Three months later, Commander Brian O'Connell, commanding officer of SEAL Team TWO and deployed with Detachment GOLF at Binh Thuy, leaned back in his chair and rubbed his salt-and-pepper brush cut. He examined aerial photos he'd just received from MACV Headquarters, gathered from a flyover of a remote region in the U-Minh Forest. The region had been reported by the local Dufflebag unit as showing considerable human activity on their electronic body temperature sensing equipment.

And now this, he thought. *The enemy has been active indeed! They've cut a clearing in the jungle and erected several huts with metal roofs, not unlike our hootches. I wonder if this has something to do with all those men going missing from the PBR patrols lately?*

He called out, "Chief Nazaro! I think it's time we make another call on our favorite VC soldier."

The scuttlebutt around the card game that evening suggested their next operation would be some sort of reconnaissance mission.

The brawny, bronze-skinned Chief Jess Nazaro informed the short and squat Julian Gomez, "You can go with us tonight, but when we get to where we're going, you stay with the boats. You know I like the idea of having a medical corpsman close at hand, but what we need for this op is just a few people with good ears and eyes, but who can't be heard or seen."

Julian saw concern in the chief's normally confident expression, but spoke up anyway, "Chief, I know the man you need on this op. He has super-human sight and hearing, and he moves with the stealth of a predator."

"Oh yeah? And just who might that be?"

"Lieutenant MacTire."

Commander O'Connell entered the room. "MacTire? Who is he?"

Julian answered, "He's from Naval Advisory Group staff. He's the command historian, sir."

"The command historian? What's he doing at Binh Thuy?"

"He came down from Naval Forces Vietnam Headquarters in Saigon to observe and document the progress of the Vietnamization Program. The training effectiveness and transfer of assets and logistics is the way he explains it. He reports directly to Admiral Adams."

Chief Nazaro interjected, "Gomez thinks we should take him along tonight, sir."

"A staff officer? Why, Gomez?" the commander asked.

"He's an exceptional man, sir. His senses of sight, sound, and smell are far more acute than the average person. Especially his night vision. I'm not saying I know why he can do what he can, just that it's so. It's been tested and proven medically. The last time he was here, Team ONE used him on ops a number of times."

"They did? Has he got any combat experience?"

"He was at Song Ong Doc the night it was overrun, sir."

"Song Ong Doc, you say! Go tell him I want to talk to him."

Julian left his cards face down on the table and exited the hootch. In a few minutes, Lieutenant Shane MacTire knocked and entered with Julian close behind him.

"You wanted to see me about something, Commander?"

The commander looked up at the tall, slender 30-year-old with thick, dark hair and said, "Yes. Gomez here says you were at Song Ong Doc. How can that be? That was about a year and a half ago."

"It was 20 October 70, sir. I was halfway through my first tour in-country. I'm now in my second voluntary six-month extension."

Commander O'Connell asked, "Is that a bit of an Irish brogue, I detect, Lieutenant?"

"Aye, a wee bit, sir. I was born in Derry. My ma is American, so I've dual citizenship. When my da was killed by the Troubles in the North, she returned to New Hampshire and took me with her. But I keep in touch with my older half-brother."

After a moment of silent reflection, the commander asked, "How did you get out of Song Ong Doc that night?"

"By doing a backward duck walk toward the water, hoping all the while that the boats would still be there when - if - I made it."

"I take it they were?"

"Several were sunk at the pier. The barges were sinking. Everything was burning. The last PBR had just cast off, but they came back when they saw me on the end of the pier."

"What did you learn from Song Ong Doc, Lieutenant?"

"I learned that the speeches about us never leaving anyone behind are a load of crap, if you'll forgive me, sir! We had people trapped on the other side of the helipad, and I couldn't get to them. No one else even tried! Charlie was already coming through the wire. I learned after the fact that the presence of a large VC force had been indicated by body movements picked up on Dufflebag, but nothing was done to investigate or counter it."

"And what would you have done to counter it?"

"I would've increased patrols to the immediate north and east to investigate and report on activity in that area. I would've tightened security on the base and moved all the fuel and munitions farther from the pier and isolated it within separate bunkers. And I would've established reliable contacts in the nearby village. They had to know what was coming."

Commander O'Connell silently took stock of Shane for a moment. "I understand exactly how you feel. Believe me, I do. I was with the team that went back in the next morning. I was there when we found those two who'd been left behind. Take my word for it. There was nothing you could have done for them. You were lucky to get out yourself." He paused. "I understand that you went on ops with Team ONE a number of times?"

Julian butted in, "He took part in the 'Big Splash,' sir."

Commander O'Connell didn't take his eyes off Shane. "Is that true?"

"It is, Sir."

Chief Nazaro piped up, "I remember you. Those odd, light-colored eyes. You were at Warner Springs, the SERE school's simulated POW camp, when I was an instructor there. I remember we made you sleep on the ground one night, headfirst into a burlap sack. During the night, I threw a bucket of cold water on you while you slept, just to harass you like we did to all the officers. You tore off the sack, sprang up, and growled! I thought you were going to tear me apart like you did that sack, but you stopped and just glared. I'll never forget those eyes!"

With a nod and a smile, Shane replied, "And I'll never forget that rude awakening."

Commander O'Connell stroked his chin. "You completed the whole SERE school, including Warner Springs. Why didn't you go through the rest of the SEAL training? You certainly look like you could handle the physical demands with no problems."

"My eyes, sir. The qualifications for SEALs include having eyesight of at least 30/20 uncorrected, which I do–and then some. But, because of a hypersensitivity to light, I need shaded lenses during the day. They considered that the same hindrance as corrective lenses, so I didn't qualify."

With a nod at Shane's black beret, the commander said, "Well, you're NAG. That's close enough for me. You strike me as the kind of man I'd value having along. We could use your help tonight, Lieutenant. Gomez says you have exceptional senses of sight and hearing. I think we can use those special eyes of yours tonight. Gomez will fill you in. But despite your rank, I want to make it clear that Chief Nazaro is in charge of this op. You'll follow his lead. Are you okay with that?"

Shane replied with a smile, "Affirmative, sir. So long as he doesn't throw cold water on me, it'll be grand."

Commander O'Connell and Chief Nazaro retired to the commander's quarters. Shane motioned to Julian to step outside. Once away from others, Shane confronted Julian, "A number of times?"

Julian replied sheepishly, "Well, one is a number!"

"What did you tell them about me?"

"Relax. They don't know about your being, you know, a werewolf."

"I am *not* a werewolf. As I've *told you*, I just have lycanthropic senses."

"I know, I know. You don't change like some on your father's side of the family. Don't worry. The only thing I told the commander was that you have heightened senses, that's all."

"Okay. So, brief me on this op."

"All I know so far is that we're to muster here at the SEAL hootch at 0400 hours in cammies. Bring your weapon and web gear but no helmet or flak jacket, they're too cumbersome. We'll be briefed on the mission then."

At 0400, Shane and Julian joined the small group huddled around Commander O'Connell. They studied the aerial photos on the table as the commander explained, "We have intel from our contact with the VC that they're building this site in the middle of the U-Minh forest for the purpose of holding captured American POWs until they can be moved north. We have had an unusual number of MIAs lately, which would seem to validate the intel. Our mission tonight is to get a close look at the site, determine if there are indeed any Americans POW's being held there, and if so, bring them out."

"Chief Nazaro is officer-in-charge on this op. Lieutenant MacTire, I'd like you to stay close to Chief Nazaro and provide him with your observations. Petty Officer Gomez, I've decided I want you to also stick close, not only because enemy contact will be imminent and injuries may result, but also because if there are POWs, we don't know what condition they'll be in to travel. I'm trusting you to deal with any medical needs. Chief, carry on."

Chief Nazaro added, "All right, we'll be going in with two skimmer boats as quietly as possible." Using his finger to trace their approach on the aerial photos, the chief continued, "We'll disembark the boats here, about half a klick northeast of the clearing and follow this waterway to within sight of it, here. Any questions? Good. Lieutenant, park your M16 there on my bunk. Here, carry this Stoner. It's a bit handier with a shorter barrel and lighter weight. It also has thirty-round magazines taped together side-to-side, rather than those twenty-round mags you have there. And it's slung in front, so you can't drop it. I'm glad to see you also carry a .45 pistol on your web belt. And Gomez, if you talk or make any noise to disclose our presence, I'll kick your ass 'till your nose bleeds! Very well, all hands lay to the pier. Let's get underway."

After cutting the engines on the skimmer boats and sliding the blunt bows onto the muddy riverbank, everyone except the two coxswains stepped off, and made their way single file through the jungle along an adjoining canal.

Shane's heightened sense of smell informed him this must be the same area he had helped blast open before Christmas. It still had that same, foul stench. After about twenty minutes, they came to a clear cut, about 75 yards wide. Beyond the clearing, they saw bright flood lights, a barbed-wire perimeter, many metal-roofed hootches, and people moving about. The steady hum of a diesel generator was evident, even from a distance. It looked nothing like the aerial photos they were shown, but rather like one of their own Intermediate Support Bases.

Crouching behind foliage at the edge of the clear cut, Chief Nazaro and Shane conversed quietly while the rest of the team hung back.

The Chief asked, "What do you make of this, Lieutenant?"

"Obviously those photos are seriously out of date. There's no way we can make it across this clearing, let alone through that perimeter, without being detected. Even if we could get inside, we don't know where, or even *if*, there are any Americans here."

"Exactly what I was thinking. I'm seeing a lot of people moving around over there. I even hear someone laughing. With those superman ears that Gomez says you have, what do you hear, sir? Do you know much of the local lingo?"

"A bit. I hear one talking about no *ba si dai, toi di lam*. He doesn't want any rice whiskey because he has to go to work. I assume he means he has the watch. Wait – now he says, *Dai Ta*, the colonel, would kill him. What do you want to do, Chief? It's your call."

"I say we were given bad intel. It can't be done. We abort and return to the boats."

"I concur. Can I have just a moment to make a rough sketch of what we can see from this point?"

"Good idea, sir. Take a minute to do so, then we'll fall back."

Traveling a bit faster this time, they made it back to the boats in under ten minutes only to find there was no one there. Everything else appeared secure, but both coxswains who'd remained behind with the boats were missing. After searching the nearby jungle and finding nothing, Chief Nazaro reluctantly decided to return to Binh Thuy and report to Commander O'Connell. Shane couldn't tell the chief how he knew, but he was certain the two men did not leave by land, because he could detect no scent trails. He focused his attention instead on the water and riverbank.

When they started the engines, backed away from the riverbank and turned, Shane saw something watching at the river's edge. He reached out and grabbed Chief Nazaro by the shoulder as he said, "Wait! What's that?"

"Where? What do you see, sir?"

"I'm not sure. It couldn't be what it looked like, and I can't see it now. It may have just been the way the mud along the bank was shaped."

"What did it look like?"

"Sort of like – a giant frog."

"Probably a crocodile. They have them here, as far north as the

Rung Sat and all through the U-Minh. Some of them get pretty big."

Shane didn't say more, but he knew it wasn't a crocodile that he saw. He'd seen lots of those sunning side by side on the riverbanks in the Rung Sat Special Zone.

This was *something else.*

It was past sunup when they got back to Binh Thuy. Shane accompanied Chief Nazaro in briefing Commander O'Connell on the aborted mission and failed efforts to find their two missing men. The chief explained, "I'm telling you, sir, those aerial photos had to be from weeks ago. It had to take that long for them to build what we saw there. There was no way we could have crossed that clear cut, let alone get through their perimeter unseen. They have floodlights, watches posted, and a sizable force there. We had no choice but to abort. Then, we searched thoroughly for the two men who stayed with the boats, right up until the crack of dawn. There was just no trace of them."

"I don't question your decision to abort, Chief. I think you made the right call. We don't even know that there really are any POW's there at this time. From what you observed, I suspect that you are right; MACV Headquarters probably didn't order a new flyover as I requested. They just sent me the photos they already had for that sector, deciding those were recent enough. Regarding the missing men, I have no doubt you did all that could be done. It's a mystery. Whatever happened to them, it's probably the same thing that has been happening to a number of men from the River Rats."

Shane hung his head and mentally reviewed the mystery of the missing men. Even his lycanthropic senses hadn't found a trace of them. *The horrible smell of that area. I can't place what it is, but it's unnatural. It must have something to do with those men going missing.*

Turning to Shane, the commander asked, "Lieutenant, do you have anything to add?"

"Yes sir, I do. I was able to overhear some of a discussion between a few of the enemy forces we observed. One of them mentioned he didn't want to drink before going on duty because he'd get in trouble with his colonel. If there's a colonel stationed there, then that would indicate at least a battalion-size force present. From the number of people moving about and the size of the compound Chief Nazaro and I observed, I'd suggest that to be a fair assessment."

"You could hear them from across a clear cut of, what was it, 75 yards? Amazing. Those exceptional senses of yours *do* come in handy. Thank you, Lieutenant, and you too, Chief. I'll pass your observations and assessment back to MACV headquarters and see what they decide should be done about it."

Shane added, "One thing further, sir. I made this sketch of their base, at least the portion we could observe from our position."

As Commander O'Connell took the sketch and began to examine it, Julian knocked on the swinging door to Commander O'Connell's private quarters, entered, and said, "Excuse me, sir, Commodore Morgan's yeoman is here. He says the Black Ponies have a bird down. The commodore sent for you."

The commander replied, "Very well, Gomez. Tell the yeoman to report back that I'm on my way." Turning to Shane and Chief Nazaro, he said, "I'd like you two to come with me." As he quickly pinned Shane's sketch to a corkboard, he added, "This will have to wait."

In Commodore Ronald Morgan's office, the commanding officers of the Black Ponies and the Seawolves, as well as the Senior Advisor of the River Divisions, were already present. Commodore Morgan commanded the Fleet Air Support Unit (FASU) himself.

When Commander O'Connell, Shane, and Chief Nazaro entered the office, Captain Frank Buhler, commanding officer of the Black Ponies, was speaking. "God damn it! Jonesy had no business being up there. He's our intel officer. Boomer should have known better than to take him up on a boondoggle."

Commodore Morgan took control of the fervor in the room. "Alright, we're all here. Everyone, pay attention! There's no time to lose. I can't stress how urgent this is. As you know by now, one of the Black Ponies' OV-10 Broncos has been shot down." Turning and pointing on the map hanging on the bulkhead, he continued, "They went down here. The wing man observed that both Lieutenant Boomgaarden and Lieutenant Commander Jones were able to exit and flee from the crash site, but the other Bronco was repeatedly driven back by heavy fire. He stayed in the area until forced to return to re-arm and refuel. The last observation of Boomer and Jonesy had them running down this shallow waterway eastward toward this river thirty minutes ago. I want every bird in the air and every boat available combing those waters, and

I want them found. Make it so! That is all. Commander O'Connell, you and your people remain a moment."

After the others hurried out of the office, the commodore faced the three men and added, "Lieutenant Commander Jones is the intel officer. If he's dead, it doesn't matter. But we can't let the enemy capture him alive. Find him before they do. If you find they already have him, make sure he's dead."

Commander O'Connell seemed suspended in time for a moment, then replied, "Aye-aye, sir" as he, Shane and the chief hurried out.

All hands of Detachment GOLF, along with Shane, Julian and the commander himself were speeding southward down the river in two PBR's when the word came by radio to abort the search and return to Binh Thuy; the two missing men from the downed bird had been spotted and picked up by a Seawolf helo.

As soon as they disembarked the PBR, Julian hurried toward the dispensary. Shane accompanied Commander O'Connell to the SEAL hootch, then took his leave, switched the borrowed Stoner for his M16, and also headed to the dispensary. When he arrived, Boomer and Jonesy were in an exam room. Julian and Doc Stephens were busy suturing the most serious lacerations on both men, while other corpsmen assisted. Commodore Morgan and Captain Buhler were also in the room but stood out of the way. Both Boomer and Jonesy seemed extremely agitated.

Boomer kept asking, "What *was* that thing? It just kept chasing us! It was some kind of monster! If the Seawolf wouldn't have shown up when it did, it would have caught us."

Doc Stephens interrupted, "Gentlemen, this is going to have to wait until we've finished. These men need to calm down now, and we have more work to do. Why don't you all go to Charlie's Den, and I'll send word when your questions can be addressed."

Shane backed out of the room, then followed the others across the dirt driveway and past the mess hall to Charlie's den. Inside, he sat apart and listened as Commodore Morgan and Captain Buhler discussed what had just transpired.

Captain Buhler insisted, "Boomer's delusional! He's just scared out of his mind. First, to be shot down, then survive the crash, and then to be chased by the enemy. It's no wonder he thinks he saw a monster!"

Commodore Morgan suggested, "Let's wait until he settles down, like Doc Stephens recommends. Jonesy hasn't said much yet. We'll wait and see what he has to say."

Shane spoke up, "If you don't mind my asking, sirs, what was it, exactly, that Lieutenant Boomgaarden said he saw?"

Captain Buhler smirked. "He said they were being chased by a giant frogman!"

Commodore Morgan added, "He's very upset and understandably so. We won't really know anything until we can question them both more carefully after they've calmed down."

Shane asked further, "If you wouldn't mind, Commodore, may I listen in when you interview them? I'm not saying I know what they saw, just that it sounds like it might correlate to an earlier observation."

"Lieutenant, if you could offer a reasonable explanation for what they think they saw, your presence would be more than welcome."

It took more than half an hour before Julian stepped into Charlie's Den to advise that the two men were out of treatment and resting comfortably. Shane had passed some of that time drawing on a napkin. He and the senior officers finished the drinks they'd been nursing and returned to the dispensary. Once there, they observed that Boomer appeared calmer and more controlled, but less forthcoming. When pressed, he stuck to his story about the monster.

Jonesy was still in pain from having his shoulder wrenched back into its socket and wrapped. Both men had numerous bandages covering lacerations and abrasions. Jonesy replied to Captain Buhler's questions with obvious caution. Regarding the reported "monster," he first turned to Boomer, then back to his CO. Finally, he replied, "Sir, you can believe what you like. But I'm saying that what I saw, what we both saw chasing us for a distance of several hundred yards, as fast as we could manage through shallow water and mud, did appear to be some sort of animal. I can only describe it as a cross between a sea lion, a crocodile, and a — well, a very large-headed, frog-faced — man, sir. I know what you must be thinking. But please believe me. At one point, that—thing was only a few yards behind us. We saw it clearly enough."

The two senior officers looked at each other, then down at the deck and remained silent. Shane spoke up, "Sirs, do you mind if I ask these officers a few questions?"

Commodore Morgan spoke. "Please do, Lieutenant."

Shane stepped closer to the two men sitting up on cots. He looked back and forth between them and said, "I think I've seen this thing you describe." Pulling the napkin from his shirt pocket, he unfolded it and showed them. "Does this look like what you saw?"

Boomer drew back, wide-eyed. "That's it! Well, at least that's its head. Your drawing doesn't show its body."

Shane turned to Jonesy and asked, "Tell me more about its body. How large would you say it is? Describe it in as much detail as you can remember."

Shane sketched while both men described what they saw chasing them. When they could add no further details, Shane showed them what he'd sketched. It resembled a fat crocodile, with human-like arms and legs, and a very large head which did indeed look like a frog, with a very wide mouth, no discernable neck, but a suggestion of flaps, possibly gills. Both men agreed it was a close likeness. As to the creature's size, they estimated at least eight to ten feet head to tail and guessed it to be more than 500 pounds. They explained to Shane how it lurched forward in short, rapid hops with its arms and legs, dragging a thick tail, and nearly matched the best speed they could manage through swampy water one to two feet deep, injured as they both were.

Boomer began to get agitated again just from staring at the sketch, so Shane folded it and returned it to his shirt pocket. Jonesy looked at Shane and asked, "You've seen it, too, haven't you?"

Shane assured both men, "I have. It was mostly submerged and stationary, but I'm sure it was the same thing that chased both of you today." Shane turned to address Commodore Morgan and Captain Buhler. "I'm certain that what they saw is real, because I saw it too, earlier this morning, and not very far from where these men were shot down. I don't know what it is, but I intend to find out."

The commodore cleared his throat, then said, "Thank you, Lieutenant. When you do, report to me everything you learn about it."

Doc Stephens entered the room and asked, "Will that do for now, gentlemen? These men could use some rest." Commodore Morgan and Captain Buhler turned and left. Shane addressed Doc Stephens and asked, "Excuse me, doctor. I noticed you had Petty Officer Gomez suturing. Is that usually within the duties of a corpsman?"

The doctor answered, "No, it's not usual. But Gomez is not a usual corpsman. Before his active duty, he was a pre-med graduate from Miami. He sutures better than most doctors I've worked with. He lacks experience in diagnosis and education on pharmaceuticals, but if I were hurt, he's the man I would want working on me."

Shane found Commodore Morgan back in his office when he knocked. The commodore looked up and asked, "Learn more about that frogman, Lieutenant?"

"No, sir, not yet. But I'd like another look at that map on your bulkhead, if I may?"

"Feel free. You haven't been here long. If there's anything more I can do to help, just let me or my yeoman know."

"Can you show me just where Boomer and Jonesy were picked up?"

The Commodore moved to the map and pointed, "Here. In this east-west canal, very close to where it connects to this river flowing southeast."

Shane noticed there was a village along the west bank of that river, not too far north of the canal. It also showed a road winding past the village and eventually leading north to the city of Can Tho. "Can you tell me anything about this village, here, sir?"

"Not much. I hardly ever get off base, myself, and I doubt any of our forces have had any contact there. That's Hoa Hao territory."

"Hoa Hao, sir?"

It's a religious sect prominent in the region. They keep to themselves. From what I've heard, nobody interacts with them; not the South Vietnamese government, the ARVNs, the Viet Cong, nobody. They're said to be fiercely independent."

"Is it safe to travel there?"

"I wouldn't do it alone, if that's what you mean. The road should be safe. I'm sure it sees traffic from Can Tho to points south. But we've been losing people from boats in those waters lately."

Shane returned to the dispensary and found Julian. He waited until Julian was finished with a patient, then asked, "What time do you get off duty?"

"Normally, around 1600, as long as things stay quiet. But I'm sure Doc would let me secure early, considering I've been up since before 0330."

"Take off at noon and check out a jeep from the motor pool. I'll clear it with Doc Stephens for you."

After entering the city of Can Tho and turning south on a dirt road exiting the Ben Sa Moi *new bus station* district, then traveling west and south about twenty klicks, Shane and Julian entered the village. There appeared to be a temple of some sort in the middle, and Shane directed Julian to drive toward it. Julian turned into its enclosed parking area and shut off the jeep. He leaned back in the driver's seat, got as comfortable as he could, slid his "Boonie" hat over his eyes, and suggested, "I'll just stay with the jeep, if you don't mind."

Shane stepped out and followed a walkway leading to a courtyard behind the building. As he did, an old man in robes rose from a bench, leaned heavily on a walking stick, and smiled as Shane approached. Both men nodded politely, then Shane asked in what little Vietnamese he had, if the man was the priest here.

The man replied, "*Toi cam bic.*" Shane knew this translates as *I don't understand.* The man spoke again, which Shane sorted out to mean *please wait here.* With that, the old man smiled again, quickly bowed, turned, and walked down a path between the building and a flower garden courtyard, which the building encompassed on all sides except for the opening adjoining the parking area. When the elderly man entered a door at the far end of the building, Shane began to wonder if he understood the man correctly.

In a minute, the door opened again, and the old man reappeared, followed by a young woman. They both walked slowly toward Shane. He observed she was rather tall and curvaceous for a Vietnamese woman, straining the button snaps down the side of the bust line on the simple, white traditional ao dai she wore.

Despite the midday sun, Shane removed his sunglasses. As the two drew nearer, the woman made eye contact with him and paused in her steps for a moment, then tilted her head to the side slightly while sweeping her long, black hair back over her shoulder with her hand.

Even from a distance, Shane's keen eyesight enabled him to observe that she was not wearing any jewelry or makeup. Her heart-shaped face, those inescapable eyes and beckoning lips could not be more…perfect. Shane couldn't help thinking, *Never in human history was makeup less needed.* Still several paces away, Shane's heightened olfactory sense told him that she did, however, wear perfume. *Or does she naturally sweeten the air as she moves through it?*

Standing before him, she held out her hand and said, "My master, Nguyen Van Phan, apologizes for having no English and only a little

French. At such times, he calls on me. I have studied very much English, and I spoke French as a child, as my father was a French plantation owner. I am Sister Anisette. How may we help you?"

"Sister? Are – are you a nun?"

She laughed, then answered, "Like the Catholic have? No, we don't do that. I was a student in the orphanage here since my parents were killed by the Viet Cong. Now I teach. Everyone here calls me Chi, which means 'sister.' Are you of the Catholic tradition?"

Shane managed to collect his thoughts and took her offered hand. "My family is. I try to keep an open mind. My name is Shane, Shane MacTire. I'm a lieutenant in the U.S. Navy, presently working at Binh Thuy. I hope I may trouble you for a little information."

"Of course. What would you like to know, Lieutenant?"

"Please, call me Shane. I'm curious about an unusual creature that I believe lives in the waters not far from your village. Can you, perhaps, tell me about this?" Shane unfolded the sketch he had taken from his shirt pocket while speaking and held it out to Anisette.

She drew in a quick breath. "You know about Ngu Tinh!"

The old man dropped his frozen smile, and he also looked at the sketch. There was a brief but intense verbal exchange between him and Anisette. Then, the old man smiled again, leaned heavily on his walking stick as he bowed to Shane, then turned and walked back the way they'd come, leaving Anisette and Shane to continue.

Shane was shocked by the reaction to his sketch but proceeded with caution. "I'm sorry, the–what? Ngu Tinh?"

"Yes. That is what we call him, after a great water beast of ancient legend."

"You know of this thing, then?"

"Yes. I know…of him."

"Can you tell me about–him–then, please?"

Anisette paced nervously. "Would you like to walk with me in the garden while I explain?" Shane fell in close by her side as they slowly strolled around the courtyard. "Centuries ago, the Ngu Tinh of legend was a big fish-like beast. It destroyed fishing boats to feed on fishermen. In 1939, Huynh Phu So, the founder of our religion, was a young man. One day, walking along a riverbank, he came upon what you drew, caught in a strong fishing net and injured. Huynh Phu So saved it by cutting it free from the net and bringing food until it regained strength."

Anisette gestured to a bench in the garden, where Shane sat by her side as she continued. "After, Huynh Phu So continued to visit. He named it Ngu Tinh, like the water beast of ancient legend. He also found that Ngu Tinh could learn to use its voice to make speech. In time, Huynh Phu So taught Ngu Tinh to speak some Vietnamese. And Ngu Tinh taught Huynh Phu So the ideals of the Hoa Hao, to live a simple, independent, self-reliant life; consistent with nature."

"So, in a way, Ngu Tinh, as you call him, taught your religion's founder the philosophies upon which it is based. Why has the outside world not heard of this wise, though strange being?"

"Many times, the world is not kind to those who are different. Also, not everything about him is good. Just like his namesake, he sometimes feeds on fishermen."

"That might explain how I learned of it–him, in part, at least."

"How do you mean?"

"This morning, he chased two of our officers for a long distance, until they were rescued by one of our helicopters. I suppose now that he may have been trying to eat them."

"That is startling for several reasons."

"Why?"

"We, the villagers have an arrangement with Ngu Tinh. So that he does not feed on people, we bring him offerings—usually a pig every week to appease him. This practice has been honored for many years. Also, he does not interact with the outside world. He avoids Americans like he avoided the French colonials before you."

"If you would, please, tell me about that. I've been led to understand that the Hoa Hao are fiercely independent and hostile to outsiders. Is that also from the influence of the Ngu Tinh?"

"We are independent, yes, but hostile? No, quite the contrary. We are tolerant toward all but simply do not participate in the ambitions of others. There was a time when we had our own army to ensure autonomy against the French colonials, the present governments of both South and North Vietnam, and, also against the Viet Cong. Similarly, we take no part in the state of war in my country. There is no war within this village."

"So, you interact with this Ngu Tinh often?"

"Every week, someone from our temple takes our offering of a pig to him."

"Does this someone speak with Ngu Tinh?"

"It can be done. Sometimes he will talk. Other times, he just takes the pig and goes."

"Anisette, a lot of my fellow American Navy men have gone missing from our boats in these waters lately. This morning, as I mentioned before, Ngu Tinh chased and tried to catch two of our officers through shallow water. I must wonder if those two circumstances are related. Would it be possible to learn what has caused this change in his behavior?"

"I'm not sure, but I will try to find out for you. Until then, I can say that it is a good thing those men this morning were in shallow water."

"Why is that?"

"Ngu Tinh is very powerful, and in deep water, he moves very fast." Rising from the bench, Anisette took Shane by the hand. "You should go back to Binh Thuy now. The road is not safe after sunset. Will you come back soon, so I can tell you if I learn about what has changed Ngu Tinh?"

As they walked back toward the jeep, Shane answered, "I shall come again in a few days. I look forward to seeing you, in any case." As they reached the jeep, he turned toward Anisette and said goodbye.

Before releasing his hand, Anisette looked into his eyes and said, "Please, pardon my noticing: You have the most amazing eyes. They are the color of the sky and seem to contain a whole world of your own in their depth."

Shane was speechless and a bit embarrassed as he reluctantly backed toward the jeep. Julian was startled awake when Shane climbed into the passenger seat. As Julian steered out of the temple grounds and turned left onto the dirt road, Shane looked back and returned Anisette's wave. He thought, *What good is a world of my own unless she is in it?*

The next day, Shane met with Commodore Morgan and briefed him on what he'd learned about the Ngu Tinh so far. The commodore, in turn, briefed Shane on the projected itinerary for the withdrawal of the Seawolves' detachments of helicopters from each of several Intermediate Support Bases throughout the Mekong Delta, all those helicopters and personnel returning to LSB Binh Thuy. The Seawolves, along with the Black Ponies and FASU, would then be decommissioned and withdrawn from Binh Thuy.

When the removal of all air operations is complete, and with the turnover of all river patrol craft already accomplished, only the few NAG still working with the River Patrol Divisions, the SEAL Detachment, and some Naval Support Activity personnel, mainly in the dispensary and the communications shack, would remain. Only about 50 personnel in all. Thereafter, the SEAL Detachment and the Dufflebag unit would also pull out, and that number was scheduled to go down to just 35 U.S. personnel left at Binh Thuy to continue supporting the Vietnamese navy.

Shane reflected, "That's quite a reduction since I was here to observe the turnover of the River Divisions last year. We had over a thousand U.S. Navy personnel at Binh Thuy then."

Commodore Morgan added, "I wish I could tell you to report back to the Admiral that the Vietnamization Program is showing positive results. But I cannot. What I can say is that we are making great strides and sticking to our projected schedule. I fear, however, that there is likely to be another turnover not long after we finally withdraw completely."

"I understand, Commodore, and I share your concerns. If I may continue to check in with you for schedule updates, I'd like to visit as many of the Intermediate Support Bases as I can to observe the withdrawal of the Seawolf detachments. I also have an errand to run for the Admiral, so I need to fly out to Phu Quoc Island, then make follow-up stops at a couple of the Advanced Tactical Support Bases we've already turned over on my way back."

"No problem. I'm sure I can persuade Captain Stromberg, the CO of the Seawolves, to provide one of his Huey's to ferry you around for a few days. Keep my yeoman informed of your travels. Thank you for the update on that frogman thing. Keep me advised as you learn more from the Hoa Hao. Carry on, Lieutenant."

After a couple of days of traveling to document the withdrawal of Seawolf detachments from the ISBs of Ben Luc and Dong Tam, as well as deliver correspondence from Commander O'Connell to the officer-in-charge of SEAL Detachment FOXTROT at Dong Tam, Shane returned to Binh Thuy.

Shane checked out a jeep and drove alone to the Hoa Hao village. He arrived without incident in the early afternoon. Anisette was busy in a large open area teaching a group of boys and girls what appeared to be a cross between physical education and dance. It's like tai chi or katas in group formation but done to music with bo staffs. Shane watched quietly until she was done, then made his presence known to Anisette. "That was beautiful. Is that what you teach here?"

Anisette smiled and answered, "Not only that. I teach Health and Fitness, English, Vietnamese History and Culture, and sometimes French, if a student requests it." She took Shane on a tour of the classrooms and the rest of the temple grounds. He was introduced to several of the children who lived there, some of whom greeted him and spoke to him in careful but grammatically proper English, between giggling and commenting among themselves in Vietnamese.

Shane learned nothing further about Ngu Tinh that day. It was still too soon since his first visit. But he found the time spent with Anisette very rewarding. He admitted to himself that he really came for her company. She appeared to enjoy his as well.

A few days later, Shane returned for another meeting with Anisette. After passing through the courtyard, he entered the door at the far end and asked the first monk he saw for Anisette. The monk directed him to a small sanctuary and indicated he should sit and wait. In a few minutes, Anisette breezed through the doorway, quickly sat beside him and smiled. After they exchanged pleasantries, she invited Shane to stroll with her in the courtyard.

At first, she seemed hesitant but began by saying, "I spoke to Ngu Tinh when we took his pig yesterday."

"You talked to him yourself?"

"Yes. I sometimes do when I accompany the monks with the pig."

"I recall you saying that someone might be able to speak with him when someone takes the pig, but you weren't sure."

"Yes. Please forgive me. My master was reluctant in allowing me to say too much about Ngu Tinh. Also, I didn't know what you would think about us—about me if you knew that we—that I talk with him."

"And now?"

"Master Phan trusts my discretion. But I feel somewhat—less sure—about everything."

"What did he, Ngu Tinh, say about chasing the men that morning, and about many other American navy men missing from our boats?"

Anisette remained silent for several steps, then she began, "Ngu Tinh is very angry. I never saw him this way before. Ngu Tinh says the Americans damaged his home, blew up his–ah–cave, some months ago.

Now he hates Americans. He admitted he kills them. He is taking part in the war. Before, I always tried to be not afraid of him. I too know how it feels to be different. I know men look at me, but they do not see me. I see them. I see they want to be with me, but they don't want to stay with me. I always feel different—like Ngu Tinh is different. But, this time, Ngu Tinh frightened me. Now, I think he is—a monster."

Shane remained silent and thought, *I was part of what changed Ngu Tinh and made him angry! What would Anisette think of me if she knew? I need not wonder what she must already think of me. It's clear she doesn't trust me, and with good reason. Just as well. I too cannot stay. What would she think if she knew how different—what I really am? She would see me as also a monster! If I don't keep my feelings for her under control, I could get my heart broken—or worse—hers.*

After several more silent steps down the edge of the courtyard, Shane said, "Thank you for the information you have been able to give me. I understand the awkward position in which I have placed you. Please believe that was not my intention." Anisette took Shane's hand. Shane could feel that control over his feelings slipping a little, but he continued, "I have some other duties which will take me away from Binh Thuy for a while. Really, I'm only there temporarily. Soon I must return to the office I work out of in Saigon. But I would like to see you before I go. I'll come back again after a few days. If there's anything more you can tell me then about Ngu Tinh, that would be fine. In any case, I don't want to leave without saying goodbye."

They walked silently to where Shane turned and slid into his jeep.

Anisette stepped back, releasing his hand and used her own to softly brush her hair back while wiping the wetness from her eyes and her now damp cheek as he started the jeep and drove away.

Meeting with Commodore Morgan's yeoman, Shane studied the schedule for the withdrawal of Seawolf detachments from the last of the ISBs. He decided to fly out to Phu Quock Island to visit Duong Dong and An Thoi, then stop at the ATSBs at Rach Gia and Chau Doc on the return trip to Binh Thuy.

A few days later, flying toward Binh Thuy, Shane passed over the city of Long Xuyen. He looked down at the immense cross atop the tall spire of Long Xuyen Cathedral below and reflected on the family in Ireland he hadn't seen in years, but with whom he regularly exchanged cassette tapes. He recorded his letters to them, and in return, he received not only greetings from his brother, sister-in-law, little nephew and niece, but recordings of them and their friends playing guitars and singing folk songs, both Irish and American. He remembered as a child how he'd regularly attended mass with his ma and da and the big brother he worshiped.

He sadly reflected on the unnatural, inhuman affliction with which his big brother, like their da, was cursed. He pondered, *Ngu Tinh is similarly afflicted. Could Ngu Tinh, too, be cursed?*

It occurred to him that the Long Xuyen Cathedral would likely keep a library, which could possibly contain local lore and legend. It would mean that he'd miss the chance to get down to Nam Can at the southern tip of the Delta for the scheduled withdrawal of the Seawolves from that ISB, but what he might be able to learn about the Ngu Tinh at the Cathedral could be invaluable.

When the Seawolves landed at Binh Thuy, Shane went to Commodore Morgan's office and learned the road from Binh Thuy to Long Xuyen was safe, and that the round trip could easily be driven in a day.

He next went to the dispensary and asked Julian, "Can you take some time off to go along with me to Long Xuyen?"

At the cathedral, Shane excitedly learned there was a library. Further, with help from an elderly Sister Eugenia, who *was* a nun, Shane learned the existence of Ngu Tinh was indeed recorded there.

In the year 1900, one of the nuns there was discovered to be pregnant and gave birth to a deformed, partly amphibious offspring. The nun was harshly condemned for her sins, which she emphatically denied. The deformed infant was proclaimed to be a child of Satan, the only conclusion possible to explain its hideous disfigurement. The nun reportedly left the cathedral, taking the strange infant with her to her family's village and was never seen or heard from again.

Nothing more was recorded until 1939, when a part-man/part-water beast was mentioned in connection with the rise of the Hoa Hao religious sect in the western Mekong Delta region.

When Shane and Julian returned from Long Xuyen, they went to chow. In the mess hall, the commodore's yeoman approached Shane,

"Excuse me, sir. I just thought you'd want to know that the withdrawal of the Seawolf detachment in Nam Can got delayed at the last minute. One of their Hueys is down for repair and needs parts. A Seawolf is departing here tomorrow to take the parts to them. I'm sure you could ride along, if you want to."

"Thanks. Advise the commodore that I'll be doing so, and I'll return with the Seawolves from Nam Can when they all arrive back here."

Stepping down from the hell hole of the Huey onto the helipad in Nam Can, Shane walked to the Operations hootch. Inside, he met the senior advisor, the wavy blond-haired Lieutenant Karl Snyder.

Lieutenant Snyder spent much of the afternoon showing Shane around and introducing him to the NAG and Seawolf personnel, as well as Commander Bai of the South Vietnamese Navy.

The short, stout man looked like an Asian mob boss more than the commanding officer of a base. Commander Bai seemed disinterested until he sorted out that Shane had the ear of Admiral Adams. Then, he monopolized Shane's time and attention with a relentless litany of everything he wanted, didn't have, and why he thought he needed it.

This continued until Snyder came to Shane's rescue by noting it was time for evening chow, and the three officers headed to the mess hall. As they approached, there was some commotion around a bunker outside the mess hall. The bunker, just half of a six-foot diameter culvert pipe cut laterally and covered over with several layers of sandbags, was barricaded at both ends by armed South Vietnamese sailors with their weapons pointed at both openings.

Commander Bai approached and began dominating the fury of many loud, excited voices all speaking at once in Vietnamese. Soon, the commander pulled his .45 pistol from his web belt, pointed it at the nearest end of the bunker and shouted. Shane caught only enough Vietnamese to know that two traitors were trapped within the bunker.

Shane and Snyder watched as one South Vietnamese sailor crawled out of the end of the bunker with his hands in a pleading gesture. The kneeling sailor began to speak until Commander Bai promptly shot him in the head.

Then, the shouting resumed until the muffled sounds of someone speaking inside the bunker were heard. A dialog ensued between the muffled speaker and the commander. Finally, all went quiet. Then, a second South Vietnamese sailor slowly crawled out. Commander Bai and several other sailors kept weapons trained on the man while he carefully stood. The man glanced down at the body of his comrade still bleeding into the sand while Commander Bai pressed the muzzle of his .45 against the man's head.

Snyder stepped forward and addressed Commander Bai, "What is this about, Commander?"

Bai answered without removing his pistol nor concentration from the standing man. "These two men VC! They put bomb in perimeter. My men see them. They run, hide here."

The standing man shifted his eyes from Commander Bai to Lieutenant Snyder and in passable English said, "No VC." Glancing at the lifeless body of his comrade, then back to Snyder, he continued. "No kill me, I tell."

Snyder addressed Commander Bai, who still had his pistol fixed against the standing man. "Commander, I advise we let him speak. He's more useful to us alive."

The commander shouted an order at the man.

The man cringed, then said softly, "No VC. I *Dai Wei (captain)*, North Vietnamese Army." Commander Bai pushed the muzzle of his pistol harder against the man's head. With his head bent to the side, the man continued, "I tell *Dai Ta (colonel)* helicopter go from here yesterday. Now *Dai Ta* bring two battalion, 750 men, North Vietnamese Army here in 30 boats. Now helicopter still here." The man pushed back against the pistol, straightened his stance and with a determined look added, "I think you all die tonight, same-same."

Commander Bai roared as he tightened his grip on his pistol. Shane stepped up to face the standing man and reached for Bai as he quickly exclaimed, "Commander! Wait! I have important questions for this man."

The *Dai Wei* turned his gaze slowly toward Shane with an expression of pure apathy. Shane asked him, "They come by river?" The man nodded. "They come from a new base your army made in the U-Minh Forest north of here?" Again, the man nodded. "Are there any Americans being held there?"

The *Dai Wei* smiled, then said, "Our man say Americans there, so if you see base, you no shoot base."

Shane was shocked with comprehension. The *Dai Wei* laughed. Commander Bai pulled the trigger.

Shane roared at the commander, "He was telling the truth!"

Bai shouted back, "He NVA!"

Shane glared at the commander for a moment, then asked, "Commander, how many South Vietnamese Navy men do you command here?"

"Almost 200."

"And how many, would you suspect, could be infiltrators?"

"We estimate one third."

Shane thought aloud, "Between a dozen NAG and the Seawolves, we have about 50 U.S. Navy personnel—and four helicopters." Then, with an air of assurance, he addressed Commander Bai. "Sir, I respectfully request that you quickly arm those of your men whose loyalty you consider certain. Use them to confine the rest of your men in the mess hall until those two battalions of NVA have been dealt with. Tell them nothing. Any who appear to already know about the imminent attack are probably infiltrators. If you do this, I will certainly inform Admiral Adams about your requests." Through gritted teeth, Shane added, "and your, ah, *decisive* actions here today."

The commander appeared pleased, "I do what you say." He then gathered the already armed men surrounding the bunker into a huddle.

Shane turned to the Senior Advisor. "Karl, I need to use your radio!"

Snyder instantly responded, "Come with me." Both men quickly returned to the ops hootch, where Shane ordered the radioman to get Binh Thuy on the horn. The radioman keyed his mike and voiced, "Bravo Tango - Bravo Tango, this is November Charlie."

In a moment, they heard the response, "Bravo Tango. Go ahead November Charlie."

Shane took the mike from the radioman and said, "Bravo Tango, I have a priority Op Immediate for Snake Charmer."

The quick reply was "Stand by, November Charlie, we'll get him."

After about a minute, Shane heard Commander O'Connell's voice say, "November Charlie, this is Snake Charmer."

Shane keyed the mike and said, "Snake charmer, this is Shamrock. Regarding that sketch of mine on your corkboard. Negative Uniform Sierra presence that location confirmed. Regarding Black Ponies' remaining surplus of zuni rockets, please advise COMFASU I recommend Black Ponies put it there."

Snake Charmer replied, "Affirmative, Shamrock. I'll tell him.

Anything further?"

"Affirmative. Regarding my earlier estimate of strength there. Double that. Those operational units presently enroute this location. Request also advise COMFASU that only support and logistics still present at location of sketch."

"Acknowledged. Do you require support your location?"

"Negative, Snake Charmer. Due to Seawolves' SNAFU, we should have matters well in hand. Nothing further from this end."

"Very well, Shamrock. Carry on."

Shane returned the mike to the radioman and turned to the senior advisor. In a thoughtful tone, "Karl, you and I need to meet with the Seawolves now. I don't know who is senior by date of rank here, but I suggest we don't have time to sort that out. I have a plan."

After getting assurance that the downed Huey was now fully operational, Shane briefed the assembled Seawolves regarding the two battalions of NVA heading toward them. With four helicopters now available, the plan was to keep the enemy force engaged with three circling at all times, while one relays back to refuel and rearm.

Seawolf personnel not needed as ground crew to help with fuel and munitions would be directed by Shane in building sandbag nests on the roofs of several hootches in the middle of the base.

Shane suspected the perimeter may be compromised and its bunkers booby-trapped against the defenders. This central, smaller, and more defensible, elevated position would be removed from that and provide visibility and clear lines of fire, should any enemy make it to inside the base. Whether, or when, to release Commander Bai's South Vietnamese sailors to go to battle stations would be a judgment call. It would then remain to be seen how many would assume defensive positions to repel the NVA or join them.

Shane addressed the senior advisor, "Karl, I'd like you to send one boat about a kilometer upriver to lie in wait and remain on watch to signal the enemy's approach."

Shane sat in his sandbag nest atop the ops hootch and watched the jungle and night sky horizon, still visible in the light of the nearly full moon. He remembered during his childhood in Ireland, that it was on such nights, for several days each month, his da insisted on being locked in the cellar alone until morning. The memory of those times was always disturbing. Shane noticed a strange prickling sensation all over in his skin and an aching in his joints, which he had never experienced before. He attributed it to nervous jitters and stood to shake it off. He realized that at least to some degree, he, too, was affected by the curse on his father's side of the family. Shane wondered, *Does Ngu Tinh, also, feel unjustly cursed and ashamed of what he is?*

At about 0300 hours, Shane saw a green star cluster pop flare, the signal for "contact imminent." With a portable radio, he released the Seawolf pack. In a minute, three of the Hueys lifted off behind him. Next, he called the three men in the mortar pit to begin slow, sustained firing of illumination rounds at the pre-established coordinates. Now, he could only sit, watch, and listen as the Seawolf pilots communicate with each other. They'd already confirmed approximately 30 sampan-type wooden fishing boats jammed with soldiers making way in tight formation down the river just north of Nam Can.

Shane saw sporadic white tracer fire reaching up toward the circling helicopters, and streams of red tracers descending from the side door mounted M60 machineguns of all three Hueys. Then, as the pilot-controlled miniguns also engaged, all three helicopters rained cloudbursts of red death upon the river below. The fourth Huey turned up its engines on the helipad.

The firefight continued through the night. Every quarter-hour or so, one Huey lifted off the helipad, reloaded with fuel and munitions to resume the attack, then another hurried back to replace it. The only change was that the battle had slowly moved closer to the base. Shane and the men with him on the rooftops could only sit on their sandbags watching and waiting. Shane caught himself panting with anxiety but restrained his need to leap up and roar from impatience.

At daybreak, the Hueys ceased firing and continued to circle as the morning light increased, then all broke off and flew toward the base. Shane hopped down from the roof and trotted to the helipad.

Lieutenant Commander Collier, officer-in-charge of the Seawolf detachment climbed out of his shut down helicopter with its blades still rotating. He unsnapped his flight helmet as he approached.

Shane greeted him, "Good morning, sir. How did you enjoy your flight?"

The pilot smiled and responded, "Fish in a barrel, Lieutenant. All boats sunk or badly damaged. The river is clogged with bodies, mostly floating face-down or feebly struggling toward shore. Rest assured, we'll not be troubled by them anymore."

Shane reached to shake Collier's still-gloved hand and said, "Well done, sir. Thank God and the Seawolves."

Shane stepped from the Huey onto Binh Thuy's helipad and turned to flash a thumbs up to Lieutenant Commander Collier up front in the pilot's seat. Then he walked toward Commodore Morgan's office. When he entered, the commodore's yeoman looked up, then said, "Lieutenant MacTire, I have an envelope here that was left by a cyclo driver for you at the gate shack this morning."

The envelope was addressed to "Lieutenant Shane Mak Teary". Shane wondered who would misspell his name like that. He tore it open and read cursive English in a fine hand:

Dear Shane, I spoke to Ngu Tinh yesterday. He said it is time for him to show he is not animal; he is man. He said next time I come, he wants me to come alone. He makes me feel very afraid. I don't like when he looks at me. When I got back to the temple, I told my master. Master Phan says, maybe this is why I am different; this is why I am here. Shane, I think I must leave the temple now. I am going to stay with my friend. She was in school with me, and she lives in the village. But she has a husband and children. I cannot stay with her long. I don't know where I will go after that. I have no more to tell you about Ngu Tinh. I am leaving the temple now. I think you have no need to come here again. I am very sorry. I hope you find what you need. Anisette

Commodore Morgan said, "I don't like it, Lieutenant, It's too dangerous. What do you think, Commander O'Connell?"

"I agree, sir. He shouldn't go alone."

Shane countered, "Sirs, I've thought it through. He never shows himself when the odds are too great against him. He's only ever attacked one or two at a time. I know where he lives, and I know how he operates. I even know what's motivating him. To some extent, I understand what he feels. But he has become a danger to those who matter more. He must be stopped! I know what I'm up against, but he doesn't. He thinks he has surprise on his side in the dark. He knows he has the advantage in deep water. But he doesn't know about the advantages I have in the jungle. He will come for me, but I'll know he is coming."

Commander O'Connell thought for a long moment, then spoke, "Well, Commodore, I'm inclined to trust the lieutenant's judgment. He's earned it and proven it at Nam Can. But I insist on sending a coxswain who knows those waters as backup with a portable radio. I'll watch his progress on Dufflebag."

Commodore Morgan relented, "Very well, I'll authorize it. But Lieutenant, I'll want a full report from you when you return."

Shane chuckled, "I want very much to be here to give it to you, sir."

The Coxswain cut the skimmer boat's engine as Shane shifted his position in the forward seat. He prepared to disembark as the boat glided toward the riverbank near its convergence with a shallow canal.

It was the same canal Shane had once helped to open. The slope on the bank they approached was not far from where they'd slid to a stop that night that they'd reconned the NVA base now in smoldering ruin half a klick to the southwest. When only about two boat lengths from the bank, Shane stood, put one foot on the boat's gunwale preparing to step off, but was flung backwards, high into the air as the skimmer boat was flipped out of the water and capsized.

Shane landed on his back in the water but lost his grip on his M16. He quickly swiveled around in his immediate position but was unable to locate his weapon. Despite his exceptional night vision and the light of the now full moon in a cloudless sky, Shane couldn't see into the murky, brown water. Ahead of him, the capsized boat continued moving forward to the riverbank.

A commotion on the surface to the rear of the boat's stern drew Shane's attention. There, the coxswain was lifted out of the water by the arms and jaws of Ngu Tinh. Shane heard a horrible thrashing and wailing and saw a gush of blood spew from the coxswain's mouth as his body was crushed and torn open.

Shane desperately swam to the bank and tried to crawl toward the jungle. But he was grabbed by the legs and pulled back into the water.

Shane jerked open the flap of the holster on his web belt and gripped his .45 pistol, pulling it free. As he did so, Ngu Tinh grabbed Shane by the right arm now holding the pistol. Shane fought to turn the pistol in his grip toward Ngu Tinh as he squeezed off two rounds.

Ngu Tinh emitted a deep, raspy roar as he dragged Shane further into the water, sliding alongside the overturned boat. Shane suspected he'd only managed to hit Ngu Tinh in the tail or lower body, the low velocity and jacketed bullets causing little real damage. Shane tried to grab onto any part of the boat with his free left arm but was pulled under.

As Shane struggled to break free while straining to point his pistol at Ngu Tinh, he couldn't shake the horrible image of the coxswain being held aloft and crushed, his vest torn open in the process. His *vest*! Shane's mind replayed the image and recalled the coxswain wore a vest with rows of small pockets in front, each designed to hold one 40x46mm grenade cartridge for an M79 grenade launcher. Shane realized the coxswain must have had an M79 as his personal weapon, and it would be somewhere on the skimmer boat within reach of the coxswain station amidships.

Now being held underwater and pulled by his right arm, Shane reached up to the underside of the boat and felt around with his left hand for the familiar shape, a bit smaller than a baseball bat. Pulled deeper, Shane desperately grasped the boat's steering wheel for leverage and held on. He managed to break free, but only by losing his grip on the pistol was he able to prevent himself from being dragged to certain death.

Shane quickly pulled himself across the beam of the capsized, partially submerged boat to its other side. Pushed up from the muddy bottom only a few feet deep, he broke through the surface and desperately gulped a breath of air. But, Ngu Tinh had now come around to this side of the boat and again grabbed Shane by his outstretched right arm, pulling him under again and toward deeper water. Shane tried with his left hand to grab onto anything solid on the bottom. Frantically, he found a tree root to grip onto. With a firm hold, he was able to counter Ngu Tinh's tremendous pull, but he was unable to get his face above the surface to breathe.

Shane knew he couldn't let himself be pulled deeper, and he couldn't hold on without a breath much longer. Using all the strength he could muster, Shane dragged Ngu Tinh closer to shore and into shallower water by inching his way up the tree root. The strain in his limbs and the burning in his chest and face was like nothing he had ever felt before. His body felt as though it was elongating. His skin burned.

Even his face seemed to take on a very different shape as he struggled to raise his nose to the surface of the water. His fingers felt oddly claw-like as he continued to work his grip further up the tree root.

Then, just as Shane's face broke through the surface and he again gulped in air, the tree root snapped. Shane erupted with a loud roar of frustration into the bright, moonlit night. He reached behind him, desperately searching for another firm handhold. His hand wrapped around a smooth, round cylinder about two inches in diameter.

From his training a few years earlier in SERE school, where he was familiarized with every personal and crew-served weapon in the U.S. as well as the enemy's arsenals, he instantly recognized the shape of an M79 shoulder-fired, single-shot grenade launcher. He fumbled with his left hand to find the trigger guard and the stock's grip. He was exceptional in training at scattering the pile of old tires, the M79 training target, at 400 yards. But he had no idea what it would do at point-blank range to Ngu Tinh—or to himself.

Shane decided it didn't matter. No matter what the cost, for everyone's sake, this thing must be stopped. He could only hope the coxswain kept his weapon loaded with a grenade cartridge in the chamber. Feeling a strange, new, super-human strength, Shane planted his feet, leaned back toward the riverbank just a few feet away to counter Ngu Tinh's pull, and thumbed the weapon's safety forward.

Ngu Tinh reversed his pull and lunged at Shane, its head breaking the surface of the water. Falling backward, Shane howled with rage as he shoved the barrel of the grenade launcher into Ngu Tinh's huge, open mouth and pulled the trigger. . .

During the 30 years of Shane MacTire's life, he'd never experienced total silence and darkness. Now, in whatever this state of being, Shane was completely at peace but aware. He began to sense something. He felt a slight touch and sort of fluttering, as though butterflies were landing on his face. No, larger, they were possibly fairies lighting and walking on his forehead. It seemed their little feet must have been sticking to his skin as they moved, lifting and tugging at it. Shane felt first tingles, then stabbing, stinging pain. He tried to swat them away from his forehead, but something grabbed his arm, restraining it.

Shane stiffened defensively until he heard Julian's voice saying, "Whoa there, down boy. Don't do that. You'll mess up some of my finest work ever."

Shane opened his eyes to peer up at an olive-green scrub shirt and Julian's face.

Julian was gripping Shane's left arm, which was bulky with splinting and bandaging. With his other hand, Julian had hold of black threads running down to Shane's head like the strings on a marionette.

Julian spoke again, "Settle down, buddy. Now that you're with me, somewhat, you can work with me to finish tying you back together." Then, much more loudly, "Doc Stephens, he's waking up. I need some help here restraining him."

Shane's world went black again.

Doc Stephens informed Shane of his condition. "You have a severe concussion. I need to keep you here for a few days. Petty Officer Gomez did a fine job of suturing the scalp wound at your hairline, and the torn webbing between the thumb and palm of your left hand. You also have a bad sprain in that wrist, but it's not fractured. We picked a lot of shrapnel out of your whole left side. Fortunately, it didn't penetrate much below your skin."

Julian added, "Good thing he has a thick hide!"

Doc continued, "And from what I see already, you also have some remarkable recuperative powers. Oddly, there also seemed to be a lot of thick, dark, hairs embedded in some of the wounds. We removed it all along with the shrapnel. I was told that beast you fought was hair-less? It must have been from something else in the water. Well, I've got another patient to check on, but I leave you in the capable hands, and unbridled mouth, of Petty Officer Gomez, here."

As Doc left the room, Shane asked Julian, "Did anyone mention whether I looked—normal when they found me?"

"I was there. O'Connell took me along. You were unresponsive and bleeding a lot. And that frog thing! It was in the water right next to you."

"Nothing else—unusual?"

"Isn't that enough?"

"Sure. Okay, good. How long have I been out?"

Julian responded, "About 36 hours. That hottie from the temple came to the gate and asked for you this morning while you were unconscious. I went and met with her. You doing that? Doggie style, I bet. Do you two make each other howl?"

Shane cringed. "You know our friendship supersedes military courtesy, but let's not push it too far."

"Oh, sorry. No disrespect intended. She said she's not going back to that village. Listen, we had a good talk about you. She seems to believe you must be upset with her for not telling you something, and because there's something wrong with her - 'cause she's different. I told her, well, I let her know that you're not exactly normal either."

"Wait. What did you tell her about me?"

"I sort of explained you have some special physical traits. I'm sorry. It seemed necessary at the time."

"It's okay. It doesn't matter anyway. I doubt I'll ever see her again. I know what she must think of me, and I don't blame her."

"Oh! After we talked, she waited while I ran back here to get her an envelope and some paper. She wrote you this letter and asked me to give it to you when you awoke." Julian reached into his pocket, pulled out an envelope and passed it to Shane. Again, it was addressed to "Lieutenant Shane Mak Teary." Shane started to tear it open when Commander O'Connell and Chief Nazaro walked in.

The commander asked, "How are you feeling, Lieutenant?"

Shane admitted, "I've been better, sir."

"Doc says you're going to be fine. I suppose you're wondering what happened. How much do you remember?"

"That thing crushed the coxswain. I couldn't help him. When I saw it, it was too late."

"We know. We were monitoring your progress on Dufflebag. We saw both of your heat signatures, then we only saw one, and it wasn't moving. I decided we had to go in. When we got there, we found you half on the riverbank, losing a lot of blood. It was a miracle you were even still alive.

"We found what was left of that big frog thing in the water beside you. Its upper body was blown apart. From what we could tell, it looked like you'd fired an M79 down its throat, which exploded and blew back, striking you on the head. We found what was left of the M79 on the bank behind you. It seems that the body mass of that thing and the water saved you from most of the grenade blast."

"We found the coxswain's body just downstream. I want you to know that I'm recommending you for the Navy Cross for your actions, here and at Nam Can. I'll write it up good, so it doesn't get downgraded to a Silver Star. And you've also earned a Purple Heart, of course."

Chief Nazaro added, "If you were an enlisted man, you'd get a Bronze Star at best."

Commander O'Connell spoke again, "Oh, that reminds me. We just came from the commodore's office, and I thought you'd want to know — you're frocked."

Shane smirked, "I'm not surprised. It seems I always get frocked, as you say. What is it this time?"

"No, I mean you've been frocked to the rank of Lieutenant Commander. It came in the morning message traffic from Admiral Adams's office. They received the paperwork from the Bureau of Naval Personnel in Washington. Your promotion came through with an effective date of rank of 01 July 72. Frocking means that in the meantime, you are authorized to bear the title and wear the uniform of a Lieutenant Commander. You just won't get the pay increase until the official date of rank."

Shane reacted to the news, "Well, I'll be frocked! That's something, I guess. Thanks for letting me know, sir."

Commander O'Connell continued, "That's not all. We, ah, have one more thing for you, which also will be entered into your service record." He turned to the chief and smiled.

Chief Nazaro asked, "Are you feeling much pain, Lieutenant Commander?"

Shane replied, "It's tolerable."

The chief opened a small box, took out a gold SEAL Trident, removed the clasps from the prongs on the back side, placed the clasps and the box on the stand next to Shane's bed, smiled, and said, "You're about to feel a little more."

After the commander and chief left, Shane strained his neck down to look at the little trickles of blood running down his chest below where Chief Nazaro had just hammered the Trident with his fist. Shane winced but left it there for now.

He reached to the stand next to his bed and took the envelope he hadn't gotten to open earlier. Inside, again in flowing cursive penmanship, he read:

Dear Shane, I am leaving on a bus today. I have been in touch with a school for girls on Pasteur Street in Saigon. I now decide to accept a job teaching there. Before I go, I want to tell you more about the Ngu Tinh of ancient legend.

The sea monster, Ngu Tinh was defeated and killed in personal combat by the great hero, Lac Long Quan. Lac Long Quan was from the low wetlands and was said to be part dragon, which gave him special powers.

After he defeated the Ngu Tinh, Lac Long Quan was made king. He married and mated with a beautiful fairy goddess named Au Co, who ruled the high mountain region. By joining, they united both lands into one country. Together, they had many children who became the people of Vietnam. This is the origin myth of my country.

Shane, we all have our peculiarities, our strengths, and our weaknesses. They make us who and what we are - each unique. I believe that everyone – and everything - has a time, a place, and a purpose. Ngu Tinh has had his. You and I are just beginning ours. It is my hope that we might unite ours and see what wonders we could create together. Affectionately, Anisette.

"Julian! How soon will I be able to travel? I need to return to Saigon!"

MI-7 mission briefing:

The troubles in Northern Ireland have become more complicated. There are rumors that the IRA has recruited extranormal members for their terrorist organization. Use the utmost caution but find out the truth of these rumors so it can be dealt with.

Love and Rockets

Rowan Dillon

Saoirse pressed her back against the crumbling concrete wall. The cold seeped through her threadbare gloves and into her bones. She clenched her jaw to keep her teeth from chattering.

The British soldier stood just around the corner. The odor of his sweat tickled her nose, making her want to sneeze. A sneeze would be fatal.

A movement caught her eye on the other end of the alley. With a nervous glance, she tensed. Just a young couple walking, hand in hand. The boy's dark curly hair reminded her of Dermot's.

She gripped the Molotov cocktail with numb fingers. Her nailbeds ached and began to grow, but she shoved the wolf back inside. Now was not the time to change.

Was he alone? Could she get more guards in that spot before she threw it? She only smelled one, but most of them smelled the same. The soap their uniforms had been washed in, the cigarette smoke, the crappy aftershave. It mixed with the ever-lingering smells of smoke and garbage.

"Oy. All quiet?"

The male voice made her jump. She hadn't sensed anyone coming. He must be with the soldier.

"Aye. Nary a peep from the street rats. Last week's skirmish must've scared them paddys into their bloody 'oles."

"Good. That's where vermin belong. Not as good as dead and

rotting in the sun, but close enough."

Saoirse's teeth ached from gritting them so hard. She should wait for more soldiers. Padraig had wanted at least four in range, but she couldn't wait any longer. In a fervent plea, she squeezed her eyes shut. *Holy Mary Mother of God, guide my hand.*

With one final deep breath, she lit the rag, lunged to the corner, tossed the bottle to the left, then spun and ran.

She couldn't run as fast in her human form as she could in wolf form, but she ran much faster than any other teenager she knew. Zipping in and out of several side alleys, the sweat dripped into her eyes despite the chill. She panted as she dove into a dark doorway. Burrowing under the pile of old rags, her heart pounded until her breathing slowed almost to nothing.

Not a soul stirred outside. She must have lost them.

Slowly, shouts and cries filtered through to her hidey-hole, but nothing close. Thinking back, she couldn't even remember if the bottle exploded. Her entire being had concentrated on escape.

This was her first mission. What if she'd screwed it up? What if the Molotov cocktail hadn't worked? What if they'd all escaped?

A siren wailed somewhere in the distance. An ambulance. *Good. At least I hurt one of the Imperial scum.*

Two hours later, the commotion had faded to silence, and she risked emerging from her hiding space. The bitter February wind blasted her chapped cheeks. She stamped her boots and rubbed her arms, hoping to bring back feeling into her hands and feet. It didn't work, but it got her moving. She crept out into the alley and scanned for people.

All clear. With a practiced nonchalance, she strode northwest, to the bridge across the river to the Catholic side of Derry.

Letting out a deep breath, Saoirse knocked on the peeling wooden door. Three knocks, a pause, then two more. Her heartbeat sped as footsteps echoed inside, getting closer. She swallowed as Padraig stood in the open doorway, tall and lean with quiet strength, smelling of whiskey and soap. "Well?"

"It's done."

His gaze darted left and right before drawing her in, his fingers digging into her upper arm. She suppressed a grunt of pain.

The interior stank of old cigarette smoke and stale beer, with a delicate undercurrent of mildew. Times like this made her hate her enhanced sense of smell. Doing her best to breathe through her mouth, Saoirse stumbled down the dim hallway while Padraig pulled her into the kitchen.

The rickety wooden table sagged under the piles of supplies for making bombs and incendiary devices. Coils of wires, boxes for housing the units, half-assembled remote controls, even some lower-end items like bottles and rags for Molotov cocktails. A couple of M16s and some sort of old Browning had pride of place in the corner.

Padraig didn't have a huge operation, but his was large enough to command a decent group of guerilla insurgents. The murder of her father and brother had brought her into this group. The poddie scum had shot them down in cold blood while they did nothing but leave the factory where they worked. She'd make them pay for that.

Another reason was Seamus' friend, Dermot O'Neill.

She hid a smile. Dermot barely knew she existed and was a year older than her. The only reason he might even notice a sixteen-year-old girl was if said girl did something spectacular. Killing a British soldier must qualify as spectacular.

Padraig sat across from her on the faded sofa and crossed his arms, glaring at her. A sunbeam caught his prematurely grey hair, making it shine. "So, you threw it?"

She nodded, swallowing again to push the lump down her throat. "And?"

She glared at him, her nerves giving away to annoyance. "I don't know, do I? I ran like you said. I didn't hang about to take a survey."

He let out a short bark of laughter and gave her a half-smile. Low, urgent voices muttered outside the sheet-covered window. "Clever girl. We'll hear soon enough how effective you were. In fact..." His gaze darted to the window. "We may get our information any moment now."

Three knocks followed by two more. When Padraig went to let them in, she glanced at a half loaf of brown bread sitting on the Aga. She felt so hungry, her stomach hurt, but he hadn't offered any food, and she daren't take any. She'd been away from home all afternoon. Even her Ma's cooking would taste good by now.

Padraig returned, trailed by Dermot, Seamus, and a blond girl Saoirse didn't know. Suddenly her elation from her accomplishment, if such it was, dimmed to near nothing. His scent of spice and musk aftershave slapped her in the face, along with sweat and dust. The blonde smelled of lilacs, gardenias, and something else… something very much like Dermot.

Her eyes narrowed and she gritted her teeth, almost letting out a growl. The bestial rage rose inside of her, the wolf trying to escape. She clamped down hard on it. Da had always drilled into her she must never let the wolf escape when anyone but family could see it. Besides, she daren't shift in front of the others. Seamus might bustle her out before they realized what was happening, but that meant she wouldn't be near Dermot. Clenching her fists so hard her nails bit into her palms, she blinked unwanted tears from her eyes.

Seamus sat on the sofa next to Padraig, apparently already bored. The newcomers settled on the loveseat. They didn't hold hands, nor appear "together," but she still wished the blonde would go drop down a deep hole. That similar smell must mean at least a snogging, if not something much more intimate.

Padraig crossed his arms again. "What's the news?"

Dermot grinned, showing white teeth with a slight gap in the middle. Saoirse couldn't remain angry with that grin in the same room. "Mass confusion! Our girl here did a bang-up job, and I do mean bang-up!"

He tossed that dazzling grin in her direction, and she nearly melted from the strength of it. Saoirse couldn't even speak to thank him. Her entire body felt rooted in place.

Seamus let out a short bark. "I told you she'd be grand. She's cut from tough stuff, so she is."

The girl piped in, her voice unexpectedly deep. "Five soldiers injured, all taken to hospital. Rumor has it one won't make it. Well done, Saoirse! I'm Diane Sullivan, by the way."

Five injured! She sent a brief prayer to Mother Mary to guide the soul of the one who might die. Did Mother Mary even deal with British soldiers? She had no idea. She'd have to ask Father Murphy at Mass that night.

With grudging courtesy, she half rose to shake the girl's hand. Her skin looked flawless, not a freckle in sight. Saoirse frowned at her own speckled arm and withdrew it into her lap, wishing she could hide it away. What sort of name was Diane, anyhow? She sounded Irish, but that name screamed "I'm Anglo."

Even Padraig's praise couldn't lift her out of her funk. "Five casualties, good job. You succeeded in your first mission."

Saoirse nodded, numb from her emotions pummeling her. Why did she think this would work? He's probably been dating her for weeks, and she never even knew. She'd never even had a chance.

Padraig said something to Diane. Saoirse risked a glance up at Dermot and found him still grinning at her. She gave him a shy smile, but had to look back down before she made an utter fool of herself.

Standing, Padraig clapped his hands. "Now for your second mission. Do you think you're ready for a step up?"

How could she possibly know if she was ready if she didn't know what it would be? Regardless, she nodded, unwilling to ask stupid questions in front of Dermot.

"Right. Dermot, come with us. Seamus, Diane, are you set on what you need to do?"

The blond girl smiled wide, clenched her fist, and punched the air. Then, much to Saoirse's intense relief, they left the house. A wave of lilacs and gardenias and Dermot left with her.

Padraig drew them both into the next room, ostensibly a sitting room. However, no furniture remained for them to sit on, only wooden crates containing Lord knows what. Some of them were marked with possibly Arabic writing. Others had English writing, proclaiming them from the United States and one in the corner, from the Netherlands. The strong odor of coffee grounds and sawdust made her sneeze.

"Bless you." Dermot handed her a somewhat grimy handkerchief. She took it and dabbed at her nose, not wishing to blow it in front of him. When she handed it back, her hand brushed his, sending an electric thrill down her arm.

"Thanks."

Padraig jumped on one of the crates, clasping his hands in front. As such, he now sat above him, like on a throne or a dais. "Now, I need the two of you to work together on this mission."

Her day just kept getting better and better.

"Saoirse Mary Aoife MacTire, you are *not* leaving this house wearing that! We're going to Mass, not a bawdy-house! Get back into your room and change this instant."

She hung her head, trying to block out her little sister's maniacal giggling. "Yes, Ma. Shut *up*, Bridey."

Walking by her mother, meticulously dressed in her striped

A-line dress and faux pearls, Saoirse stuck her tongue out at Bridey, who continued to giggle. With grumbling reluctance, she changed from her shorter red skirt, which didn't even reach to her knees, to a more appropriate frock. She hated the soft, ugly thing. Flower print, in pastel colors. Old, horrible, and the farthest thing from sexy she owned, except maybe her pyjamas. Besides, the shorter skirt would make it far easier to shift, should she need to. The longer frock would get tangled in her legs. Ma never thought about such details. She wasn't a shifter like Da was. All the kids inherited the ancient family curse in one form or another, but Ma married in and when she finally found out about it, made it quite clear she didn't approve. They only gained the ability to fully turn if they experienced some massive trauma by the time they hit puberty, but in Derry in 1982, trauma was pretty much a given.

What if Dermot didn't approve? It would probably horrify him. She mustn't let him know until they were married, like Da did.

Properly attired, Saoirse stepped out for her mother's approval. She got a curt nod, and they walked out the door.

The street, never in the best of shape with potholes and occasional piles of debris from stray bombings, seemed particularly quiet tonight. Identical red-brick row houses spat out their families, all dressed for Mass, and they flowed toward the church in a steady wave. Her toes turned numb in the chilly air, as her dress shoes weren't sufficient for March, but she had no others that fit. She'd outgrown her boots this season, and Ma wouldn't buy more until next winter.

Their family walked along the sidewalk in a string. Her mother led the way, followed by her brother Seamus, her sister Siobhan, herself, and then Bridey, just ten years old. Their father had been killed last April, along with her brother, Sean. She wanted to walk next to Seamus, to ask him about Diane and Dermot, but not only did she not dare walk out of place, but she wasn't certain she wanted to hear the answer.

Seamus usually ended up being her confidant by default. Bridey was too young and Siobhan too self-centered. Now that they'd both joined the Provisional IRA, he became the only one she could speak with.

Uncle Shane had helped them with money sent from the States for a little while, but he didn't have much, either. He'd been in the Vietnam War, and couldn't hold down a job, despite their shared family heritage. Ever since then, money had been really tight. Her meager pay from Padraig's group would help bring some food in, at least. Seamus's work had kept them from starving all winter. Well, it had kept them from reverting to their ancient bestial habits, at least. Saoirse didn't know if she could kill as a wolf, even if her victim was a British soldier. However, if it came to that to feed her family, she would have to try.

As they crossed the last street toward St. Columba's Church, several British soldiers stood on either side of the street, blocking car traffic. They stood stock still, holding their guns across their chest, eyes locked forward. She swallowed hard, hoping none of them would arrest her for her actions that afternoon. How dare they make her so afraid on her own street? *English, Queen-loving scum of the earth!*

The pig next to her twitched his weapon. For a horrible moment, she thought she'd said all that out loud. When she had passed the last one, she breathed again. She sent out a heartfelt prayer as she stepped across the threshold into the sanctuary of the church. With a glance to the newly installed marble altar at the front, she thanked Mother Mary for protecting her before they took their regular places. She always found solace and peace within the church, despite the chaos outside.

Chaos both frightened her and excited her. That was partly due to their family heritage.

When she was eight, she had made the mistake of asking Ma if their family was cursed. She'd been completely unprepared for the volley of prayers and Hail Marys she'd been made to say after such a question. Later, Seamus had pulled her aside to explain.

"Of course, we're cursed. Did Da never tell you the story?"

She'd put her hands on her hips in exaggerated anger. "If he had, would I have risked going through all *that*?"

He chuckled, putting an arm around her shoulders. "Let me see if I can remember all the details. It dates back eons, to Saint Patrick, so the story goes."

"Saint Patrick? Are you kidding me?"

"Shut up and let me remember, right?"

She rolled her eyes. "Fine. Remember."

"From what Da said, there was this massive battle between the Faeries and some humans. Only, some of the humans fought with the Faeries, and Saint Patrick didn't like that. He cursed that family. Ever since then, they turned into wolves in the dark of the night. To help alleviate it, we're mandated to be protectors of others."

"But we don't turn only at night! We can turn when we want. And some of us can't even turn all the way."

He shrugged. "Well, that's the story. Maybe we've evolved."

She gasped. "Ma would wash your mouth out with soap if she heard that word!"

"Yeah, well, she isn't here, is she?"

School the next day seemed to be the longest day Saoirse had ever endured. That afternoon, she was to go with Dermot and harass some black-and-tans along the riverside. Just a little taunting, Padraig had said, nothing dangerous. This was to prove a distraction so another group could raid one of their armories for some much-needed guns. A new shipment had just come in, and Padraig wanted to get his hands on some of them.

She would be able to spend at least an hour with Dermot. Her hands grew cold and sweaty. What if she said something stupid?

She practiced the things she'd yell at the British pigs. "Go back to London!" seemed much too mild. "Feck off, you gibbering scum!" would be better. It couldn't be too strong, as she didn't want to goad them into shooting at them. She could run fast, but Dermot might get hit.

Maybe if she took a bullet for him? Her curse made her heal fast. That would certainly make him grateful. He might even fall in love for saving his life.

Her head in the clouds, she didn't even notice when Sister Mary Christopher stalked to her desk. When the ruler slammed on the wood, she jumped, again almost losing control of her feral nature. She must pay more attention to that! Why was it so hard to keep it reigned in lately? Could it be part of growing older? She wished Da were there so she could ask.

The huge white clock on the wall ticked slowly. Each minute lasted at least an hour. She fiddled with the edge of her uniform jacket, where it was beginning to fray. She must have Ma sew that bit up. Just because they were Catholic and poor didn't mean they had to look it, Ma always said.

Despite her anticipation, the bell caught her by surprise and she jumped again, amidst the bustle of students getting up from their desks and gathering their books. She strapped her backpack on and sauntered with practiced nonchalance to the place where Dermot said he'd meet her, right in front of the chippy down the street.

The heavy odor of fried fish and old oil assaulted her. As much as she loved fish and chips, they couldn't afford the treat often, and the smell of the place just made her want to run away. Dermot came out, holding a huge newspaper cone filled with chips and she reconsidered her reaction.

He held it out for her. "Have some? I just put on fresh salt and vinegar."

She smiled and picked a tiny one out, nibbling on the still-steaming end. How could she eat in front of him? So unattractive.

He shoved three at a time into his mouth and closed his eyes. "Nothing like a hot, steaming chip on a cold day, aye?"

With a nod, she picked another out. The salty flavor stung her tongue and made her mouth almost as happy as the rest of her. This felt like a date. Could she call it a date? It was, after all, a prearranged meeting. No matter that Padraig had arranged it, and not them.

As Saoirse reached for a third steaming chip, the rat-tat-tat of shots echoed down the street. She grabbed Dermot's arm and pulled him behind the shop to crouch behind the rubbish bin. She breathed through her mouth to keep from gagging. He managed not to spill the chips as they both hid in the alley. No more shots came, but they remained where they were.

He sat close next to her, so close their thighs touched. She daren't move a muscle in case he shifted away. He craned his head, looking out the alley, while she swallowed, trying hard not to do anything stupid.

He turned back to her, his blue eyes dancing. His lips were only about a foot from her own. She would just need to lean in a little bit. "Right, I think it's clear. We'd better go do our job."

Dermot rose and offered his hand to help her. She cast him a shy glance from under her eyelashes and placed her hand in his, imagining him as a prince pulling her up into a dance. When she stood, they were very close, just inches apart. She couldn't breathe but also couldn't stop staring into his eyes.

Clearing his throat, Dermot smiled and, their hands still linked, drew her out of the alley. Her hand sweated, but no force on Earth would make her break that contact voluntarily. They walked along the river, hand in hand, like lovers on a summer stroll. She felt ten feet tall and invincible.

Shouting on the other side of the river caught her attention. Some British soldiers were running, but they didn't look frightened, at least from this distance. Just six of them jogging along the edge, guns in hand, like they were doing a drill or something. They disappeared into an industrial complex and she paid them no more mind.

After almost ten minutes of bliss and a bridge crossing across the river, they approached their target. A warehouse on the other side of the armory, guarded but not heavily. Four black-and-tans stood sentry at the warehouse gate, and another two at the door inside. A truck pulled up to the entrance and, after some talking and papers exchanging hands, the driver was allowed in. Dusk set in, and the yellow sulfur streetlights flickered on.

Before they got close, Saoirse pulled Dermot back. "Hey, Dermot, I have an idea about this distraction."

He raised his eyebrows, inviting her to continue.

"What if, instead of yelling at them or throwing things, we distracted them in a different way?"

"I'm listening…"

She swallowed, praying he wouldn't laugh at her suggestions. Or worse, recoil in disgust. "What if we… gave them a show?"

Now his eyes narrowed. "What sort of show?"

Taking a deep breath, she plunged in. "A snogging show."

He stared at her, a slow smile spreading across his face. "That might work pretty damned well. And if it doesn't, then we can pretend to get into a fight. Besides, it would be much more fun!"

He agreed! He didn't shoot it down as a disgusting thought! Her head soared far above them, joy infusing her soul. She couldn't trust herself to answer, so she only nodded and squeezed his hand. He squeezed back.

Dermot and Saoirse, still holding hands, walked near the gate guards. *Showtime.*

She stopped and pulled off her backpack. The guards came to attention, holding their guns across their chest, watching her intently. She calmly took out the lip gloss from a side pocket, applied it, and replaced it, looking up at Dermot. After she shrugged the backpack back on, he took her in his arms and kissed her.

The soldiers fell away from her notice. So did all of Derry. Instead, she lived only for Dermot and his lips, his arms around her, his body up against his, warm and smelling of musk and chips. His lips were salty and delicious. His tongue darted into her mouth, just a flicker, and she moaned with desire. She wanted to drag him off then and there,

Padraig's mission be damned. Still, the plan was important, and they had a vital part.

"'Oy! You two! Clear off. This ain't no 'otel."

Dermot's hand drifted down to her bottom, squeezing slightly as she pressed up against him. His strong back under her hands flexed with the movement. She ran her fingers through his silky dark curls, something she'd ached to do for so long. She could feel his desire grow between them and a response tingled through her body.

"'Oy, do you hear me? Away with you both!"

The clack of the gun next to her ear made her freeze, making her desire screech to a halt. Dermot stopped and took a deliberate step away, his hands held up in clear sight.

Saoirse glared at Dermot. "See what you've done? Now we're in a right mess. You and your 'needs.' What did I ever see in you?"

Dermot's eyes grew wide in an expression of shock, but he caught on quickly enough. "My needs? Is that what it is, now? You're the one who couldn't wait to get away from yer Ma. 'Let's go down by the river,' you said. 'It'll be fun, we can have some time alone.'"

"Alone? Do you call this alone? With these pervy bastards watching our every move?"

By now, they had all four external guards surrounding them, and the two near the door had stepped closer. *So far so good.* But she needed something bigger, something more spectacular, to get the others away from the doors. Padraig had emphasized they needed to be far enough away not to hear the work in the armory next door. She stole a glance at Dermot's watch. The hands said it was five. Now was the time.

His eyes twinkling in the growing darkness, Dermot crossed his arms. "You know we don't have a place to be alone. Your family hates me! I can't even go to your house!"

"Don't you bring my family into this! Oh, so you'd rather put on a show for these lads? What about it, boys, want a real show?" She spread her arms, and she had everyone's attention.

Da said never, ever change in public. But surely just a little, for the greater good, could be alright. Besides, the night had deepened enough the guards would never be certain what they truly saw. They'd be labeled as drunk or mad for even reporting it.

Saoirse glanced at Dermot, wishing he wasn't there, mentally urging him to flee. She didn't want him to see her beast, not yet. She shouldn't let the entire wolf out, only her face and hands. Otherwise, her clothes would rip.

Turning her body away from him, she faced the youngest guard. She drew up all the anger and rage at their occupation in her home. *Invading our country, telling us where we can and can't go in our own neighbourhoods. Think they're better than us stupid Fenians, but we'll show them!*

Her wrath fueled, she released the ancient, cursed form. The growl grew deep in her throat as she lunged at him. Her bones ached as they lengthened, her skin itched as it stretched. Her canines lengthened and her fingernails grew into talons.

From the startled look on his face, he must have peed his pants from fear. Her trick worked, as his gun went off into the air. The other guards brought their guns back up and the two near the door ran forward.

"Run!"

She swiped at the nearest guard, a bare feint to frighten him, and then ran into the darkness.

A howl escaped her lips as she loped into the dim alleys, her backpack grasped in her claws. She led her pursuers down first one alley, then a second, occasionally pausing while they caught up, panting and sweating, stinking of fear and adrenaline. She would let out another howl and lead them further into the industrial warehouses and empty factories.

Finally, judging them well away from the armory, she found a place to hole up so she could regain control over her bestial self. She calmed her breathing and prayed Dermot had found an escape. Calming breaths. In and out. In and out. Just the way Da taught her.

Once her breathing was human again, she listened for pursuit. Nothing but a few trucks driving by and some drunk singing off-key. The slam of a door. A shout in the distance.

She emerged, straightened her school uniform, and ran for home. Ma would kill her for missing Mass. If she sprinted, she might just make it on time.

When she arrived out of breath, her mother glared at her with her hands on her hips. "What have you to say for yourself, young lady?"

Trying hard not to pant and wishing the sweat on her forehead had dried, Saoirse bowed her head. "I'm sorry, Ma. I just got talking with a friend and didn't notice the time. I came running as soon as I realized how late I was!"

"That is patently clear. You're a right mess. Get into your room

and change, quick as you can. I'll not be late for Mass because of you…
again."

Properly chastened, Saoirse did as she was bid. She changed into her frumpiest Mass dress, the one Ma liked the most. Maybe that would help.

The shuffle toward Mass seemed quieter than normal. She caught a glimpse of her brother, Seamus, but he walked a bit away from the group. Dermot walked next to him, and she let out a sigh of relief. Not only had he escaped, he'd made it home for Mass. However, her relief fell flat when she noticed Diane walking next to him. She said something to him, and he put his arm around her shoulder and gave her a squeeze. *How dare he! He just kissed me like we were married, and now he's walking out with* her!

Saoirse wanted to release the wolf and rip something to shreds. She wanted to scream and run down the street at top speed. All the emotions, fear, and worry from the day battled within her brain. Her nails grew thicker, and she pulled back on the maelstrom of emotions, worried she'd change right here in the middle of the street, right in front of the church. She barely even noticed the additional British soldiers on the street today. All her attention was focused on Dermot and Diane, walking twenty feet in front of her, cosy as you please.

When they sat in their spots in church, she tried to concentrate on the Mass, but to no avail. She tried to smell if he'd gone straight to her after they'd kissed for something more than a kiss, but she couldn't tell. They still smelled similar, but no sex odors lingered on either of them. She supposed that was something, at least.

After Mass, she should have gone to Padraig to report, but he knew she couldn't always get away from her Ma. Tomorrow would be soon enough. She hoped they'd succeeded in their mission, and the hit on the armory had been successful.

Padraig actually hugged her when she came in, after drawing her into the living room. "You did brilliantly, my girl! Couldn't have asked for better! Whatever you did drew them away like a treat."

She beamed at the praise, and glanced over to Dermot and Diane, already sitting on crates. Dermot with that heart-breakingly gorgeous half-smile on his face, and Diane grinning fit to break her face.

Padraig sat down at the old metal desk. "Now, I've got to plan the next hit. It shouldn't take me more than about twenty minutes, so if you hang out for a bit in the kitchen, I'll call you in with the details. Shoo." He waved them away and they shuffled off. Dermot opened the tiny, antique fridge and pulled out three beers. He gave one to Saoirse and another to Diane.

Taking the cold can, Saoirse's eyes widened. She'd only ever had beer once before, when she snuck one of her Da's… back before he'd been murdered. Her jaw set, she opened it and took a deep swig, almost choking from the bitter, fizzy taste.

Dermot patted her on the back with a laugh, and her face grew warm. Whether her flush came from the beer or sheer embarrassment, she had no idea.

Then Diane's eyes narrowed and she walked to sit next to Saoirse, facing her with an intent expression. "Can I ask you a favor?"

Startled, Saoirse nodded, resisting the urge to glance at Dermot.

"I want to do something with your hair. It's so gorgeous, but you always have it back in a ponytail. Can I style it for you? I have these gorgeous blue sparkly hair combs. They'd look stunning in your red hair."

Self-consciously, Saoirse ran her hand around the red ponytail. She'd always hated her hair, so tried to hide it. Not quite straight, not quite curly, just muddled in between. "Now?"

Diane chuckled. "No, of course not now, silly. I haven't got any of my tools here. We need curlers, a hairdryer, hair spray. Give you some lift, some body. How about after we finish this mission, sometime next week? You'll look like Farrah Fawcett when I'm done!"

Again, Saoirse touched her hair. A small warmth, a feeling of friendship and camaraderie, began to displace the envy and jealousy which had been eating at her heart. This time, she did glance at Dermot, almost asking his permission. He shrugged and flashed his half-smile again. With a shy nod, she agreed.

"Grand! Come over Monday, after Mass. We'll have a girl's evening."

"Come over… where do you live?"

She laughed. "Why at my house, of course! Just three doors down from you, toward the church."

The warmth she'd felt disappeared into a hole in her heart. Did she mean where Dermot lived? Or across the street, at Miss Esme's house? Neither seemed likely.

Padraig came in. "Right. I've got the plan set. Here's what we do."

That Saturday, Saoirse gripped the homemade device in her hands, and once again, the cold bit into her fingers. This time, however, it was a detonator for a small bomb planted near the British barracks. They only managed to get it to the entrance, but if they could gather enough troops to that area, it would be most effective.

Padraig had warned her to wait for exactly the right time. He wanted as many troops as he could get in place before she flipped her switch. She sat on the steps of the empty building down the street, just within sight, ostensibly studying the schoolbook on her knees. She glanced over several times, but never found more than one or two guards near the gate.

Diane and Dermot would be part of the distraction this time, and she seethed at the betrayal. Hadn't she done a fantastic job last time? Why should she be punished by being isolated from Dermot for this mission?

She monitored the area when she smelled them, and glanced the other direction to see a group of six young men and women, including her brother, Seamus, strolling along with apparent ease. They laughed and joked amongst themselves, unconcerned with the guards on the other side of the barracks fence.

None of them glanced at her when they passed. She continued to "study" her book, her hands now sweating on the grip of the detonator.

One of the boys, someone she didn't know, shoved Seamus. He let out a cry and shoved back. Then Dermot shoved the instigator, and a general tussle began. Angry shouts, more shoving, and then one punch to the gut later, the guards from the barracks came out.

"Move along, ye paddy shites. None of that here."

They ignored the guard's command, and continued to pull out a right Donnybrook outside the gate.

Saoirse gritted her teeth. They needed to move further away! They were way too close to where the IED had been planted. She couldn't trigger it with them so near.

More guards spilled out of the barracks. Eight, no, ten now. *Move, Dermot. You know you need to move. Move them all away!*

Twelve troops gathered, all with guns and grim expressions. Their words had no effect on the knot of fighting boys. Diane stood to one side, her arms crossed and her face set in a somber assessment.

Suddenly, one of the guards grabbed Diane and held her arms behind her back. When she struggled, another guard gripped her by the neck and they pulled her to the gate.

"Hey! All you lot! We've got your girl. Shove off and we'll let her free."

The fighting stopped. Dermot wiped his nose, where a small trickle of blood had dripped from a punch. Seamus straightened, a purple bruise already showing on his cheek.

Twenty soldiers now stood around them, all in range. *Come on, move off, all of you!*

A voice behind her whispered. "Good. Almost enough. Just a few more."

She jumped and swiveled her head to see Padraig leaning casually against the wall on the building next to her. "I can't do it now! It'll get our people!"

He nodded. "That may not be something we can avoid."

"My brother is there! Dermot! Diane!"

Padraig just nodded again. "You have to do it, Saoirse. For your Da. For Sean."

She swallowed, glancing back at the knot of people. Twenty-four soldiers. Some of the boys had backed off, just out of range, as well as she could tell. Dermot looked safe, as did Seamus. One boy she didn't know, the one who had shoved first, still stood too close. And Diane was at ground zero.

"Now, Saoirse."

She closed her eyes, urging Diane to run, run away. It didn't matter if she was Dermot's lover or not, she didn't deserve to die like this. Da had always told her to protect others. Diane, despite being with Dermot, should be protected. But he also said to protect the greater good. That's why they were doing this, right? To protect the greater good? *Run! Run!*

Padraig gripped her shoulder and, without opening her eyes, she squeezed the button.

The world exploded into a chaos of smoke and fire. The concussion of sound boomed through her head, and she covered her ears, screaming at the pain. People ran, shouted, and guns fired into the confusion. She darted behind the building, her book and the remote forgotten. Padraig had disappeared.

Her beast wanted free. It wanted to attack, to rend apart every soldier into quivering, bloody bits! Maybe she should rip Padraig apart as well. Tears pushed through her rage, dripping down her cheeks. She gasped and sobbed, trying to pull the wolf back into her heart, into its daily cage.

Had she killed Diane? How about the other boy? Maybe she'd misjudged the range and gotten all of them, Seamus and Dermot alike. She knew better than to look. She had to flee to safety, as the plan had dictated.

With growing dread, she wended her way through the streets of Derry, not knowing what she would discover when she got home.

British soldiers ran through the street on her journey. Four times, she had to flatten herself against a wall or hide in a doorway. They weren't looking for her. But the bomb had obviously disrupted operations considerably.

Barely daring to breathe, she walked up the concrete steps to her front door. Her hand shook as it touched the doorknob. She listened for a moment, hoping to hear voices; specifically, Seamus' voice. Nothing came through.

Once inside, the house remained eerily silent. With a household of so many people, that in and of itself was strange. She reached the sitting room, where her mother sat next to Seamus. Saoirse let out a deep sigh of relief to see her brother, alive and well, in her house. A bandage wrapped around his head, perhaps, but alive.

She blinked several times at her brother. "Seamus? What happened? The streets are full of soldiers."

His voice came slow and sad. "Someone set off a bomb near the barracks. We'd just happened to be nearby."

Pointing to the bandage, not certain she wanted the answer, she asked, "Were you the only one hurt?"

Her brother shook his head. "No. A few of the lads got shrapnel wounds. But the guards held Dermot's half-sister, Diane."

Sister? Dermot's *sister*? Sweet Mother Mary, Diane was his sister?

Tears came unbidden down her face. "What... what happened to her?"

Seamus only shook his head and dropped his gaze. Her mother patted his shoulder, pity in her eyes. "You were sweet on her, weren't you, son?"

He gave one desultory nod before the world crashed around Saoirse. Gray filled her vision and she collapsed on the floor.

Mother Mary, what have I done?

The funeral was held a week later. Saoirse's entire world had turned numb. Even Seamus couldn't snap her out of her shell. Her mother was no use, alternatively screaming at her and hugging her. Saoirse just stood stiff in her arms, refusing to speak.

Father Murphy tried asking her to confession, but she just sat in the cubicle. Even Bridey hugging her tight did nothing to change her mood.

Dermot came to visit her three days after the funeral, still dressed in black. She swallowed, wanting to emerge for him, but still unable to make herself do anything. He sat next to her in the sitting room and took her hand, holding it in silence. After about ten minutes, he stood.

"I know Padraig made you do it, Saoirse." Then he left.

She glanced at the table. Something lay there, wrapped in pink tissue paper. Slowly, she picked up the package, unwrapping it with trepidation.

Two sparkly blue hair combs.

That released the tears. The grief, the hatred, the frustration, the anger. Everything that had built up inside of her when she realized what she'd done poured out of her.

This time, she didn't hold back her full beast. Her nails lengthened into wicked claws, fur bristled all along her spine and arms, then the rest of her skin. Her teeth poked into her lips, and she howled with rage and despair.

Her mother rushed in and tried to take her in her arms. Saoirse struck out, her claws ripping her mother's dress.

"Leave me alone! Don't touch me!"

Pulling back, her mother retreated to the door in tears. "Saoirse! How could you! You promised never to change in the house!"

Saoirse didn't care about changing in the house. She didn't care about her mother's idiotic prejudice, or propriety, or anything right now. She just wanted to rip something, destroy something, to make something else feel as destroyed as herself.

She slashed at the chintz sofa, ripping great rents in the white and seafoam green stripes. Turning around, she glared at her mother, who beat a hasty retreat.

Her rage still burning through her veins, Saoirse loped out the front door. Someone stood in her way on the front walk and she plowed over them. She recognized the voice, deep in her bestial mind, and turned around.

Dermot picked himself up from the asphalt, brushing his knees. His eyes grew wide when he saw her. "Ah, bloody hell, Saoirse. I forgot we share a great-grandfather. You never said you could turn, too!"

The Office of the Aberrant briefing:

Rumors of an emeny power looking to replace leadership of a strategic partner with one more aminable to their political ideology is a danger to American interests in South America. The country in question is suspected to have untapped oil reserves and other crucial resources that most not fall under this emeny influence as they had the potential to become the most potent navel power in the world. The President has requested we deploy Jack Risen to handle this matter quietly.

Deep Cover

Patrick Thomas

Anton Hernandez's chest puffed up with pride, standing extra straight in his cleaned and pressed dress uniform. Just one week as a soldier in the Surinam Army and he was already assigned to a detail guarding the president and his family. Anton did not realize that he was chosen for the detail simply because the president knew he was just in from the jungle and so had not had time to be either co-opted, bought, or bullied into one of the varying factions in the army. The fact that divisions existed in his nation's military would have shocked and dismayed the young man.

Not only did Anton have much pride at the assignment's prestige, but he was privy to a show the likes of which his life in the rain forest had never provided him. What seemed like the very shapeliest of young women swam in the large lake the presidential summer residence was built near. Anton simply could not take his eyes off the beauty, who was barely covered by a bikini that seemed to have less material than one of his socks. The raven-haired goddess was tall and slender with curves that the young soldier yearned to hold in his arms. In his youthful mind, he had often imagined the perfect woman, basing her in part on his childhood crush. All memories of that girl had been incinerated by the goddess who stood in the water, her practically naked and wet body glistening in the sunlight.

Anton had to fight in order to force himself not to stare—one, because his duty was to monitor a stretch of the estate for intruders, and two, because this particular goddess was the president's daughter, Jantina.

It was a losing battle, but he managed to divide his time equally between his duty and staring longingly at his dream woman.

The president himself did not swim in the lake, sitting instead on the patio making a series of phone calls, one after the other. The president's wife had not joined them. Instead, he had brought his much younger secretary with him. Anton heard the whispers that the secretary was also the president's mistress but had been taught by his mother from a young age to never speak ill of others, especially if it was only rumor. His mother and he had suffered enough in their small village from vicious gossip and he took the lesson to heart.

The rainforest loomed almost an acre away from Anton's post, the land in between cleared. The private assumed he had plenty of time to notice anyone approaching, which conveniently allowed Anton to justify his sidelong glances at the bathing beauty. His shock was total when he turned away from the glistening girl to find an old man leaning on a cane in front of him. The private's resulting jump backward embarrassed the part of him that had become a soldier but he was also proud that he was able to catch the shout in his throat before it escaped his lips.

"Something scare you, boy?" asked the gray-haired man, who was dressed in a suit and tie, topping off his ensemble with a fedora-style hat. The temperature was well past sweltering and the humidity was far past the point of soaking skin. The old man was likely the only person in all of the Paramaribo District wearing long sleeves—let alone a suit jacket—out of doors. And he wasn't even sweating.

"How did you just appear like that?" asked Anton.

The gray-skinned man smiled and leaned on his cane. "Trade secret. One that would do you well to learn when performing guard duty so you can be on the lookout for it."

Anton realized that he was being derelict in his duty. A private in the army of the Republic of Surinam should not be conversing with an intruder, but subduing him. Anton raised his rifle from his side and pointed the business end at the old man. Instead of a look of fear or worry, the old man's smile widened going all the way up to his eyes.

"You are trespassing. You are hereby placed under arrest for invading the presidential grounds," said Anton, cocking the trigger on his rifle back.

"Now son, let's not go doing anything that either of us is going to regret," said the man. He spoke Dutch with an American accent. Unlike most of the other countries in South America, Spanish was not the native language. That was the problem with Surinam. Although Dutch was the national language, in the capital city of Paramaribo alone there were at least a half dozen languages spoken extensively, including Hindi, Japanese, Chinese, Spanish, English, and more than one native tongue. Quite a lot for a country of less than half a million people. Anton had a gift for languages and spoke most of them.

"My name is Jack Risen and I am with the CIA. Your president is expecting me."

Anton was not sure of whether or not to believe the old man, but he did have him within his sights. There was no harm in him checking, although the soldier hesitated to interrupt his president's phone call.

"Mr. President, this man says his name is Jack Risen and claims that you are expecting him," Anton shouted.

Across the way, the president hung up with whomever he was speaking with and slowly rose to his feet. His first expression was one of worry, but it was quickly concealed with a big smile.

"Ah, my American friend Jack. Welcome, welcome. It is always a pleasure to see you," said the president in English.

"It is always a good thing to bring pleasure to others with their arrival," replied Jack, likewise in English. "Do you think you could ask your soldier to stop pointing his rifle at my head?"

The president's face assumed a look of dramatic horror and he threw up his hands. "Private Hernandez, stop pointing your weapon at our honored guest this instant."

"Yes, Mr. President." Anton uncocked and pointed his rifle at the ground. "I am sorry, Mr. President. I was just doing my duty."

Jack Risen leaned in to whisper in Anton's ear. "Listen, kid, never apologize for doing your duty. Save the *mea culpas* for the times you screw up, not the times you don't. Trust me, there will be plenty of both."

Jack Risen walked slowly towards the president. Anton could not help but notice that the old man did not seem to really need the cane. The two men embraced.

"My friend Jack, can I get you a drink?" said the president.

"A double scotch. And don't be stingy," answered Jack.

"With you? Never," said the president, pouring the old man's drink himself. Anton noted this with interest. This Jack Risen must be someone truly important as the president didn't even pour his own drinks, instead having one of his soldiers or secretaries tend to the task.

The two men sat down at the table to talk and whisper things Anton could not make out. After a quick glance to make sure no one else was invading the grounds, the soldier turned his attention back towards the scantily clad young woman swimming in the lake. Jantina had moved closer to shore and was standing so the water barely came up to her hips. She seemed to realize that Anton and the other soldiers were all concealing their lustful stares and appeared to be enjoying the veiled attention. In a blatant display of exhibitionism, she reached her arms up toward the sky, stretching what little there was of her bathing suit to the limit. Anton could not have turned away if terrorists had chosen that moment to storm the compound with guns blazing. Jantina's body moved in ways that Anton was sure would be revisited in his dreams for many nights to come.

This voyeurism did more than feed a soldier's desire and a young girl's ego. Since all of Anton's attention was focused on the president's daughter he could not help but notice when something green and scaly rose up and dragged her below the water. Alligators were not common in this part of the rainforest and rarely found their way into lakes, but that didn't mean they weren't there.

"Jantina has gone under the water!" yelled Anton, throwing his rifle on the ground. Not even bothering to strip out of his uniform or army-issued boots, he raced toward the water, diving in head and hands first. The arc of his dive was easily ten feet long in the direction the girl had been pulled.

Anton had always been at home in the water. As a child, he could swim better and faster than any adult and stay underwater for lengths of time that made everyone but his mother believe he had drowned. Anton also had the uncanny ability to be able to see, hear, and even smell with amazing accuracy while in a watery element. It sometimes alienated him from his peers, one of his reasons for leaving the jungle for the big city.

That which made him a freak in his village was a blessing here. In seconds, Anton had found the missing girl. What was with her sent chills down his spine. It was not an alligator. Two men held either side of Jantina, if you could call them men. Even in the dark water, Anton could see they had green scales for skin as well as webbed hands and feet. A brief glimpse might let them be mistaken for alligators, but a good look would not.

Despite her struggles, they dragged Jantina through the depths of the lake. Anton worried she would drown, but there was something placed over her mouth that bubbled and seemed to allow her to breathe.

Anton wished he had not been so quick to throw down his rifle, even if he did not know if it would work beneath the lake. Shooting underwater was not something covered in soldier training. Fortunately, he had a knife stashed in his boot, a suggestion from the sergeant who trained him. Removing the blade, he swam faster toward the reptilian kidnappers. Because they were expecting no pursuit, they did not notice Anton until he was almost on top of them.

For an instant, the reptilians repelled back from him.

You take the girl. I'll take the soldier. Anton heard this from the kidnappers, but inside his head rather than with his ears. He had often heard voices in the past, but at least this time he knew where they were coming from.

The one closest to him let go of the woman and flipped around toward him, swimming faster than he had ever seen anything else move in the water. Suddenly his claws were raking toward Anton's face. If not for an instant of sheer panic-filled reflex, Anton would never have gotten out of the way in time. The act of blocking brought Anton's blade into play. Instead of having his face torn off, Anton managed to plunge his knife into the side of the reptilian creature.

Argh!

This cry of pain echoed inside Anton's head. As the creature sped away, Anton kept a death grip on the hilt, pulling it free from the scaly flesh. Anton didn't chase him, choosing instead to go after the girl. Her remaining captor had not bothered to look back, probably lulled into a false sense of security by thinking that no human would be able to stay under water long enough to either follow him or survive an encounter with his partner. This overconfidence allowed Anton to sneak up behind him and stick his knife between the creature's ribs.

This time Anton left the knife in the wounded reptilian, mainly because he needed his hands free in order to grab hold of Jantina. The young beauty grabbed him back hard, holding on for dear life. As

Anton felt Jantina's mainly bare flesh press up against him in a way he had only dreamed of, thoughts of danger and escape were momentarily overwhelmed by a lightheaded bliss. Jantina's terrified eyes looking back over his shoulder brought him back to the deadly reality they now shared. Holding onto Jantina with one arm, the young soldier swam away so fast he caused wakes in the water.

Unlike the creatures, Anton was not so confident that he didn't look behind him. The sight of two green shapes surrounded by growing clouds of red spurred him on to even greater speeds.

When they arrived at the shoreline, Anton did not slow down, instead picking his waterlogged goddess up in his arms and running toward the land. The change from water to shore caused Anton to stumble and land on his knees, but he did not drop the girl.

Her father raced toward the fallen soldier, taking his daughter from Anton's arms into his own.

"We need to move sir. They're right behind us," said Anton on hands and knees, gasping from the exertion.

"Who is behind you?" demanded the president.

As if in answer, the two creatures emerged from the shallow water racing toward the girl they had lost. Their reptilian appearance caused the other soldiers to freeze in disbelief. Jack Risen stepped forward, pulled a handgun out of his jacket, and put a bullet between the eyes of each creature. Both reptilian men fell to the knee-deep water unmoving.

"You men retrieve those corpses. I want to make sure they are dead," said Jack, stepping into the water wearing shoes that cost more than Anton would make in a year. He offered the younger man his hand. Anton took it.

"Well done," said Jack, pulling the soldier to his feet. When their hands separated, Jack looked down and noticed webbing between Anton's fingers that had appeared during his time in the water.

Anton pulled back his hand and was looking at Jack in a new way. "Your hand is so cold. Are you not well?"

"I'm as well as someone in my condition can be. How about you?" he said, pointing towards the new folds of skin on Anton's hands. "That something new?"

Anton looked rather sheepish. "It doesn't happen often."

"Hmmm." Jack rubbed his chin thoughtfully. "Mr. President, this soldier is a brave man, not hesitating to leap when others stood still. His actions saved your daughter." Jack then noticed the president struggling with the organic-looking blob on Jantina's face. The old man walked over, took a lighter out of his pocket, and held it over the lumpy mass. Moments later it shivered and fell off her face, leaving behind some slight discoloration, but other than that the girl appeared fine. Jack used his shoe to grind it into the ground. "I would like him to be my personal attaché during my time here, if that is okay with you."

"If it is okay with me? This man is a national hero, he shall have any reward he desires." The president stood up to embrace Anton, kissing him once on each cheek. "Thank you, Captain Hernandez, thank you."

"Mr. President, I am only a private."

"Not anymore," said the president, turning to his daughter. "Are you okay, my dear?"

Jantina nodded, still shaken up by her attempted submerged kidnapping. "Thanks to him." The president's daughter stepped forward, gently placed her open palms on Anton's chest, and stood on her tiptoes. "You have my eternal gratitude." She kissed the soldier on his cheek. "Perhaps later I can see you alone and show you just how thankful I truly am," she whispered in a tone that made Anton's knees go weak.

"We need to get you to the doctor," said the president snapping his fingers. A servant ran to get the estate's physician. The president led his daughter gently by placing her arm in his and led her toward the house. He looked back over his shoulder at the old man. "Jack, you'll take care of this for me?"

"That's why I'm here, Your Excellency," said Jack. "*Captain* Hernandez, you are with me. You four ..." Jack pointed to a quartet of soldiers who moments earlier outranked Anton. "...bring the bodies to the wine cellar."

"What do we do now?" Anton asked.

Jack Risen's gray face was unable to hide a smirk. "Odd choice of question. Most people in this situation might first inquire as to what those creatures are. I think perhaps you might have a little insight into that yourself, eh Anton?"

The newly made captain did not reply, but his refusal to look Jack in the eyes answered the spy's question just the same.

The wine cellar was built a hundred years prior, deep beneath the presidential estate, its walls made from rock that a talented stonemason had lain down to fit together seamlessly. The temperature there rarely rose above fifty degrees. It was not refrigeration, but it would slow any decay.

A pair of folding tables were brought down and the soldiers placed the creatures' corpses upon them. Their task complete, Jack said, "Leave us."

Once the door had closed behind the exiting soldiers, Jack twisted the tip of his cane and pulled out a hidden sword blade. This was not a flimsy bit of metal, but finely honed and crafted steel. The old man took a swing at the necks of each of the reptile men, detaching their heads from their shoulders.

Anton found himself slightly sickened by the act, but also fascinated, looking at the exposed flesh and blood. "Why did you do that?"

"Because deep ones are notoriously hard to kill and can live centuries so long as they don't sustain a mortal wound." The old man pointed to the neck stump. "They can breathe like a man on land and these gills let them breathe underwater." The spy turned and looked at Anton's neck so intently that the young captain found himself tightening the collar of his still-wet uniform. The old man eased back. "Why back in nineteen twenty-eight, the US torpedoed Devil's Reef off the coast of Massachusetts and even that wasn't enough to destroy that entire colony."

"Were you the one who did that?" Anton asked.

"Exactly how old do you think I am boy?" snapped Jack. Anton stammered and Jack waved him to stop. "What I'm trying to say is, if deep ones can survive that kind of damage, I figured it was best if they didn't sit up and try to kill us while we examine them."

Anton curled his brow. "That could happen?"

"That and even more. The deep ones have been around for a very long time and have always tried to influence politics on a small scale, usually choosing an isolated town or village to infiltrate. Of late, their ambitions have been growing. It appears as though they are looking to make themselves major players in the world scheme starting with the takeover of your country."

"Why Surinam?"

"Your nation is relatively small and is literally a melting bed for a dozen cultures. It makes their infiltrating easier," Jack said. "And recently oil deposits richer than those in Venezuela have been discovered. Your poor country is about to become very rich and strategically important."

"But they are green and have scales. How exactly would they manage to infiltrate us? They can hardly hide in plain sight," Anton said.

Jack wiped the blood from his sword, which had an odd green tint to the normal red. "Excellent question, but one I think you may have the answer to, eh my boy."

"I…" stammered Anton.

The old man held up a hand. "Please, don't insult either of us by trying to make up some lie." The old man reached out and lifted Anton's right hand. "It appears that your fingers are back to normal. Interesting, wouldn't you say? Perhaps we could start with you explaining that."

Anton took to the defensive. "How about we start with exactly why you're so cold? And your skin isn't like any I have seen before. You are the color of a corpse."

The old man laughed. "Good. Your observation skills match your reflexes and courage. A very encouraging sign. Okay boy, I will tell you a little about myself, but be warned what you're about to hear is so highly classified that it makes top secret look like yesterday's washerwoman gossip. I have worked for the CIA for a very long time. I am over eighty years old and once, not that long ago, I tried to retire. It seems my superiors were a little concerned about some of the knowledge I carried around inside my head and they decided the best retirement for me would be the grave.

"However, right before my decision to leave the CIA, I'd stopped what would commonly be referred to as a mad scientist. He had been working to combine the Frankenstein elixir of life process with a zombie virus, creating a new even more dangerous entity. Said scientist got the drop on me and injected my body with something fowl. Even so, I managed to stop him and blow up his lab, but not before his process started to work on me. The key to the whole thing was death by electric shock. The person sent to eliminate me was told to make my retirement look like an accident, so he knocked me out and put me in a bathtub, which was followed by the throwing in of multiple electrical appliances. The shock was more than enough to kill me, but it also jumpstarted and finished the work the mad scientist had begun. I died, but came back as something … else."

"That is unbelievable," said Anton.

"Most of the good stories are. Now you best not share that with too many people because my government is never one to waste an asset and eventually brought me back into the fold. I officially work for The Office of the Aberrant, but the OTA subcontracts me out to the CIA, as it is easier to explain. They would be willing to kill you to stop that information from getting out, so I advise you to never speak of it. Now why don't we talk a little about you and your amazing ability to stay underwater extended periods and that wonderful webbing that appears between your fingers when you get wet? And I for one would love to know exactly why you were not the least bit startled by the appearance of two deep ones."

Anton shifted from foot to foot uncomfortably and was having trouble with not looking away from the old man.

"I am going to guess that you have had some experience with deep ones before?" said Jack Risen.

"I grew up deep in the rainforest and practically lived in the water. I could out swim anyone, even some of the fish and alligators. There have been occasions where I have noticed people like them watching me from a distance, but whenever I would approach them they would vanish or would swim away faster than I could follow."

The old man rubbed his chin. "Tell me about your father."

The newly made captain shrugged. "Not much to tell. I've never met him. He and my mother were never married and she has never really told me anything about him other than he is not like other men and that he was very important."

"You never pressed her for more?" asked Jack.

"I did, not that it did me any good. There was some talk in the village that my mother had done … unnatural things with unnatural creatures, but it was only spiteful rumors."

"And how do you explain your aquatic gifts?"

Another shrug. "It's just something I have always been able to do. I was an adolescent before I realized everyone couldn't do them. Now tell me more about these deep ones."

"They are an ancient race who worship the dark sea god Dagon, whom they call 'father,' and his consort Mother Hydra. Some of them even worship an elder god that sleeps and dreams, but so far we have been able to keep him out like a light under the Pacific."

"Gods? You can't be serious."

It was the old man's turn to shrug. "I know I had a similar reaction many years ago when I was told the truth, but I learned. Boy, did I learn. One other thing you should know: their method of infiltration involves mating with humans, mainly the males with human women, and producing offspring which for all intense purposes look human, but maybe have some extra … aquatic abilities. At certain ages, which can vary from puberty to old age, the children change their appearance and begin looking just like their deep one ancestry. I felt that was something you would want to know."

"Are you saying my father is one of these things? That I am going to turn into one of them?" demanded Anton.

"Perhaps. It would be an explanation, although obviously not one that you would much care for."

"But that means the reason they're after Jantina ..."

"Exactly. The grandchild of the president would very likely one day have a shot at ruling this country. Having him be half deep one would certainly help the rest of the reptilians out, don't you think? They'll all still be around, so the waiting is only time to them. It could be just a simple kidnapping and they were planning to use the girl as a bargaining chip to try to get something they wanted. Sadly, I've found that when you consider the darkest possibility, you're never disappointed with the actual outcome," the old man said.

The spy examined the bodies, looking under their clawed fingers and toes, in between the webbing, turning them over to check every nook and crevice.

"But for them to take her in a lake makes no sense," said Anton.

The old man raised an eyebrow. "Why so?"

"Well, the lake is not terribly big and it's not fed by a river. Where exactly were they going to go? Stay at the bottom of the lake until dark and then try and sneak out?"

"That is one possibility. Another would be that the lake has some other outlet that we don't yet know about, but we'll need to find."

"How are we going to do that?" Anton said.

"We could just call up a mini-sub and take it down and see where it can lead us," said Jack.

"That would be amazing," Anton said, his pupils wide with excitement.

"Yes, it would, especially since your entire navy does not have a submarine of any sort, let alone one that is small enough to use in the lake."

"Then how are we going to do it?"

"You and I are going to go down and see what we find," the old man said.

It took three hours for scuba gear to be brought to the presidential summer residence. Although Jack could have gotten by without it and was reasonably certain that the young captain would be able to as well, it was best to keep up appearances. Besides the facemask would be useful in terms of looking, for Jack at least.

In addition, Jack had requisitioned a few other things including a pair of spear guns, large knives, plastic explosives, and several detonators.

"What about guns?" Anton asked.

The old man shook his head. "Too unreliable, at least the guns that are readily available here. Even with a decent gun, the currents and the other factors can play havoc with marksmanship. The spear gun is a much more efficient weapon."

"But it is only good for one shot," Anton said.

"Yes, so you better make sure that you don't miss," Jack said, handing one to the soldier.

The president had ordered wetsuits to be brought to the men. Anton declined, choosing to wear a pair of bathing trunks. Jack Risen simply took off his hat, coat, and tie.

"It may not be waterproof, but I'm comfortable in it."

The pair donned the scuba gear and walked into the murky waters. Knowing he would be unable to see far, Jack was more than happy to let Anton take the lead. Before going in, they had gone over a map of the lake, making it into a grid that they searched bit by bit. The process took hours underwater and in the tradition of lost items everywhere, they found it in the last place left to look. At the far end of the lake, it bordered a small rock cliff. The stone continued under the water. Jack had insisted they search the entire rock face with their hands. It was Anton who accidentally brushed against the trigger, causing a single part of the stone to flip inward like a door. The water within was black as ink and there was no lighting in the tunnel.

Using hand signals, Jack asked if Anton could see and he put his thumb and index finger together about an inch apart, indicating a little. Next, he mimed if he saw anything inside and Anton shook his head so Jack nodded and motioned for him to go in first.

Nervous but unwilling to look afraid in the eyes of the old man, Anton swan onward. Jack followed. The tunnel was small enough that if either man extended both arms out, they could touch both sides of it at the same time. Plunging ahead in a slow and careful manner, they made steady progress swimming by touch, using the walls to guide them forward. Their sense of time not only got lost but jumped the track entirely. The tunnel easily extended for miles. It was a good thing that neither was actually using their air tanks because they would have been in danger of running empty and drowning. After what must have been hours of slow and steady, Anton jerked to a halt, extending one hand behind him onto Jack's chest, so he did the same.

Slowly, Anton moved forward. As Jack followed, he realized there was a light in the distance. It was one of the reasons they hadn't brought a light. Deep ones could see in the dark and Anton shared that skill. That dim light shone like a beacon in the night as the pair advanced through the murky blackness. They followed it and emerged in a pool, their heads breaking the water when they stood.

Jack gasped for breath. Anton looked at him.

"Don't have to breathe, but the body gets used to it," Jack said, looking around. They were in a bunker of some sort. The walls were cement and box-like, a single light bulb hung on the ceiling and provided the light that guided them in. Jack pointed to Anton's neck which had sprouted subtle skin folds. "We can't all have your advantages."

Anton raised a hand to his skin folds and tried to change the subject. "Where are we?"

Jack stepped out of the pool onto the cement floor and stripped out of his scuba gear. He brushed the water off his clothes as if it were lint. The spy was still soaked, but the action seemed to make him feel better. "I'm not sure, but I bet you if we go through that door, we will find out."

"Is that wise?" asked Anton, removing his air tank.

"We just swam through a tiny tunnel built under a jungle into what is likely an enemy stronghold. Why turn wise now?"

There was no lock on the door. Those that built this place probably didn't see the need. The access tunnel was filled with water and even the best-trained scuba divers or Navy Seals would likely run out of air before they reached the end. They thought their bunker unreachable by any but them. They were wrong.

Jack examined the door from the knob to around the frame very carefully,

"What are you looking for?" asked Anton.

"Booby traps. You'd be amazed at what nasty surprises you can hook up to a door. Electricity, poison, even explosives. All great fun if you trip them. However, this one looks clean. Would you like to do the honors?"

Anton hesitated. "Are you sure there's no booby traps?"

The old man laughed put his hand on the knob, then turned and pushed. The door creaked but nothing else happened, not even a small explosion. "I am now. There are no guarantees in this life or the next. You take a chance when you think you've got a good one."

The hallway was decorated in the same cement block architecture style. Its length was decorated with three more single bulbs hanging evenly spaced from the ceiling.

"I don't see any cameras. Of course, these days I wouldn't if they were any good. I miss the old days when you at least had an idea of what you were walking into," said Jack.

There was another door at the end of the hallway. Jack repeated his inspections and again opened it. Behind door number two, there were three men waiting for them, although only two of them qualified as human in the strictest sense of the word. The humans were in military uniforms. Between and behind them was another reptilian man. The deep one held an automatic handgun and the soldiers held rifles. Anton raised his spear gun and pointed it at the green man. Jack barely reacted except to narrow his eyes.

"I'd ask you what you are doing here," said the man in scales, his voice guttural and raspy as if his throat and mouth weren't designed for human speech. "But I'm afraid you'd answer me and I wouldn't be able to torture it out of you. And where would the fun in that be?"

"I'll shoot you first," said Anton, holding his spear gun.

"You could do that, son," said Jack. "But the other two soldiers have Type 56 riffles. It's an old Chinese knockoff of the AK-47, but it shoots over six hundred rounds a minute. He would have a large stick poking through him and you'd be dead and the consistency of hamburger."

Anton took his finger off the trigger and held the weapon forward. The soldiers were more than happy to take it from him.

"Take them to the interrogation room," the deep one said.

The two soldiers herded the intruders using a generous helping of gun barrel battering to indicate direction, leading them down a new hallway and into another room. "Interrogation room" sounded frightening but relatively safe. What awaited them was anything but. There was no table or even a mirror for anyone to observe questioning. Instead, the cement room was furnished with surgical tables, complete with steel clamps for wrists and ankles. A chair with leather straps sat to the side.

Anton was too frightened to speak.

Jack didn't have that problem. "Not really into this kind of thing, especially on the first date. And you have horrible Feng Shui."

The deep one pistol-whipped him across the right cheek. The old man's skin opened and something that didn't much resemble blood trickled out. "Ouch," he said deadpan.

"Silence!" demanded the reptilian. "You will speak only when I tell you to speak or you will know pain like you have never known before."

"As threats go, not terribly original. You use the word speak twice in the same sentence. Couldn't you try something a little more original? Substitute talk or maybe utter for speak," said Jack.

The reptilian brought his knee up into the old man's groin. The spy doubled over in pain.

"Get him into the restraints," ordered the voice from the deep. The two human-looking soldiers obliged, binding Jack and then raising the table so that he was at an angle most of the way toward standing.

"Bind the other one." The green man from the deep walked over so he was almost touching Anton, then bent his head forward. Anton leaned away. What passed for a nose on his reptilian face wrinkled as he took several sharp inhalations, then smiled. "But be gentle with this one. He's family."

"What do you mean family?" said Anton.

"Do you think that a human could swim through our tunnel? The old man smells of death, but you…" He held up Anton's hand. The webbing on the fingers was much less then when he first got out of the pool but had not faded completely yet. "You know you are more than human. You are a child of Dagon and Hydra. And we will show you where your true loyalties must lie—with your family."

The soldiers secured Anton to the chair with leather bindings for his wrists and ankles. Next, they dragged out a gas-powered monstrosity of an engine-driven generator. It was nothing fancy, although it did sport a pair of jumper cables.

"So, what are your plans here? Start a Surinam chapter of AAA?" said Jack.

The reptilian took one of the clamps on the end of the jumper cables and attached it to the jowls under the old man's neck. "I told you; I will ask the questions here."

"Well, that's hardly much good for a conversation, isn't it?"

The reptilian gave an abrupt laugh. "Strip him." The soldiers obliged.

"You're really not my type. I'm not into sushi or long walks underwater. It's not you, it's me. But we can still be friends," said Jack.

"Humans and the deep ones can never be friends. There can never be peace between our races until one of them is eliminated."

"All right, if that's the way you feel about it. I'd like to say we'd miss you, but I'd be lying," said Jack.

"In a moment you will be screaming," said the creature, taking the remaining clamp and attaching it to a much more delicate area that was significantly lower down than Jack's neck.

For the first time, a look of fear crossed Jack's eyes. "You son of a bitch."

"Never insult Mother Hydra," the reptilian said, throwing the switch on the generator. Electricity shot through the wires out onto the metal clamps and through Jack's body, making the muscles spasm and convulse. The old man screamed, first in pain, then anger. The look on his face made the two soldiers involuntarily take a step back. Jack's face had become something inhuman.

"Stop it! You're killing him!" Anton screamed, straining to be free of his chair's restraints.

"That's the idea," the reptilian said. He turned his attention back to Jack and shut the switch off. "Now, why don't you tell me what you're doing here?"

Jack coughed up something that again was not quite blood. He gasped for air and it took him a moment to get enough breath to speak. He used that time to hide his inner monster's fury back under the veneer of an old man. "We were looking for a nice two-bedroom on the waterfront and we heard this place was for sale, much like Mother Hydra herself. I hear for a buck she'll go down on the whole fleet and give back change."

"Blasphemer!" The reptilian flipped the switch and let the electricity flow twice as long, the current not allowing Jack's exhausted muscles to rest, making them fire into constant states of contractions and convulsions.

"Now I ask again and for the last time, what are you doing here?" The deep one leaned in close to Jack's face and the old man spat his not-quite blood into the reptilian's eyes.

"Bite me."

The deep one opened his jaws showing two rows of sharp teeth. And they were surrounded by a dark grin. "I'd love to." The reptilian leaned in.

"Stop! Leave him alone. I'll tell you what you want to know," Anton said.

"Captain, you don't have to tell him anything. I am perfectly fine," Jack said. The old man may have been the toughest person Anton had ever met, but even the young soldier could tell he was in pain.

"We know you tried to take the president's daughter. We know you had plans for her," Anton said.

The creature turned from the old man and smiled. "Of course we do. Do you know what those plans are?" Anton nodded. "Do you know that you yourself are the offspring of similar plans many, many years ago?"

Anton's face was ashen as he nodded.

"Were you the one who wounded our brothers?"

Anton's head again moved up then down.

"You are lucky. They will be fine by the tides of the next new moon. You had not been brought into the fold before now, so this transgression shall be overlooked this once and you will be allowed to live and serve your people. We will one day rule this land and you will help us. Having saved his daughter, you must now have the trust of the president. We can use that to our advantage," the reptilian said. "But first you will have to prove your loyalty."

"How exactly?" Anton said.

The deep one simply turned his head and looked at the shackled Jack Risen and pulled his finger along his throat.

"You want me to kill an old man?" Anton asked.

"I want you to kill an enemy of our people. One who seems to know far too much to be allowed to live. The deep ones survive because humans do not believe we exist."

Anton's eyes narrowed. "What's in it for me?"

The reptilian's eyebrows rose. "You get to live."

"That's not enough. You want me to come work for you, then you have to make me an offer. This morning I was a private in the president's army, now I am a captain. You want me to throw that away and do something I find morally repugnant, then you've got to give me a better reason. You say I would be doing this for the family. What would my position be in the family? Soldier, officer, cannon fodder?"

The deep one laughed. It was a deep and frightening thing. "You are far too valuable for cannon fodder. Not many of our offspring exhibit the abilities you have shown so far at such a young age. Why we even have some family able to shift back and forth between their true forms and that of a human." A single eyebrow rose on Jack Risen's face. Apparently, this revelation was news to him. "You may be one of them. That means you would have a high ranking with the deep ones. Did you know that you will live for hundreds, maybe thousands of years if Father Dagon and Mother Hydra smile upon you? You're not going to rule even a small village right away, but given time and work, someone with those abilities has the potential to rule this country. Or, better still, be one of the high council, those that answer to none but Father Dagon and Mother Hydra. That is the reward you should try for. Is that enough for you?"

Anton grinned and held his hand out. "Oh yeah. Give me something to kill the old man with." The deep one handed the young soldier his gun. The other two soldiers carefully trained their rifles on him. Anton pretended not to notice. He walked over to the surgical table that Jack Risen was strapped to and pointed the gun between the old man's eyes.

"Kid, do you really want to do this?" said Jack.

"Not particularly, but I don't want to die. And maybe someday being in charge of this country? President Hernandez. That's got a nice ring to it, don't you think? Close your eyes, Jack. I will make it quick."

The old man shook his head. "Nope. You think I'm going to make it easy by not watching you? You want to kill me, you have to watch the life go out of my eyes."

Anton shrugged. "Suit yourself." Anton cocked the hammer back, put his hand on the side of the table and spun it, turning as it did so he fired the gun and his bullet caught one of the soldiers in the throat. Diving to the ground, his next shot caught the other soldier in the chest. He fired off the third shot but only got the deep one in the kneecap. The flesh wound was enough to make him run for the door.

"You are no brother of ours. There is no forgiveness for this."

Anton crawled for the soldier with the bullet in the head and reached inside the pocket where he'd seen him put the keys for the shackles and took them out.

"Good work, kid. Make sure you take their guns away. They may be deep one offspring like you and may not be dead and dying men have no problems trying to take others with them, especially the one who killed them."

Anton took their rifles away.

A few moments and some fumbling with the keys later, Jack Risen was free from the shackles and the clamps. He picked up his clothes, checked their pockets, and put them back on. Anton handed him one of the rifles.

"We have to go after him, otherwise he will raise an alarm and we have no idea what we are facing here." The old man walked to the door and put his hand on the knob. "It could just be the three of them or …" Jack opened the door and on the other side of it were a dozen more deep ones, a river behind them. All of them were holding firearms. Firing off a short burst made the reptilians scatter. Jack then slammed the door as the deep ones returned fire and rained bullets on the metal door. He slipped the bolt and jammed it with the rifle. "Too late. They called their friends. We need to find another way out."

They searched the building for another land-based exit and came up empty.

"Damn it. We need to go back out the water tunnel."

"Won't they follow us?" Anton said.

"Most likely, but deep ones are very strong and very resilient. In a gun battle we would be in a lot of trouble. We would need to make all head shots."

"Why head shots? Wouldn't a shot to the heart or one that made them bleed out be just as good?" asked Anton holding onto his 56 with the same intensity he had wanted to embrace the president's daughter.

"Because if they got into the water, especially salt water, it'd speed up their healing. Most things die if you put a bullet in their heads."

"Most things? What do you mean things?" said Anton.

Jack took the plastic explosives out of his pockets. The deep one had been so intent on torture, he hadn't bothered to order the spy's clothes searched. Sloppy. The old man began placing the explosives and detonators in strategic places in the bunker. "Zombies for one thing. You have to hit the cortex. That stops the signals from going in and that usually stops them. Vampires and weres can survive a shot to the head, especially if it's a full moon for the weres or if the vamps have recently fed. However, the bullet still takes out brain matter which can play havoc with their memories, personalities, and affect their motor function."

"What about you? What would happen if I put a bullet in your head? Would you survive?"

Jack stopped and stared down the soldier. "Yeah, I might. Especially if I was as jazzed up on electricity as I am right now. Makes me much stronger. Still hurts like hell. If my restraints had been leather instead of steel, I'd have ripped through them like tissue paper."

Outside, torn-down tree trunks were battering at the bunker.

"That door won't hold for long. We need to evac," Jack said.

"Can you keep up with me?" Anton said, getting in the pool.

Jack had picked up the jumper cables that had been used to torture him and ripped apart the rubber that joined the two cables. He tied two of the four ends together, then fastened one end across Anton's waist then did the same to himself with the remaining end. He then put on his scuba tank and mask and tucked the spear guns awkwardly into either side of his belt.

"No, and in a space that confined they'd rip me apart, so I'd appreciate it if you'd tow me behind you. I'll bring the harpoon guns and try to slow down our pursuers."

The two men went back under the water as the bunker door bent inward. Anton swam furiously in the tunnel and Jack did his best to follow. On the way in, they had moved slowly and cautiously. Now Anton was swimming for their lives, which sped up matters considerably. It wasn't long before the deep ones came up behind them. Waiting until the lead reptilian was close enough to give him a good shot, Jack fired the first spear gun and quickly returned it to his belt, removing the second one. It caught the scaled man in the shoulder and penetrated down between his ribs. The tunnel wasn't wide enough for his fellows to easily swim past so that slowed them and Anton's rapid strokes let them take the lead again.

In what seemed to Jack to be much too short a time, their reptilian pursuers narrowed the gap, forcing the old man to fire the second spear. This time his aim improved, catching the lead swimmer full in the face and out the other side of his skull where the barb caught a second deep one in the chest. It was his struggle to get free of the spear that effectively blocked the tunnel long enough for them to get far enough ahead that neither man could see anyone chasing them. It too was slipped back in the belt.

With two wounded or dead, the pursuers hung back just out of sight.

It seemed like an eternity, but was actually took a little less than an hour to travel over five miles, effectively halving the world record for swimming a mile five times.

The tunnel door was still shut and the pair frantically searched for a switch or button but came up empty. The deep ones hung back no longer, quickly narrowing the gap. The old man removed his unused air tank and pointed it toward the creatures, adding a small piece of plastic explosive and a detonator to it. With his bare hand, he grabbed hold of the valve on top and ripped it right off the metal. The compressed air propelled the tank like a torpedo. The deep ones flattened against the tunnel walls to let it go past, but Jack waited until it was amidst them and pushed a waterproof detonator in his hand. The tank exploded, metal shrapnel tearing into many of the deep ones.

Knowing it was only a momentary reprieve, Jack handed one of the spent spear guns to Anton and wedged the other one between the rock where he knew the door opened, Anton followed suit and they were able to wedge the door open a little bit. Anton could barely budge it against the springs, but Jack pushed and it moved. The gray-skinned man was able to hold it long enough for Anton to squeeze through. The old spy, however, was stuck—if he let go it would close, if he tried to go through it would crush and trap him.

They're stuck at the tunnel's end. Get them!

Anton looked back and saw deep ones approaching fast. Jack tried to motion with his head for Anton to swim away, but the newly promoted captain shook his head and wedged his spear gun between the rocks. Anton grabbed a hold of the old man's belt and yanked him through. The spear gun held an instant longer than Jack needed it to before it snapped in half. The stone door slammed shut. Jack paused to nod his thanks and placed the remainder of his explosives on the door, half on the stone that would move and the rest on the rock that would stay, and linked them with a trigger that worked on the same principle as a trip wire. When the door opened, it would blow.

The two of them swam for shore as fast as they could, Anton still pulling Jack along with his jumper cable tow rope. As they crawled from the lake, shouts from the soldiers announced their arrival.

Jack stood and made his report. "Mr. President, we are coming in hot! Have your men ready to shoot anything that comes out of the lake behind us."

As he finished speaking, there was an explosion from beneath the lake spraying water high into the sky. A second and third explosions followed from miles away, deep within the jungle.

The president looked shaken and confused.

"We rigged some booby traps behind us, but it may not have been enough to stop the deep ones."

Nothing came out of the water. Jack ordered the soldiers to drag the lake, but no bodies were found. Within the hour, Jack led Surinam's crack troops to the bunker, but it had been abandoned. Again no bodies, human or otherwise, were found.

That night, Jack met with the president to discuss matters. He was planning to recommend the young captain be transferred to intelligence. Surinam was a small county, but the superpowers and many of the not-so-superpowers had so-called monsters working for them as spies, soldiers, and more. Jack himself was a perfect example. Surinam would need every advantage it could muster against the other countries of the world as they tried to come after its oil, not to mention a much quieter invasion by the deep ones. Anton Hernandez could help on both fronts. Anton was wet behind the ears but had great potential. The United States was trying to ingratiate itself with the government of Surinam and Jack had orders to do whatever was necessary to make that happen so long as it didn't compromise US interests. Boosting their homegrown resources and people certainly fell under those orders.

As was his habit, Jack went to the open doors of the balcony to check above and below for any possible dangers or lurkers. There were none, but his dead eyes saw amazingly well in the darkness. Across the grounds the president's daughter was sneaking off in lingerie that may have had more material than her bathing suit, but was so sheer it gave the illusion of having less.

Jack watched to see where she was going. When he saw Anton step out from behind a tree, the old spy's face got a wry grin. Smart kid, taking what looked like a good chance. The girl was beautiful although a bit too young for his tastes these days.

Anton's eyes must have been almost as good as Jack's, because he looked up into the dead spy's face. Jack smiled and saluted him. Anton nodded back before turning his full attention to his goddess. Their kiss held the passion that only the very young can muster. Anton lifted the woman into his arms and carried her off to an empty bathhouse.

Jack smiled remembering younger days. then shut the balcony doors. The president didn't need the distraction of hearing the moans of either his daughter or his new national hero. Although Jack did decide he'd better have a talk with the young soldier to make sure the plans for the president's grandchild to be part deep one didn't happen even without their direct intervention.

From the writings of Abraham Van Helsing, founder and Lord Protector of the Sway:

Humanity should know better. People should recognize the danger that monsters pose to them but frigtheningly most do not.

Even more troubling are those who choose to give up their humanity and become monsters of their own free will. These betrayers of humanity are perhaps the most dangerous of foes for they know what it is like to be human and how to overcome it.

Troubling Thoughts

Max Birkett

BANG BANG. In the bleary drift between reality and dream, Captain Edward Rem couldn't tell whether the pounding was coming from the door or from inside his own skull. With a groan, he rolled over in bed. The movement disturbed the tangle of limbs sprawled over his naked body. With monumental effort and maximum reluctance, Rem propped himself up on his elbows. The sleeping women covering the overlarge bed murmured unconscious protests.

The hammering noise continued. With unfocused eyes, Rem regarded the door with hatred. It was dark in the room, but the light of a full moon shone in through the open balcony. Even the gentle blue light was too much for Rem in his present state. The stink of sweat, sex, cheap incense, and fetid waste from the street below all mixed together in the humid night. It threatened to make Rem sick. Rem's usual constitution was, well, superhuman. But in his current condition, every single molecule of him felt fragile.

The captain squinted and tried to orient himself to time and space. He was in a whorehouse in Thailand. He'd been at it with tequila and beer. Then, as the party had stretched on, had come cocaine, hash, and Ecstasy. The girls passed out one at a time over the evening until finally Rem himself burned out his horrible hungers and could submit to oblivion. Of course, thanks to the serum, he recovered from his self-poisoning faster than any of the prostitutes.

And there was the knocking. Unable to ignore the infernal, endless knocking, Rem staggered to his feet, trying his bleary best to avoid disturbing the women. He cast about for something, anything to cover himself. Rem was a modest sort and deeply sensitive to propriety. He was forced (COMPELLED) to these horrible debaucheries but found no pleasure in them. Quite the opposite in fact.

Rem hated the filthy whores. He loathed alcohol and the way it made people lose control (INHIBITIONS). And the drugs—a habit of the feeble-minded and failures. All of it made him miserable, miserable even as he partook of these illicit (REVELS). The girls last night had laughed and teased him about his ever-present scowl. He had gone about the business of the night with a grim sense of duty.

Finally, after a seeming eternity, the captain reached the door. He'd found a discarded shirt and wrapped it around his waist. Rem cast a baleful glance back at the incriminating naked pile on the bed. It wasn't like he could hide any of this. Reluctantly, Rem opened the door.

To his horror, a boy was waiting for him. The child couldn't have been more than ten. If the situation behind Rem was shocking to the boy, he gave no indication. He just stared at the secret agent with eyes that seemed too old.

"Edward Rem?" asked the child, his tongue tripping on the foreign name.

The situation was so shocking that the polite Englishman simply nodded. The boy produced a plain letter and shoved it at the man. Rem took the letter, still on autopilot. His task complete, the boy turned and slipped away into the brothel.

Rem found himself profoundly disturbed by the brief encounter. On the list of people that he would never want to meet while naked in a whorehouse at three AM, a child had to be right on top. The sin and filth of this terrible place had reached new depths. In a sudden fury, he stomped across the room, collecting his clothing. Edward couldn't stand the thought of spending another moment in this sewer of humanity.

In his rage, Rem almost forgot the letter. It was only when he stood before the door again that he remembered. He tore it open and scanned the contents. It was a simple and business-like message. He had another mission. He was to leave immediately.

Rem crumpled the note and reached for the door but momentarily a mirror on the wall caught his eye. He couldn't say exactly what made him pause but for a moment he considered his reflection. His face, aristocratically thin and handsome, looked gaunt in the pale light. His eyes were sunken, haunted. And then the reflection twisted and grinned at him.

(TIME FOR SOME ACTION, EH?), it said.

Hugh Altier. That was how his altered (UNLEASHED) ego referred to himself. Hugh reveled in all the sins that Edward disdained: envy, lust, greed, gluttony, sloth, and wrath. Only pride was kept to Rem. Rem was only human, he had passions and dark thoughts. But he was a righteous and rigid person. From a young age, Rem had never allowed himself to acknowledge his baser impulses, let alone indulge them. That discipline and vigilance had served him well in the military. But once the serum took hold, a life's worth of repression suddenly found expression and form.

Rem slipped through the streets of Bangkok as a light drizzle fell from the dingy sky. Even at this late hour, the city was alive with activity. He made his way towards a private airstrip on the outskirts, weaving around women and dealers plying their trade. The flickering streetlights twisted Rem's trailing shadow into strange and unsettling shapes.

Marching past muddy alleys and ramshackle tenements, the captain brooded on the circumstances that had brought him to this low place. Already his head was clearing and the aches of his abused body were fading. All thanks to the damned serum. That and the devil's bargain he had struck.

He had been at the height of his career. The British Army had appreciated a soldier as zealous, professional, and loyal as Rem was. He secured a promotion to special operations and from there was approached by a secretive little section of military intelligence known as MI7. As an agent of MI7, Rem was able to make a real difference in the country's security. He took grim satisfaction in eliminating (MURDERING) dire threats to his homeland. Rem protected the solid and morally superior English citizenry from extraordinary dangers and unnatural enemies.

It had been on one of his first missions for MI7 where it had all gone wrong. Rem's target, a mysterious mercenary scientist known as Dr. Proteus, had escaped and Rem was grievously injured in the battle with the Doctor's flunkies. When MI7 rescued him from the burning laboratory they offered him a choice right there under the clear night sky, by the light of the building's fire. They had a serum, very rare, very special. It would ensure Rem healed up quick and right, put him back on his feet and ready to fight once more. There was a side-effect, a serious one. But they believed he was the right type. He could shrug it off. (GOT THAT WRONG, DIDN'T THEY?)

Half unconscious from the pain, bleeding out into the dirt, and delirious from the terrible scenes of science gone wrong he had just witnessed, Rem had agreed. And the rest, as they say, was history. The serum did its work and instead of spending months in recovery, it was weeks. The mixture changed Rem, made him tougher and faster. He no longer got sick and rarely tired. Amazing benefits and all it cost was half his mind and body.

The blackouts started soon after he'd returned to work. When Rem dutifully reported the side-effect, he received the full story. The so-called "Hyde" potion divided a person in two. The fact that it had worked on Rem and had not killed him slowly meant that he must be distantly related to the serum's inventor, one Dr. Henry Jekyll. What Rem knew as "blackouts" were actually full transformations. In a recorded message on his personal phone, he was introduced to the despicable Hugh Altier. His own personal demon.

The face in the video was completely different. And yet, horribly familiar. The ugly truth of it was that Rem was not quite clear where he ended and Altier began. They were not cleanly partitioned off. It would have been much easier, simpler for Rem if Altier had been a total stranger.

(EACH ONE OF US HAS OUR OWN LITTLE CORNER UP IN HERE. BUT WE SHARE SO MUCH! REM MAY HATE ME, BUT I BEAR HIM NO ILL WILL. I JUST WANT MORE IS ALL. MORE TIME OUT AND FREE.

(AT FIRST, REM WAS READY TO FIGHT, TOOTH AND NAIL. BUT WHAT WITH HE AND I BEING TWO SIDES OF THE SAME COIN, I KNEW THAT DEEP DOWN, HE WASN'T PREPARED FOR TOTAL WAR. NEITHER OF US WANTED SCORCHED EARTH IN THE OL' NOGGIN. DIDN'T TAKE LONG BEFORE REM UNDERSTOOD THAT HE HAS NO REAL HOLD ON ME, NO MORE THAN I ON HIM. WE COULD WRESTLE BACK AND FORTH, SEIZE CONTROL FOR A TIME. BUT THAT WASN'T

GOING TO WORK, NOT IN THE LONG RUN. SO, WE STRUCK UP A DEAL.

(I LET PENCIL-DICK RUN THE DAY-TO-DAY. AND HE LETS ME OUT TO PLAY AT ALL THE BEST PARTS. IN RETURN FOR MY GRACIOUS COOPERATION, ALL I ASK IS A LITTLE COMPENSATION. SOME RIDE-ALONG BENEFITS. AIN'T THAT KIND OF ME? 'OHHH NOO, POOR OLD REM HAS TO ENJOY HIMSELF FROM TIME TO TIME. THE POOR SOUL HAS WILD SEX AND PARTIES DOWN, WHAT A TERRIBLE, TERRIBLE CURSE.' PLEASE. DO I ENJOY FORCING A STUCK-UP PRICK LIKE REM TO SULLY HIMSELF WITH HAVING ACTUAL FUN? 'COURSE I DO.)

Outside of the city center, the crowds began to thin. Rem felt exposed without the mask of the masses. Each passerby stared openly at the tall, white man marching purposefully down the narrow dirt lane. Rem could imagine what they all were thinking. That he was some degenerate foreigner on a sex vacation. *Which was entirely accurate,* thought Rem unhappily.

Just then a pack of motorcycles roared toward him. The few furtive individuals on the lane threw themselves out of the way. Rem himself was forced to dive for cover. One of the cyclists came within a millimeter of him, as he plastered himself against the wall. The wheels hit a puddle, splattering the captain with mud. For a split second, Rem heard a crackle of laughter as the motorcycles zoomed by.

Then Hugh Altier took over.

Rem's arms became burly with ropey muscle and covered in black hair. The face that turned to track the bike gang was no longer Edward's. The jawline thickened, hair went lanky and coarse, the thin nose potatoed out and swollen. It was Hugh's face now. Only the eyes remained the same.

Hugh reached out and grabbed a bottle of sake from a nearby drunk. The old souse stared at the transforming man in shock, eyes like saucers. Hugh squinted, quickly gauging distance and speed. Then he threw the bottle, a perfect spiral, arcing gracefully only to shatter on the head of the lead biker. The man was instantly knocked out and the bike flipped up and over, taking out another motorcycle in the process. The other four bikers skidded to a stop. They stared at Hugh. And then all of them dismounted and started towards him.

Hugh Altier was a pale-skinned brute. He was a little shorter than

Rem but had triple the bulk. He was all muscle and, enhanced by the serum, it made Altier inhumanly strong. The olive-skinned Rem was glamorously handsome—Altier made do with being interestingly ugly. He gave a crooked grin when it became clear the bikers were going to confront him.

The motorcyclists were a slick bunch with matching jackets and tattoos. Their swagger and bearing marked them as professional criminals of some sort. The four cracked their knuckles and balled their fists. One of them shouted something sharp in their native tongue, but Rem was the linguist, not Altier. Altier spoke the gangsters' language all the same though, the vocabulary of violence and force.

The four formed a loose semi-circle around the casually loitering brute. And then the fight was on. The gangsters rushed in, looking to throw the big man to the ground with sheer force of numbers. Hugh Altier was ready though. He dodged the first punch thrown, grabbed the outstretched arm, then swung both arm and attached body around, slamming one attacker into another. The next up got a kick in to Hugh's gut, but the big man merely let out a little grunt. A swift stomp crushed the foot of the offending opponent and Altier followed it up with a vicious uppercut that lifted the hapless thug off his feet. The final gangster had gotten around behind Hugh. He jumped onto Altier's back and began to choke him. It was a bit like trying to choke a tree trunk. With a roar, Altier reached both arms behind him and grabbed the man. With casual ease, the brute lifted the man over his head and lobbed him through a shop window.

Altier dusted off his hands and looked with satisfaction at the mayhem he had caused. Unconscious bodies and shards of glass surrounded him. Without ceremony, he transformed back into Rem. The captain sniffed disdainfully at the mess but then looked down at his mud-splattered pants.

"Wildly unnecessary, Hugh." Rem said to the empty air. "But perhaps this criminal scum might think twice about their life choices now."

Rem reached the airstrip without further incident. It was a dimly-lit quarter mile of packed earth with a rust-eaten hulk of a tin hangar loitering nearby. There was but a single soul there that night. A woman. She approached the captain with a distracting sway to her hips. She was small, with short brown hair and a supple figure. She supplied the correct call signs, and Rem replied with the countersigns. Their mutual legitimacy as MI7 agents established, the woman got right to the point.

"You got my message," she said. "If it's all the same to you, Agent Hyde, I'd like to fill you in on the mission in the air. I don't know how long our quarry will sit still."

"You have me at a disadvantage, ma'am," Rem stated. "And I prefer my own name and rank rather than the MI-7 designation."

The woman blinked then smiled up at him. "Very well, Captain. I'm Agent Mallon. An analyst with MI7, but I've begun to dabble in fieldwork. Pleasure to make your acquaintance."

(I'D LIKE TO ACQUAINT MYSELF WITH HER PLEASURES. COULD THROW HER DOWN IN THE DIRT RIGHT HERE AND DABBLE IN HER FIELD.)

"Are you alright, Captain?" Mallon asked, studying the man curiously.

Rem, he of perfect posture, was somehow even more upright and rigid than normal. He shuddered and forced himself to relax his body slightly. Rem made extra certain that his eyes never once focused on the curves of her breasts or the shape of her thighs. "I'm fine. I… I assume you've heard about me or read my file? You know my condition?"

Mallon laughed, a light little sound that seemed to fill the heavy black night. "I know about Hugh Altier. But as incredible as your power is, that actually isn't why I requested you for this mission. I chose you because of your past history with the target."

She produced, of all things, a business card. "I came across this while following a lead in Dubai."

The card read: *Doctor Proteus. Neurologist for Hire. Specialties in Information Extraction, Subliminal Messages, Applied Lobotomy, Mind Control. "You provide the bodies, I provide **results**."*

Rem felt a cold chill sweep over him, even as dawn's first rays crept across his face. "It's good you brought me on. Anyone else might laugh this ridiculous card off as a joke. But I know Proteus too well by now. The Doctor thinks himself clever. He's left dozens of lives shattered from Glasgow to Moscow and the bastard still thinks of all this as an amusing game. He is taunting us."

Rem crushed the card, his cold manner a poor mask for his burning zeal. "We'll end it this time. We'll get Proteus. No escape."

The MI7 jet they flew out of Bangkok on could not be more different than the dirty rundown airstrip they took off from. It was clean, slick, and high-tech. The supersonic craft was small but the inside had luxuries befitting a prince. Rem's standard cover was that of a corporate executive scout, a profiteering bloodhound. Even third-world countries tended to roll out the welcome mat for potential investors. The jet subtly backed up that story.

Aside from the pilot, Mallon and Rem were the only passengers. As they lounged in the leather seats across from one another, Rem was intensely aware of the woman's gorgeous body. Although at the moment, Mallon wasn't exactly putting on the charm. She rubbed her temples while grimacing. When she looked up at Rem, a trickle of red came from her nose. The agent quickly wiped it away.

"It's the pressure change. Sorry, I was going to fill you in on the situation. It all began when Machine//ghost (Machine//ghost was MI7's tech expert. A seemingly sentient digital entity, everyone at the agency assumed Machine//ghost was some sort of Artificial Intelligence or a genius agoraphobic hacker. No one wanted to believe the official story behind //ghost as it raised all sorts of unpleasant questions about the afterlife and the soul.) detected some anomalous videos uploaded to the internet. We managed to quarantine the files before they could spread far. Which was a big stroke of luck, because despite looking like an *avant-garde* music video, these uploads were incredibly dangerous. Each image contained a thousand books worth of information, each tone would key up specific chemical reactions in the brain."

Rem nodded. "A deliberately mind-altering video. Any idea what the effect is?"

Agent Mallon shook her head, "We are still debriefing victims who were exposed. The effects seem to be all over the place. Personally, I think this was just a small test of a prototype payload. What I can tell you is within twenty-four hours of exposure, over 73% of the victims committed some sort of violent crime.

"Machine//ghost managed to trace the uploads back to Dubai. I was sent there to investigate. Long story short, I found evidence of Dr. Proteus's involvement. I know, I know, he is supposed to be dead. I read the report on your last encounter with him. But this sort of mental manipulation with just sound and image… well, you have to admit, it's Proteus's signature style."

Rem leaned back and closed his eyes. He pictured Proteus: the abnormally large grey brain floating in its tank, pulsing and quivering. Oh yes. The doctor was a thing of nightmares. The whys and hows of Dr. Proteus's origin had been lost to time. Who Proteus had been, how he'd lost his body, whether the sinister grey matter had ever been a man at all—all shrouded in mystery. The living brain's first recorded appearance had been in Glasgow in the '60s. Like a bad penny, the rogue scientist kept turning up ever since, all over the globe.

And every time Dr. Proteus would surface, Rem would be there to put the slimy horror down. Twice now Rem had thought he'd destroyed Proteus. But the brain just wouldn't die. In one form or another, Proteus always came back.

Rem realized Mallon was waiting for a response. "The location makes sense. Dubai has cutting-edge technology and a whole class of people who can go missing without there being too many questions. Proteus's two requirements for any location."

The alluring woman smiled, "Well, this should be easy enough. We smash our way in, grab the brain jar, and get out."

Rem didn't respond to that. He had no intention of taking Dr. Proteus alive. This was one point on which he and Altier agreed. Given half a chance, they would eliminate their nemesis once and for all. Morally, the captain could never allow the mad scientist to be brought in alive. Some beings were too corrupt, too hideously evil. In Rem's opinion, Proteus was beyond any redemption. Any utility the insidious creature could provide was overshadowed by its monstrous crimes.

Altier just liked to kill.

In theory, the Doctor was the perfect captive. After all, he was completely dependent on whatever government seized him. A bodiless intelligence, what could be more harmless?

But it always ended the same. The Doctor's only interest was in forbidden research, to do things to the human mind that were by any definition a violation. To produce results, Proteus's captors always needed to supply the living brain with subjects. Undesirables, prisoners, the desperately poor—it depended on the country. In Britain, it had been the incurably insane. Those victims always became thralls of Proteus, slaves to his will.

And then the real nightmare would begin.

Rem deliberately changed the track of his thoughts before they turned too morose. He refocused on the stunning beauty seated across from him. Mallon regarded him back, with a look that made the captain flush. Searching for something, anything to say, Rem spoke up.

"So have you laid eyes on the Doctor yourself? How exactly did you find his lair? Details are important. It might give us some idea of what to expect…"

Rem found his voice slowing and finally drifting into quiet. Mallon stared straight at him the whole time he was speaking. And he found himself completely lost in her gaze. She had one green eye and one blue. They were enrapturing.

"Can you transform at will?" asked Mallon, ignoring Rem's questions. "Is Altier in there right now, watching?"

Rem was offended that this strange woman would be so forward. But there was something about her that compelled him to answer gently. "Sometimes I can feel Hugh paying attention, like an itch behind the eyes. But he is lazy and bores easily. There needs to be something that titillates his base interests. A plane ride hardly qualifies."

"So what about you? What happens to Edward Rem when Hugh takes control?"

"It's… hard to describe. Sometimes it's a complete blank, a patch of amnesia. And maybe I'll get flashes or fragments of what the little creep has gotten up to over time. And at times I, hrmph. It's a bit like a lucid dream. Like I'm watching me, but not me."

"Incredible."

There was something about the wonder and interest in Mallon's gaze that made Rem tingle. Or maybe it was just the way when, she leaned forward to study him, her blouse revealed… Rem had to remind himself that Agent Mallon wasn't *good*. An ally, yes. But she no doubt flaunted her loose sexual mores as a matador flapped his cape. To use her body like a beacon to attract the enemies of MI7, to dash themselves to pieces on hidden dangers. (MIXING METAPHORS, EH? MUST BE SMITTEN.)

For her part, Mallon was still talking. Rem only tuned in for the last bit. "…you really are unique. That's why I find the mind so interesting. Each psychology is so different, a snowflake. And yet for all our variations, we are all like you and Hugh—different configurations but all running off largely the same wetware."

"What?"

But Mallon once again changed the subject. "I really shouldn't ask… we've only just met. But could you transform for me? I know, I'm sure everyone you meet asks. And it's not like it's a party trick. But can you?" She seemingly unconsciously toyed with the neckline of her shirt.

Rem's face twisted into a bitter scowl as he prepared to fire back a venomous response. But his face just kept twisting, morphing like a wax

Picasso until it was Altier's visage. The big lout leaned forward even as his muscles billowed out from beneath Rem's skin. He smiled. "Ta da."

Mallon clapped her hands in delight. If she was at all disgusted or disturbed by the sudden appearance of Hugh Altier, she gave no indication. "Absolutely marvelous! Cor, you're a big one aren't you?"

"Lady, you've no idea," said Altier with a smirk.

To his surprise, Mallon reclined back in her plush seat and beckoned with a waggling finger. "Well, why don't you show me?"

A disoriented Rem stumbled down the stairs from the jet. He didn't remember what had happened during the flight. He must have fallen asleep, but hadn't he been talking to Mallon? There was some smear of a sexual dream lingering in his memory, but no details. Captain Rem found himself temporarily blinded as he stepped out. The sun was beginning to set in Dubai.

Mallon was waiting impatiently for him and the two made efficient time to the Main Terminal. They moved through Customs with little trouble. Hugh Altier was a wanted fugitive in eleven different countries. He was listed as one of Interpol's most wanted. Edward Rem's record, however, was the purest white.

Mallon seemed a little off. Their dynamic had shifted but Rem wasn't clear how or why. He tried once or twice to talk to her, but she remained closed. Rem searched his memories of the flight, for some cause of offense. But he'd been so tired from Thailand that it was all a blur now.

The pair of spies took off in a rented car, leaving the airport and heading down a broad highway towards the city proper. Rem drove and Mallon navigated. The steel and glass spires of Dubai glittered in the fading light like gossamer creations of some fairy race. The sun was swollen red and cast the gleaming futuristic city in a warm, rosy glow. The heat and the endless desert all around made the panorama dance and bend, completing the impression of a magical Arabian utopia, something out of a storybook.

"All of this beauty and grandeur, and beneath it the toil of hundreds of thousands imported slaves," mused Rem as they drew closer to the palatial towers. Dubai, it seemed to him, was indeed like something out of a story. But not some fable. No, the city was more like a medieval kingdom masquerading as something modern. A vast pyramid where a base of foreign indentured servants worked endlessly to ensure that the chosen few occupants of the city lived in luxury. And above the pampered citizenry were the royals in their skyscraper penthouses.

And so Rem passed the time in taciturn silence. Mallon seemed to have her own weighty thoughts to process. Shadows lengthened until they became the night itself. It was only the jolt of the parking car that brought the two of them back to reality.

"This is the place," said Mallon.

It was a three-story office building. The structure was unremarkable, though it had little in the way of windows. It blended in with the surrounding residential blocks so perfectly as to be invisible. The only indication that this might be more than some office drone nest were heavy-duty antennas sprouting from the top and the occasional glimpse of an armed guard roaming the roof.

Rem paced up and down the block, passing in and out from the streetlights' spotlight. Mallon leaned against a wall watching him. Finally, Rem stopped and spoke. "That's all you've got? This location? Nothing on how many guards are inside? What defenses we can expect?"

Mallon shrugged. "I was told that this is what you do, Rem. That the agency gives you a location and you do the rest."

"I'm tougher and stronger than normal. Not bulletproof. I don't like walking into a fight blind. Ideally, we would take out Dr. Proteus without going through an entire building."

Agent Mallon sighed. "Two guards on the roof. The lobby is the only entrance; with three guards always on duty. Camera coverage of the surrounding block. Safe to assume there are more inside. The only good news is they are unlikely to receive any sort of backup. The doctor isn't running the sort of operation that can just call the police."

Rem looked across the street at the unassuming office. He sighed and ceded control to his other half. For a moment, Altier replicated Rem's distant stare, frowning at the possible hideout, then flashed a cocky grin at Mallon. "Hey babe, no plan, no sweat. Hugh Altier is gonna make this all alright. Watch."

Mallon folded her arms and raised an eyebrow.

The burly man walked over to a telephone pole and gave it a once over with a critical eye. Then, with a wink to the waiting MI7 agent, Hugh loosed a tremendous kick to the pole. There was a snap and crack like a gunshot, echoing up and down the street. The electrical pole swung violently forward, across the road, the transformer and snapped wires hitting the office's roof. In the same instant, all the lights in the neighborhood went out. There was a scream from above as the guard up top took a livewire to the face.

With a satisfied grunt, Altier lounged against the wall, next to a dumbstruck Mallon. In a conversational tone, he said, "See, this is why we're the best, love. Between Rem and I, we are a one-man kill team. Now me, I'm the wreckin' ball. Rem, he's the scalpel… Hang on a tic."

Two guards from the building had rushed over to the stump of the pole. They shouted questions at the pair of spies in heavily accented English. Both soldiers were clearly spooked, tightly gripping their machine guns. Altier strolled forward to greet them, his hands raised and opened to show he was harmless. Mallon, thinking fast, moved into the shadows. The gun barrels rose to meet Altier, who stopped just a couple of feet away. Suddenly, both guards heard someone shout behind them. They spun around with a yelp, to confront Mallon. At which point Altier darted forward and bashed both men's heads together. The two dropped to the pavement, out cold.

"And now we have weapons," crowed Altier as he hoisted a pilfered assault rifle. He handed the other to Mallon. As she took it he noticed her arm was trembling a good bit. "You already rattled?"

Mallon stared at her uncontrollable tremor and then snarled up at Hugh, "I'm fine, forget it."

Altier shrugged and slipped a grenade off an unconscious soldier's belt. "Where was I? Oh yeah, wrecking shit. That's the key to leveling the playing field. Keeps the enemy guessing on what the situation is. Keeps them off balance."

The burly brute casually popped the pin and chucked the grenade through a ground floor window in the office. The subsequent blast left a hole in the side of the building. But instead of heading for it, Altier power-walked around the side of the block and made for the front entrance. Mallon trailed behind him, her rifle raised and ready.

"Ideally, now the guys inside are spread out all over the place. So we can just pick them off like we're the monster in a haunted house," Altier explained as he opened the door to the office and walked into the lobby like he owned the place.

A single guard was behind a metal desk, the man's eyes wide with confusion and fear. He almost shot Altier the moment the door opened but had a second thought. The poor soldier never got a third. Altier filled him with holes without a moment's hesitation. Mallon swept in from behind, only lowering her gun when she saw the tiny lobby was otherwise deserted.

She knelt by the dead guard and checked his belongings. She flashed a keycard to Altier and then scooped up a strange pistol as well. She looked at the weapon with skepticism. "Some sort of dart gun? Odd."

Altier was already pushing through the first set of security doors, into a winding antiseptic hallway lit by red glowing emergency lights. He looked back impatiently at Mallon. "Probably tranq rounds. These wankers must do double duty rounding up test subjects for Dr. Proteus."

Mallon pocketed the tranquilizer pistol and hurried after the human juggernaut. The two of them stalked through the compound, a maze of identical hallways. The power seemed to be largely knocked out, with the only illumination coming from intermittent red lights that cast the gloom in a blood red. Twice they encountered guards, but Altier was always quicker on the draw. Finally, in the center of the office, they discovered the true nature of the place. The building's monstrous heart that wore the drab surroundings like an ill-fitting skin.

It was hard to miss: a large open room ringed with windows, which easily fit over forty metal desks. On each desk glowed a large monitor. This was the room where backup generator power had been routed, shining in the dark. A variety of colors and abstract shapes flowed across the forty screens, creating a kaleidoscope flicker on the walls. And by the light of the screens, Altier and Mallon could see the subjects, Proteus's victims. Their limbs were bolted to their chairs, and the chairs to the floor, trapping them. There was an IV stand next to each subject. The top of each person's skull was open, their brains exposed. Around the rim of their heads was a sort of metal tonsure, with insectile mechanical limbs which curved around to each brain, gently prodding here and there.

If Altier was bothered by the tremendous sight of the experiment it did not show. He pressed his face against the glass, studying the scene. The victims were of Indian origin and almost all of them existed in a desiccated state, wearing ragged clothes. The men and women were alive. Altier could see their eyes twitch back and forth, staring at the monitors. Whether the images on the screen were caused by their brain activity or the reverse was unclear. But Altier's course of action was crystal in his mind.

He punched his arm through the window, startling Mallon. She opened her mouth to ask a question but then saw that Altier had produced a second grenade from somewhere. He lobbed it into the center of the experimental chamber and motioned for Mallon to move away.

Mallon backed off and then just kept heading down the hallway. At the roar of the explosion, she stopped for a moment but did not look back. Altier hurried after her. "Where you off to?"

Mallon stopped and glared at him. "You know you just killed forty people in there? What the hell was that?"

Hugh shrugged. "I don't think those living cadavers were gonna have a very high, what's the phrase, quality of life. Look, I didn't saw off those poor sods' skulls. I forgot you're just an analyst. This is what science gone mad looks like, Luv."

"I'm not a delicate, goddam flower. I know the damage was already done for those bastards in there. But the only way to make them count for anything was to salvage whatever data we could from the experiment. You blew it all up!"

Altier's little smirk disappeared. "Destruction is what I do, Agent. This whole thing has been a cock-up from the beginning. Until we found that room, I was thinking you'd just led me into some random deathtrap. There hasn't been any other sign of the Doctor here."

Mallon whirled around and stalked off down the hall. She made a left and then another left, bringing the pair to an elevator. Mallon tapped the guard's keycard against the controls, summoning it. "While you were wrecking things, I found a map. There is a sub-basement below the building. I've got a hunch we'll find plenty more evidence of Proteus down there."

Altier grunted. In uncomfortable silence, the two entered the elevator. Mallon was pressed into the back by the burly Altier, who filled most of the little chamber with his muscle. He jabbed the basement button and they began their descent.

Mallon cut the quiet with a command. "We'll need Rem for this next part. A scalpel, not a cudgel. Also, he'd give me a little more room to breathe in here."

"I see how it is. If my presence is no longer desired, I'll bugger right off. OK, princess?"

By the time the elevator doors opened, it was Captain Rem who stood at the ready, finger on the rifle's trigger. He stepped out into the dim concrete corridor, which was empty. There was a sudden sharp sting in his back. Followed by five more. Rem whirled about, but the sedative coursing through his system was already taking effect. The momentum of his turn kept him spinning and the captain found himself on the ground. He looked up, vision beginning to blur. Above him stood petite little Agent Mallon, holding the tranquilizer gun. The last thing he heard before unconscious overtook him was Mallon huff, "Finally."

Rem woke syrupy slow. Awareness came in fits and starts as his body fought off the effects of the sedative. Facts seemed unconnected to one another. He was lying on a tilted table. The dim ceiling above was crisscrossed by pipes and wiring. Big room. There was Agent Mallon. Standing next to the tank with a brain floating in it. Machinery cluttered the area. He couldn't move his body. A strange Jacob's Ladder was in front of him pointed at his head.

Rem just couldn't make heads nor tails of it all. "Hey, Mallon," he croaked. "What's happening?"

Mallon looked at the brain in the jar. "He's ready, Master."

The brain had two eyeballs in the glass canister with it. They were attached to the grey mass by pink flesh tethers and secured in a lateral configuration by a metal rod. The veiny white bulbs seemed to look deep into Rem's soul.

"We should be sure he is fully aware before beginning. He needs to be conscious for the process to be effective," came a mechanical voice like a text-to-speech bot. Rem realized it came from a speaker at the base of the canister.

Rem studied the brain closer. It seemed abnormally large and throbbed repulsively. The thing had a pallid grey color, like something dead. And it glowed ever so slightly in the poorly lit basement. Wires and cords flowed out of the brain and into the top of the tank. As horrible as the thing was, it seemed very familiar. Rem was sure he knew this particular brain.

"You're Doctor Proteus," declared Rem, immensely satisfied with himself for figuring it out.

The floating eyes rolled. "Yes, let's give him a couple of minutes. Besides, when you no longer have a body you learn to savor these moments. The pleasures of the flesh were never of much interest to me. Having an enemy like the Captain here, helpless? Priceless."

It had begun to dawn on Rem that he did not like Proteus. "What are you doing? Mallon, I can't move."

Mallon's expression was stony. Instead, the brain answered, "Agent Mallon works for me now. I caught her snooping around and well... I can be very persuasive. Also, I invented mind control."

Dr. Proteus paused for an awkward second. Rem noticed there

were more people in the room, Indians with shaved heads and glassy eyes. They had all stopped what they were doing and stared blankly at the brain.

"Laugh," commanded Proteus. "It was funny!"

Mallon and the Indians all laughed. It ended as abruptly as it began. Rem, becoming more alert by the second now, saw that the Indians all had livid scars and sutures across their shaved heads. Thralls. The word popped into his head.

"Whatever. Mallon is some of my finest work. It took a week to break her. A new record for me. Not an easy thing; do you have any idea how annoying it is to listen to nonstop screams for a week? I haven't quite mastered the technique. You may have noticed some signs of neurological degradation."

As if on cue, one of Mallon's eyes drifted off, pointing in some entirely different direction. With a scowl she slapped the side of her head, jolting the two orbs back into sync. Rem winced. Mallon had betrayed him, true. But whoever she had been, the woman before him must be suffering now.

"So that's what you're up to. You plan to make me into one of your puppets," he said.

"The thing I miss most about my body is being able to laugh," Proteus said. "No, you imbecile. I have plenty of puppets, like my loyal assistant there. But the cutting and electrodes only take you so far though. My thralls do their best, but after the procedure their capabilities are… not great. And while Mallon has been an invaluable weapon against MI7, I'm after something more than a minion. As you may have noticed, I lack colleagues. I have no one to talk to, no one with any sense of humor."

Rem began to struggle against his restraints. The solid metal had no give. He couldn't even move his head. Proteus continued.

"I've developed a way to copy my brainwaves and memories and transpose them onto another mind. The copies never take though. They go mad, or demented, or fail to take root. I've improved the process, but the wetware just isn't tough enough. Similar to what Miss Mallon is currently going through, my 'others' neurologically decline over time.

"But I've come up with a solution. The problem isn't the process. The problem is the subjects. They just aren't sturdy enough for the trauma. I need someone with a frankly superhuman constitution."

A thrall approached Dr. Proteus and gave the brain an affirmative.

The unblinking gaze of those floating eyes made Rem shudder.

"You're mad, Proteus. This won't work. MI7 will be right behind me. I—"

"Activate the Transposer," came the affectless mechanical voice. The great strange device in front of Rem's face glowed and crackled. Then it fired a mind annihilating beam of light and electricity into the captain and he knew no more.

Rem's eyes fluttered open. The Transposer had been removed but Proteus still floated before him. "Incredible, incredible," he murmured.

Proteus wasted no time. "Who was the first girl we ever operated on?"

Rem smirked, "Jenny Merkwitz."

"Ah, if I could shed tears. Doctor Proteus, I presume?"

Rem laughed and laughed. "Right back at you."

Thralls came up and undid the steel restraint that had bound Rem. He sprung up off the operating table and rubbed his wrists. Rem didn't move like he once did or hold himself the same way. He was a new man. He felt like a new man. Rem grinned at the brain floating before him.

The Doctor (the original that is) began to talk of additional testing. But Rem's smile was short-lived. He stared at his arms, frowning, as if he'd never seen them before. And then he doubled over, gripping his head.

"Something is wrong! There's—there's something else in here!"

Arms and legs thickened, torso compressed, and Hugh Altier's face emerged as if Rem's had been but a poorly fitting mask. Proteus queried the transformed man, in the hopes that his copy had hold of Altier as planned. The mad scientist got his answer in the next instant as Altier snapped out a punch, KOing the wary Mallon in a single hit.

In response, the thralls all about the room muttered and howled. Hugh ignored the lobotomized minions and strode forward. The brain of Proteus shone brighter for a moment and a metal bar sprang from across the room towards Altier's head. The telekinetic missile was easily intercepted though. Altier snatched the pipe out of the air like it was a softball. He looked at the heavy metal pipe in his hand, then at Proteus, and smirked. Then came the smashing and shattering and stomping and crushing until the brilliant mind of Dr. Proteus was smeared across the dirty concrete floor. The whole thing had taken less than a minute.

Hugh retreated to the elevator, Agent Mallon slung under his arm, easily fending off the pathetic assaults of the confused thralls. He himself barely understood what had just happened. Altier had been in the elevator, Rem had taken control, and then he'd found himself in front of the slimy scientist.

"Guess that's finally the end of old Proteus," Altier muttered under his breath.

(NOT QUITE.)

The Authors of the Abyss

John L. French is a retired crime scene supervisor with forty years' experience. His first story, "Past Sins," was published in Hardboiled Magazine and was cited as one of the best Hardboiled stories of 1993. John's first book was *The Devil of Harbor City. Past Sins* and *Here There Be Monsters followed.* His other books include *Souls on Fire, The Nightmare Strikes, Monsters Among Us, The Last Redhead, The Magic of Simon Tombs, The Santa Heist* (written with Patrick Thomas), *When the Moon Shines,* and *Mortal Sins.*

Melora Johnson is a writer who daylights as a librarian because that is where she hears the *best* stories, but also because sanctuary, and sometimes salvation, can be found in the stories we share. She has written something in just about every genre while living in Upstate New York with her husband, daughter, a black cat, and quite a few chickens. You can read more of her work in *A Sanctuary Built of Words: Poems of Peace, Grief, and Passion.* She is currently hard at work on a murder mystery.

Elyssa Mikaela Bolt is an avid hiker, social worker, and tarot reader based just outside the Adirondacks. Her life journey has taken her from the cornfields of the Midwest to the backwoods of Appalachia to the deserts of Arizona with stops in Hungary, Greece, and China. She is also the author of the Homer Trilogy (The Apple of Discord, Dance of the Hyenas, and Wrath of the Wounded) and the stand-alone The Dark Heart of the Raven.

Thomas Karwacki is a videographer and scriptwriter. He has written and produced short films that have shown at festivals in Philadelphia and Indianapolis. He was a creative script writer for Bill Diamond Productions in New York. He has also worked as a model maker for McFarlane Toys. This is his first published short story.

Born at West Point Military Academy on the eve of Christmas, 1960, **G.H. Monroe** spent the larger part of his adult life working in the information technology field, but he never strayed far from his true passion, which is writing. Situated in the Finger Lakes region of central

New York, near the Pennsylvania border, he is currently contemplating his next project. His work includes the poetry of The Ramblings of a Lonely Stranger, the coming-of-age novel The Hanley Chronicles, and the time travel book The Wormhole Café. Visit him at GHMonroe.com.

Dave Muffley is a formalist poet and novelist who writes of war and peace with passion, precision, and purpose. As a young man, he served four continuous tours of duty with the U.S. Naval Advisory Group in Vietnam. The scenes and events depicted in his story here are based on his experiences. Through the Department of Veterans Affairs' Disabled Veterans Rehabilitation Program, Dave earned a Bachelor of Arts degree in Mass Communication. If you enjoy his story in this anthology, you'll love his historical novel, *Belle of Lisbon,* a romantic sea adventure set near the end of the Anglo-Spanish War in 1603. Like his story in these pages, his poetry collection, *Admonitions of Ares* recounts his experiences in combat. Both are available through Amazon and other major booksellers. As Dave says, "The recalling is easy. The retelling is difficult and is best done in writing."

Rowan Dillon is a pen name for Christy Nicholas. She is a wordsmith extraordinaire, weaving tales that blend history, fantasy, and a sprinkle of magic into a literary cauldron that bubbles with intrigue and delight. With a penchant for strong themes, bittersweet endings, and complex characters, her books are a rollercoaster ride through the corridors of imagination. When she's not busy conjuring worlds and characters, Christy can be found traversing the globe, following her muse wherever it may lead, at least when she can afford it. Currently stationed in Connecticut, she daydreams of emerald landscapes and the haunting melodies of Irish music, wishing she could trade her skyscrapers for rolling green hills of Ireland.

There's been a debate among certain obscure and drunken literary scholars about whether **Patrick Thomas** was raised by Cthulhu or a leprechaun in a Manhattan bar. What there is no arguing about is that Patrick is the award-winning author of 50+ books including the beloved fantasy humor *Murphy's Lore* series and universe of books, the darkly hilarious *Dear Cthulhu* advice empire, the *Bikini Jones* series, the *Mystic Investigators* paranormal mystery series, the Jack Gardner

Mysteries (with John L. French) and is the creator of the *Agents of the Abyss*. Patrick's book *Nightcaps* was thrown at a suspect on the show *CSI*. *Dear Cthulhu* is a part of *Destinies: The Voice of Science Fiction* radio show on WUSB. His *Soul For Hire* story *Act of Contrition* was made into a short film.

As Patrick T. Fibbs, he writes middle readers including the *Babe B. Bear Mysteries, The Undead Kid Diaries, Joy Reaper Checks Out,* as well as the *Ughabooz* kids' picture and chapter books, and the YA *Emotional Support Nightmare.*

Please visit him at www.PatThomas.net and www.PatrickTFibbs.com.

Max Birkett travelled from the distant future to this era, to live an incredibly normal life. He lives in upstate New York with his beautiful wife, two wonderful children, and a cat.

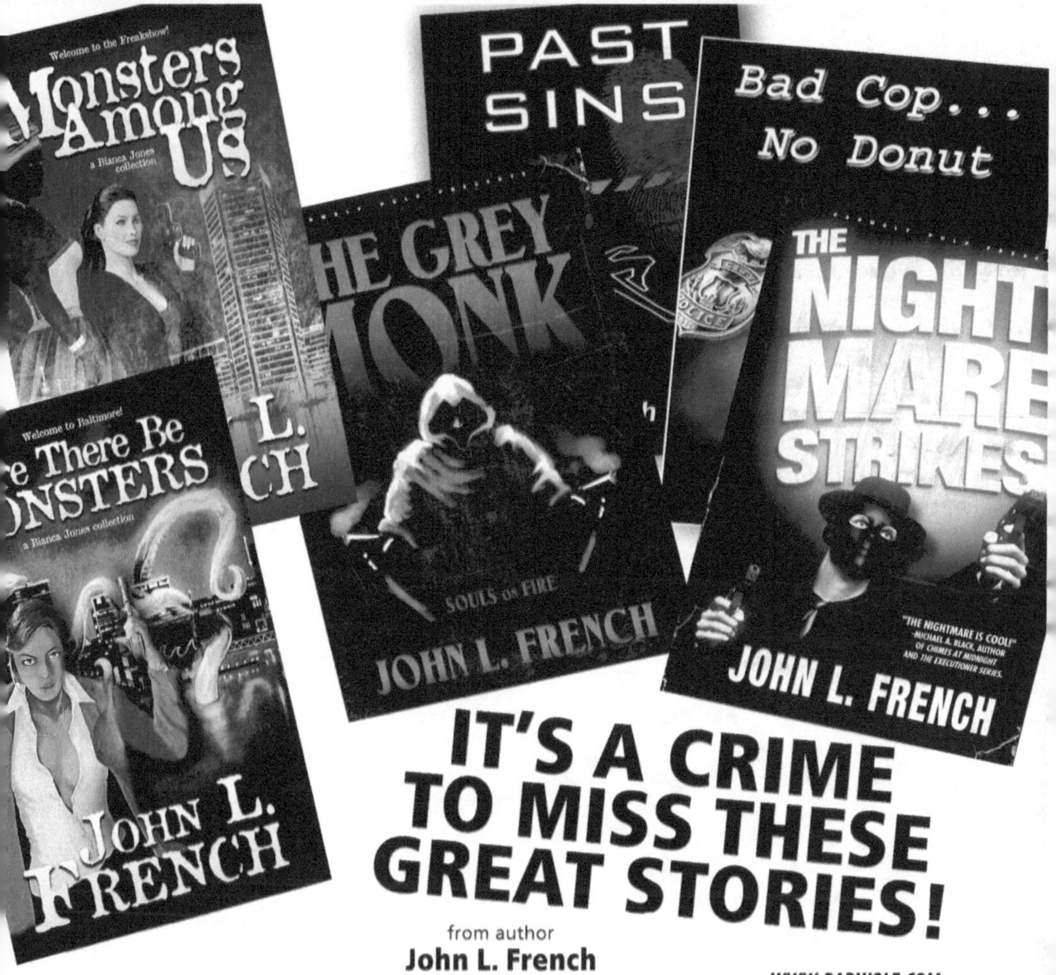

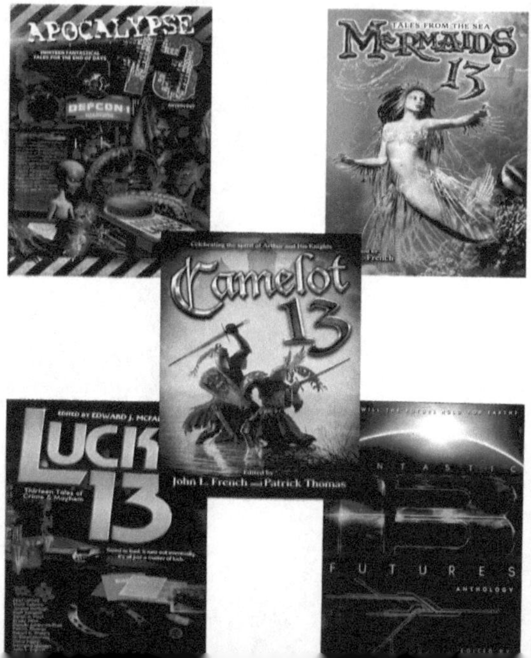

One Last Chance to Save Happily Ever After

Can a group of heroes including Goldenhair, Red Riding Hood and Rapunzel help General Snow White and her dwarven resistance fighters defeat the tyrannical Queen Cinderella? And will they succeed before a war with Wonderland destroys everything?

Their only hope to stop Cinderella's quest for power lies with a young girl named Patience Muffet who carries the fabled shards of Cinderella's glass slippers.

Roy Mauritsen's fantasy adventure fairy tale epic begins with *Shards Of The Glass Slipper: Queen Cinder*.

"Fantastic... A Magnificent Epic
-Sarah Beth Durst author o
Into The Wild & Drink, Slay, Love

"The Brothers Grimm meets Lord Of The Rings!"
-Patrick Thomas, author of the Murphy's Lore series

"Shards is a dark, lush, full-throttle fantasy epic that presents a bold re-imagining of classic characters."
-David Wade, creator of 319 Dark Street

"Roy Mauritsen's enchanting epic comes at a time when fairy tales are back in the forefront of our collective imagination."
-Darin Kennedy, short fiction author

PADWOLF
P U B L I S H I N G

In paperback & e-book
Find out more at
shardsoftheglassslipper.com
padwolf.com

BIKINI JONES
Vs. THE BRAINNAPPERS FROM OUTER SPACE
From the Author of Murphy's Lore and Dear Cthulhu
PATRICK THOMAS
BIKINI JONES
Vs. THE SEA MONSTERS
From the Author of Fairy With A Gun and Dear Cthulhu
PATRICK THOMAS
BIKINI JONES
Vs. THE EMPIRE OF PLANET Z
From the Author of Fairy With A Gun and Fairy & Dynamite
PATRICK THOMAS

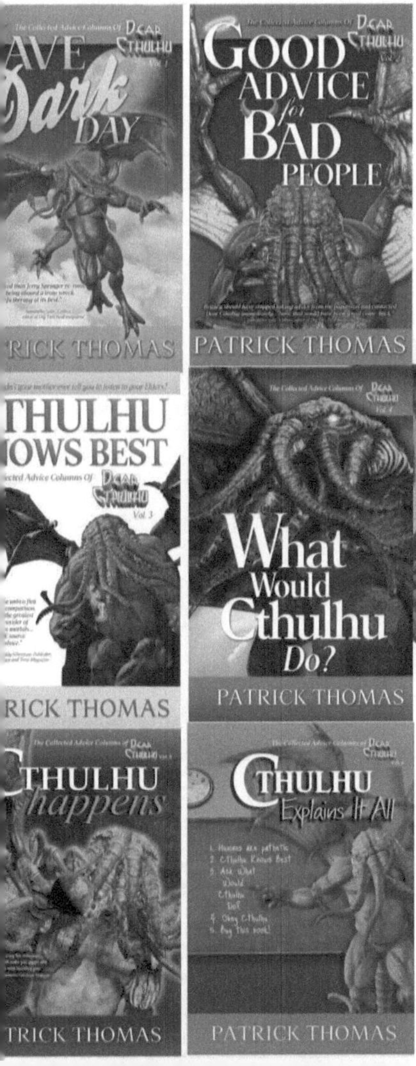